A Royal Competition

Amanda Schimmoeller

A ROYAL COMPETITION

Copyright © 2023 by Amanda Schimmoeller

All rights reserved.

No part of this book may be reproduced in any form or by any electronic or mechanical means, including information storage and retrieval systems, without the written permission of the author, except for the use of brief quotations in a book review.

This is a work of fiction. Names, characters, ideas, places, and incidents either are the product of the author's imagination or are used fictitiously. Any resemblance to actual persons, living or dead, events, or locales is entirely coincidental.

Cover design by germancreative

Edited by Emily Poole and Jenn Lockwood

Visit www.authoramandaschimmoeller.com for more information.

For my husband, Wade. I adore writing love stories, but ours will always be my favorite.

CONTENT WARNING

My books are closed-door romances (nothing beyond kissing) and will always have a happily-ever-after. However, there are some topics touched on in this book that I want you to be aware of (if you want to be) before jumping into the story.

The male main character has lost both parents (one when he was a teenager, from a horseback riding accident, and one recently to sarcoidosis). Although neither of these deaths occurs on the page, the character is still grieving their deaths, and the funeral for his father does happen on the page.

There is also one scene in which a character intends to harm another character with a knife.

But remember…there's a happily-ever-after at the end. :)

CHAPTER ONE
LIAM

Everyone hopes for the day that their dreams become a reality. But actually living out that dream can look a lot different than originally expected.

Prince Liam had aspired to be the king of Wistonia for nearly his whole life, but it had always felt more like a far-off dream since he was the spare rather than the firstborn heir. That is, until his older brother, Barrett, had abdicated the throne to marry his true love, Jules, a few weeks ago. Then, his dream finally seemed within reach.

But his brother had been training to be king of Wistonia for practically his entire life. He, on the other hand, had always made sarcastic jokes about how his father should pass the throne to him. He had never truly studied or prepared for the role, and now that Barrett had abdicated and the throne would actually be passed to him, he was panicking. He wasn't even close to being ready to ascend the throne.

As much as he tried to avoid reading the tabloids, he'd seen enough to know that the media had labeled him "The Royal Heartbreaker." His reputation as a playboy prince, jumping from one relationship to the next, was mostly fabricated. He *was* a flirt. And he wasn't too proud to admit that.

But most of the pictures of him in the media were with random women who would sidle up next to him at events right before the cameras arrived. In his real dating life, he supposed there was some truth to what the media said. He was never photographed with the same woman more than once. But the truth behind him being a one-date wonder lay with the vow he had made to himself four years ago—that he would never let himself fall in love again. *Not after what happened with Mila.*

He didn't want to spend enough time with someone that feelings could develop and he could get hurt. Liam also didn't want to hurt someone else through his inability to ever love them. He was doing them a favor by not asking them on another date and setting them up for actual heartbreak. Yet, girls always seemed to go to the media, saying he broke their hearts, making their one encounter out to be more than it was.

He was disheartened by the person the media portrayed him to be, especially when compared to his brother, who they referred to as the "Perfect Prince." *Will the people ever see me through the same lens as they see him?*

He shook off the negative thoughts. The media might depict him in a negative manner, but at least he knew who he really was.

I can only hope the Wistonian people will accept me as their king. I'll do everything I can to earn the trust of my people before I ascend the throne.

The truth was, he still needed time. Time that he no longer had because his father had suddenly passed away a week ago, leaving him without any living parents. And leaving him without the time he needed to prepare to take the throne. Liam wasn't much for memorizing policy, but Article 2, Section 17 of the Wistonian constitution had been ingrained in him by his parents from a young age.

To continue the royal lineage, the king's successor must be married to ascend the throne as King of Wistonia. The individual the royal heir marries must be of royal standing. If the king's successor is not married when the residing king becomes deceased, the King's Council will rule for a period of ninety days. If the Crown Prince does not marry within the allotted ninety-day period, the next married royal heir in line will ascend the throne.

So, not only was he dealing with the grief of his father's passing, but now he was on an accelerated timeline to marry. A *very* accelerated timeline. Less than ninety days remained before he must marry. Otherwise, the throne would go to the next person in line—his cousin, Prince James.

He had no other choice than to find a woman of royal standing—and marry her. But nowhere in his wildest dreams of becoming king had he ever imagined he would be hosting twelve royal women at the Wistonian Palace for a televised dating competition.

In the final days before his father passed away, he'd told Liam it was his greatest wish for him to marry. Barrett had found Jules, and his father wanted Liam to find someone who made him happy and could live the rest of his days with him. Someone to proudly lead Wistonia at his side.

The king had suggested the idea of a televised dating competition because of their family's love of watching *The Perfect Match* together. It had been his mother's favorite show, and she'd convinced his father to watch it with her once they'd married. He and Barrett had joined in watching as well. Even after his mother passed away due to an unfortunate horseback riding incident when he was thirteen, they had continued the tradition of watching the show together.

"I still don't know how a competition where I date multiple women is supposed to help with my playboy-prince image," Liam muttered under his breath as he waited outside the doors to the ballroom. "But I'll do it…for Dad."

To say Liam had concerns about how this competition would be received was an understatement. But the King's Council and the head of the Wistonian Royal Press, Lindsay, had ultimately decided it was his only option for finding a woman of royal standing to marry on his short timeline without forming an arranged marriage with someone from another kingdom.

"It's time, Your Highness." Lindsay popped her head out of the ballroom, her brown hair swishing around her shoulders with the motion.

Liam's stomach dropped at her words, making him wish he hadn't eaten Mexican food for dinner. *It's showtime. There's no turning back now.*

He nervously brushed the shoulders of his charcoal-gray suit and tugged at his emerald-green tie, the ensemble chosen by a stylist for the welcome ball. Liam nodded and followed Lindsay into the ballroom. They entered through the second-floor doors—the entrance used by royal families and dignified guests—allowing him to take in the whole space.

The ballroom was already regal enough that it only required minimal decorations. The back wall was floor-to-ceiling windows that let in the night sky, making the moon and stars sparkle off the glittering white marble floor. The other walls were lined with white pillars, and a plethora of crystal chandeliers hung from the vaulted ceiling. The only additions appeared to be some cocktail tables with gold linens, a few tables of hors d'oeuvres and desserts, and modern couches.

The palace's head butler, Wadsworth, stopped him at the top of the grand marble staircase, pulling him into a fatherly hug. "You will do great, Your Highness." When he pulled back, he excitedly pointed to the cameraman set up next to him. "I can't believe I'm going to be on television."

"Maybe you'll catch your big break." Liam chuckled and clapped him on the shoulder before strolling down the grand marble staircase to the first floor and taking his place on the spot the camera crew marked for him.

"Your Highness, this is Alec." Lindsay gestured to a tall, middle-aged hipster with a man-bun and clear-frame glasses. He had a headset hanging around his neck and was holding a clipboard against his white V-neck and plaid blazer. "Alec is the production director for *Royally Yours*. He will be the person you work with to set up dates and film individual interviews for the duration of the show."

Alec extended his hand, and Liam grasped it, giving it a firm shake.

"It's a pleasure to meet you, Your Highness," Alec said with a deep bow.

"The pleasure is all mine." Liam knew this was a person he wanted to butter up since he would have a lot of control throughout the filming process.

"It's time for us to begin, Your Highness. Each woman will pause at the top of the staircase, where Wadsworth will announce her name. She will walk down and greet you for a quick moment. You'll then escort her to that seating area in the corner, where she can enjoy a glass of champagne and hors d'oeuvres while chatting with the other women until everyone has arrived. The actual ball itself will be fairly short. We want to get some good shots of you dancing with different women but don't want you up all night."

Alec tapped his clipboard with his pen and looked up. "Any questions?"

Liam shook his head, so Alec attached a wireless microphone to the back of his waistband and gave him a small earpiece before walking off to prepare the camera crew.

"You've got this." Lindsay shot him a quick thumbs-up before joining the rest of the crew.

Suddenly the cameras were rolling. No prayer or deep breathing exercise could calm his racing heart as the ballroom doors opened. Liam rubbed his cufflinks with his thumbs as Wadsworth made the first introduction.

"Presenting Her Royal Highness, Princess Rosalie of Findorra."

Liam had been quickly briefed about the format of the competition after his father's funeral. Twelve ladies had been selected by the King's Council members, and they were coming from all eight countries throughout their continent of Fenimore, a large land mass off the coast of Europe. They had each been selected for their achievements, qualifications, charitable endeavors, and influential families—the women whom the council thought would make the best candidates for Wistonia's future queen.

Rosalie would likely be the youngest in the competition at the age of twenty-two. She was also the only princess who would be part of *Royally Yours*. The rest of the ladies held noble titles as daughters of dukes, marquesses, earls, viscounts, and barons.

He'd had a decent amount of interaction with Rosalie at previous events, since their countries neighbored each other. He probably knew all the women in the competition, to some extent, within the royal sphere. He would have to tread very lightly throughout the process if he wanted to maintain good connections with the families of the women he didn't choose after the competition was over.

Rosalie glided down the steps in a light-blue gown, her auburn hair flowing behind her. There was no denying she was beautiful—anyone with eyes could see that—but he had never pursued anything romantic with her because she was a few years younger than him. But that age gap seemed less pronounced at this stage of life.

"You look as graceful as ever, Rosalie."

"Thank you, Liam." Rosalie squeezed his hands and smiled softly. "I can't believe this is all happening. It's surreal for me, so I can't imagine what this experience must be like for you."

"It's not a situation I ever thought I'd find myself in." Liam chuckled. "But I'm ready for this journey." He saw Alec motion to wrap it up over her shoulder behind the camera crew. "I'm looking forward to spending more time with you here." He offered his arm to Rosalie. "I saw some delicious food was prepared. I'm jealous you get to eat while I have to stand here and greet people."

"What a hard life you live," she teased, swatting at his arm.

He exaggeratedly held a hand to his heart. "It's a sacrifice I'm willing to make for my country."

"How giving of you." She smirked and shooed him away. "It's not kind to keep a lady waiting."

"Now *that* is good advice." He grinned at her and walked back to his mark.

"Presenting Lady Raina of Bristol."

How could anyone forget Raina? he thought, knowing he would have to watch what he said with the mic attached to him.

Last fall, when she had visited with his cousin, James, Raina had backed him up against their horse stables, flirting with him and telling him how great they would be together. He should've known she would make her way into this competition because of her influential family ties.

She sashayed down the stairs in a tight red dress that left little to the imagination.

"Liam, darling." She pulled him in and gave him a loud kiss on each cheek. He discreetly wiped at his face, hoping she hadn't left any lipstick marks behind. "Thank you so much for having me. I cannot wait for all the time we'll spend together." Raina smiled saucily at him and strutted away before he could get a word in. The whole interaction was so very Raina.

Liam met woman after woman until they seemed to blur together in a mix of elegant fabrics and sweet perfumes. He was trying to be hopeful. But he'd watched enough seasons of *The Perfect Match* with his family to know that most couples who met on dating shows didn't make it in the long run.

I only need to find someone I can get along with enough to have her rule beside me. I can't let this experience flop. I will find a wife and make my parents proud.

He vaguely heard Wadsworth announce, "Presenting Lady Tiffany of Meldovia."

Liam looked up just in time as Tiffany stepped in front of him, wearing a navy dress with a skirt that fluttered behind her. "Lady Tiffany, it's a pleasure to see you again."

"The pleasure is truly all mine." She smiled up at him. Her eyes wandered over to the growing group of women. "It looks like you have a…decent group of ladies here already."

But the party can officially begin now that I'm here." Her hand slid up his arm, wrapping around his bicep.

Liam forced a smile. "I'll let you go ahead and get the party started, then." He escorted her over to the other women and pressed his lips together as he walked back to his mark.

Are women always this flirty, or do they just want the crown?

He attempted to make his smile authentic as he welcomed the next few ladies, though nothing much stood out about them.

"Presenting Lady Sienna of Bristol."

Her long brunette hair was styled in a fancy updo, little curled pieces bouncing around her face with each step she took. She smiled at him the whole walk down, her eyes never leaving his. The maroon dress she wore fit her perfectly, and her dark eyes sparkled when they reached him.

"It's so lovely to see you again, Your Highness." She curtsied.

"Please, call me Liam."

"I haven't been to Wistonia in years. I forgot how beautiful your country is."

"I'm glad you're here." Liam took her hands in his. "I look forward to catching up with you soon. It's been far too long."

Sienna's cheeks turned pink at his words. "I can't wait."

He escorted her over to the couches and genuinely smiled as he walked back to the stairs. *Maybe there's some hope after all.*

There had been a few ladies who'd stood out so far. Lady Piper, Lady Tiffany, The Honorable Olive, and Lady Raina had all been extremely flirtatious when their time came to speak with him. Others, like Princess Rosalie, Lady Sienna, and Lady Bridgette stood out for their sweet-natured conversation and composure.

When he arrived back at his mark, he heard Alec in his ear, letting him know that this would be the final contestant.

The ballroom doors opened to reveal the last girl. He looked up and tried to maintain his composure as he looked into the eyes of a woman he'd never expected to see here.

His jaw dropped as she walked down the flight of marble steps toward him in what felt like slow motion. He quickly closed his mouth as the world seemed to stop while he took her in.

Her blush-pink dress looked like it was created for her. She looked like a goddess. It flattered all her curves in all the right places, and he wasn't even trying not to stare.

As she got closer, he discreetly wiped the side of his mouth to make sure he wasn't drooling. Because she wasn't just anyone.

She was the one woman he had tried to avoid as often as possible since the vow he made to himself four years ago.

The one woman he would've fought hard to exclude from this competition.

The one woman who stirred up feelings he wanted to shove far down and never feel again.

The one woman who had the power to break down all the walls he had built up around his heart.

When she finally stood in front of him, his hands reflexively reached out and grabbed hers. His lips pulled up into a coy smile of their own accord. And, before he knew it, words were falling out of his mouth in a husky voice he didn't recognize.

"Hello, Charlotte."

CHAPTER TWO
CHARLOTTE

One week ago

"You really won't give me more time to find a suitable husband?" Charlotte shook her head. "I'm trying. I can't help that Prince Barrett chose to marry someone else."

"No." Duke Vincent Croft's strong voice bellowed throughout their sitting room with a tone of finality. "A prince chose to marry your assistant over you."

Her father's words pierced her heart. He hadn't always been like this. She remembered times in her childhood when he would take her to the fair or dance with her at events. But as she'd grown older, her father had started using her as a puppet to gain more popularity—more control.

He'd grown more demanding of her when she'd become a teenager, and it had only gotten worse from there. Her father knew how to cut her down with words and get her to bend to his will. Charlotte had learned to brush off most of his comments. But today, his remarks were even harsher than usual.

"That was the eye-opening event I needed to remind me that what I'm doing is for the best. You will not receive your inheritance if you don't get married by your thirtieth birthday."

"My thirtieth birthday is in a little over three months. How do you expect me to get married by then?"

"I don't." Her father smiled as he looked out the window. "I've been wanting to add a tennis court to the property. Those funds should be sufficient."

Charlotte stared at him in shock and took in a sharp breath.

Azalea. Bluebell. Calla lily. Daffodil.

As a public figure, she always had to do her best to remain composed. Gardening and flowers were Charlotte's happy place, and alphabetically listing the names of flowers in her mind had become her way of maintaining her perfect façade. Her way of being the calm, faultless figure everyone else wanted—*expected*—her to be.

Before she'd learned her method of naming flowers to calm herself, she had found a different way to take out her pent-up aggression—going to a local paintball facility and playing until her mind was clear. Luckily, naming flowers worked just as well, and it was a more fitting, proper method for someone of her station.

She let out a long sigh after her father left the room. If she lost her inheritance, Charlotte would be losing a lot of funds she could use to do so much good. Her charitable endeavors would suffer without her inheritance money. She would sell everything she owned before she would quit supporting orphanages and adoption agencies.

People had found a husband in less than three months before. Surely she could, too.

Pulling out her phone, she scrolled through her contacts, wondering who she could call to vent to. All her "friends" were really more connections her father had forced on her for political gain.

The only person who felt like a real friend was Jules, her previous assistant who was now engaged to Prince Barrett. Despite what her father had said, she truly was happy for them and glad Jules and Barrett had found true love rather than convenience. But the whole situation was a bit awkward. They hadn't had a chance to talk since Jules no longer worked for her. *Maybe I should reach out to her first.* It had only been a few weeks, and Charlotte already missed her.

Before she could convince herself otherwise, she hit the call button under Jules's name and held the phone to her ear. On the second ring, Jules answered.

"Char!"

Jules calling her by a nickname allowed Charlotte to breathe again. It was like no time had passed at all.

"Jules, I'm sorry it's been so long. How are you? I can't imagine it's been easy since King Henry's passing."

Jules sighed, and her voice turned to a whisper. "I wish I could do more to help support Barrett."

"I'm sure your presence alone is enough for him." Charlotte paused. "How's wedding planning going?" *Might as well bring up the elephant in the room right out of the gate.* She'd never thought of Barrett in a romantic way, and she wanted Jules to know there truly were no hard feelings.

"You really don't mind talking about it?"

"Not at all. I miss your friendship."

"Oh," Jules cried out. "I miss you, too." Jules went on to tell her how Barrett had surprised her with her parents showing up to help plan their wedding and that they had picked a date in April for the ceremony.

"That's so sweet. I'm really happy for you." Charlotte really was happy for her friend. Knowing Jules had found happiness with Barrett gave her hope. Jules was unapologetically herself, while Charlotte had always done what her father had told her to do. Her deepest desire was to be seen. *Chosen.* Charlotte was still the little girl who dreamed of being wanted as a person, not for her title or money.

"Enough about me. How are you? And how are things back in Findorra?"

Charlotte's countenance fell. "You know, things are…going."

"Oh, no! It sounds like you need a good vent sesh. Spill, girlfriend."

"My parents only returned from a trip to England yesterday, and my father already made it a point to reiterate his strict conditions for me to receive my inheritance. He won't budge, Jules."

"But wasn't his qualification—"

"That I have to get married by my thirtieth birthday that's in just over three months? Yeah." Charlotte rubbed her forehead with her palm.

"I feel awful. If I hadn't gotten in the way—"

"It's not your fault, Jules," Charlotte interrupted. "Barrett and I were never more than friends. You know better than anyone that I've had my eye on someone else for a while." She shook her head, trying to wipe the image of her longtime crush from her mind. "You and Barrett were clearly meant for each other. You can't help who you love, and you shouldn't feel bad for it."

"You truly are the best, most understanding friend a girl could ask for." After an uncharacteristically quiet moment, Jules added, "But what're you gonna do?"

"I have no clue. I mean, how am I supposed to find a man who wants to get married that quickly?" Charlotte asked with a hollow laugh.

"You could always get a mail-order groom."

"Are those still a thing?" Charlotte giggled.

"I have no clue. I'll keep thinking on it. You leave it to me. I will make sure you have a good man *and* your inheritance."

"I really appreciate your help, but it's my mess. I'll figure it out. You just worry about planning your wedding and being there for Barrett."

"You never have to walk alone through hard times, Charlotte. That's what friends are for." Jules's words were like a warm hug. "Will I see you at the king's memorial service in a few days?"

"Yes, my family will be attending." Charlotte and her family had been invited to King Henry's private funeral along with many other royal and influential families from around the continent of Fenimore and the rest of the world. She had been unsure at first if she should attend but ultimately decided to go in support of Jules, Barrett, and Liam.

"I'll find you there, then."

"Let's talk again soon."

"Definitely. I'm so glad you called," Jules said.

After Charlotte ended the call, she felt something for the first time since she had been home.

Hope.

CHAPTER THREE
LIAM

Five days ago

Liam breathed in slowly through his nose and released the breath just as slowly, trying to keep his emotions at bay. He had been biting back tears the entire memorial service—because that was what was expected of him. To put on a robotic, royal front. To keep his emotions at bay and show strength. To show that Wistonia would be strong, despite any hard times that may come. But all he wanted to do was cry because there were so many more questions he wanted to ask his father. He needed more advice. More training before he became king.

King Henry's funeral honored his life and reign in such a beautiful way. It was filled with tradition and fitting for royalty, recognizing everything his father had sacrificed to lead Wistonia over the past thirty-four years. He'd had to step up and be king at the young age of twenty-seven when he'd suddenly lost his father.

And now Liam was in a similar position. He would have to step up and take the throne at an even younger age than his father had. But there was one main difference between their circumstances. His father had already been married to his mother when his own father passed away. Liam, on the other hand, was single as a Pringle, and due to Wistonia's marriage law, he had less than ninety days to correct that issue.

He bit his cheek to rein in his emotions as his mind went back to his last conversation with his father.

"Liam, thank you for coming to see me," the king said through slow, labored breaths.

His father lay in bed, looking pale and fragile. Liam swallowed down the lump in his throat as he sat on the edge of his father's bed. It took him right back to the moment he'd lost his mother. He hadn't been especially close to his father, but the thought of losing him—of losing both parents by the time he was twenty-five—was more than his heart could handle.

Liam gently placed his hand on his father's arm. "You couldn't keep me away if you tried." He tried to lighten the mood, but his voice came out melancholy.

"I want to talk"—his father paused—"about your future."

The king motioned for his glass of water, and Liam quickly picked it up and held it to his lips.

"Thank you. I know we've had our differences, but I hope you know I love you." A wracking cough overtook his father before he continued. "I don't have to worry about Barrett anymore now that he's found Jules. But I worry for you. It was always our greatest wish to see you and your brother find love and get married." He took another deep breath. "Now that you're going to be king, it's of the utmost importance that you find someone who will lead beside you. Someone with whom you can share your life."

"You don't have to worry about me. You'll be around, leading Wistonia, long enough that I may never lead." Liam lightly squeezed his father's arm.

His father shot him a sad smile. "My body is failing. My time is coming to an end."

"Don't say that," Liam interrupted, holding his hands to his head.

"It's true, and I want you to be happy." He paused to cough again, wiping his mouth with a handkerchief when the coughing fit ceased. "Which is why I've submitted an idea to the King's Council. It's a little bit unusual, but I think it will be a great way for you to gain popularity with the Wistonian people. And I know it would've made your mother so happy."

"Well, go on," Liam urged.

"I want you to host your own televised dating competition. Just like The Perfect Match."

"And how exactly will that help with my popularity? The people already think I'm a heartbreaker. How will dating multiple women in a televised competition help remedy that?"

"It will allow them to see the real you." The king rasped, reaching for his water. He took a long sip. "To see the you that we know and to find your future wife and queen."

"Please don't worry about me finding a wife. Just focus on getting better." Liam took in his father's eyes as he struggled to keep them open. "You should get some rest. We can talk more about this tomorrow."

Only, the opportunity to talk again didn't come. They had lost his father that evening. And now he was going to be starring in a reality dating show to find a wife in under three months' time. It sounded like a bad punch line.

He stood tall by his father's casket, trying to believe that everything was going to be okay again. But life as he knew it was changing, and there was no stopping the events of the day to come. Right after the funeral, he and Barrett would attend a press conference where they would announce Barrett's abdication to the general public, as well as the news of Liam's dating competition. He wasn't sure how the people would react to the news. But he could only hope to do what his father had said—gain the love and loyalty of his people.

After the service ended, Barrett left to stand by Jules. Liam remained by his father's casket, wanting to say one final goodbye. Once the crowd had dwindled, he let his tough exterior slip for a moment. He crossed his arms on top of the casket and laid his head on top of them.

"I love you, Dad. I'll make you proud. I promise." He stood, swiping his fingers beneath his eyes before putting back on his stoic front. Liam turned to leave when his eyes connected with Charlotte's. She stood in the back of the chapel, but even from that far away, he could see that her eyes were filled with empathy. He was catapulted back in his memories to his mother's funeral when he was thirteen.

Liam slammed the closet door behind him as angry tears streamed down his face. He was angry that his mother had been taken from him so suddenly. He was angry that he had to stand through the funeral service, acting strong, when all he wanted to do was break down. He was angry that he had lost the one person who truly understood him.

A knock sounded at the door, cutting off his sobs.

"Your Highness? It's Charlotte." She tiptoed into the closet, shutting the door softly behind her. "Are you okay?" Charlotte stepped closer to him and likely spotted the tears on his cheeks. "Oh, Liam." She threw her arms around him and pulled him close.

Her touch was so kind—so caring—that he allowed the sobs to erupt out of him again, letting out all the sadness, anger, and grief he had been holding in. They were childhood friends who had grown up playing tag and attending the same royal events. Charlotte had always had a heart of gold, and today she was like an angel, sending him a message in his moment of need that he wasn't alone and that everything would be okay again one day.

It was in that moment, in Charlotte's arms, that a small crush had formed—a flickering of feelings in Liam's heart for the girl who saw him when no one else did.

His angel on earth.

He started to walk over to Charlotte to thank her for being here today when Lindsay appeared at his side, grabbing his arm and pulling him toward a waiting black Mercedes sedan. He shot Charlotte an apologetic glance over his shoulder before getting into the car.

"Are we headed straight to the press conference?" Liam asked his driver, Dean.

"Yes, Your Highness."

He sighed and leaned back in his seat. There was never time for rest as a royal. Lindsay and his bodyguard, Marcus, joined them in the car before they left.

As he rode to the press conference, Lindsay briefed him on the kinds of questions he would likely be asked. She told him what things to say and what not to say. But there was never enough prepping for this kind of event, especially one that was completely unprecedented.

When they arrived at their destination, he took a steadying breath, putting back on his stoic, strong face. Then he stepped out into the flashing lights.

Everything sounded like a muffled echo as Liam walked to the podium. A crowd of at least fifty press members stood at the base of the stage with hundreds of the Wistonian people behind them. Barrett already stood at the podium, waiting to make their big announcements. As soon as he reached his brother, sweat beaded at his brow from the lights shining on them from every angle.

Lindsay joined them at the podium and cleared her throat. "Thank you all for joining us today for this press conference. The Wistonian Royal Family has some grand announcements they would like to make. They will take questions after they have both shared their news." She gestured to Barrett to begin.

"Thank you, the people of Wistonia, for taking time on this heavy day, when we honored my father's life and reign, to come listen to us speak. We are blessed to have such caring, loyal people. I have loved my time as your Crown Prince, and I love Wistonia. However, after much consideration, I have come to the difficult decision to abdicate the throne."

The cameras immediately started flashing again, and press members began shouting questions as Barrett continued.

"I have chosen to follow my heart and marry for love rather than duty. I know this might come as a shock, and I apologize for any hurt this may cause. That was never my intention, but I know I am leaving the throne in capable hands. I believe my brother, Crown Prince Liam, will do a wonderful job leading Wistonia." Barrett clapped Liam on the back, and questions began ringing throughout the crowd again. "Now, I believe my brother has an announcement of his own to make."

Liam stepped up to the microphone, his hands turning clammy. "As my brother said, I have taken on the role of Crown Prince of Wistonia. With my father's passing, this means I will be ascending the throne to be your king much sooner than expected." He took a deep breath before continuing. "Due to Wistonia's marriage law, I must be married to a woman of royal standing to ascend the throne. Therefore, in accordance with the King's Council, I will be hosting a group of women at the palace over the course of the next three months for a dating competition. The events will be televised so that you—the people—can get to know me more, as your future king, and whomever I choose to lead Wistonia by my side, as your queen. We realize these are unprecedented events but hope you will join in watching the fun when the show premieres in a few days."

The crowd's questions were so loud it rivaled a teenage heartthrob's concert.

"Your Highness, how do you plan on juggling a large group of women at once?" a press member asked.

"Like he hasn't done it before," another member of the press scoffed, drawing a laugh from the crowd.

Liam looked over to Lindsay, and she nodded her head, letting him know he could address the question.

"Very carefully. As you so *expertly* pointed out, I've done it before. What makes you think I can't do it again?" He gave a winning smirk, drawing light chuckles from those in attendance. "In all seriousness, I plan to treat each woman as if she is the only one there. The selected women are all giving up their time to be here, and I will make every effort to get to know each of them. Whomever I marry will not only be my wife, she will also become your queen, and I don't take that decision lightly."

The press stood in stunned silence for a moment before the person who'd asked the question thanked him.

"Any other questions?" Lindsay asked, and dozens of hands shot into the air. She selected a woman, who stood up taller as she spoke.

"Your Highness, I appreciate your sentiments, but how do you plan to treat each woman like they are the only contestant? You have such a short time with them. How will you keep each of your relationships straight?"

"Thank you for your question. I know I will not get everything right in this process. You all know very well that I am human, and I make mistakes. I will learn from my mistakes, as I always have. I can't predict my actions throughout the competition because I have never been in this situation before. But what I can say is that I will do my best to treat these women as they deserve to be—with respect and dignity and kindness. I want to truly get to know them on an emotional level. One way I plan to keep my relationships straight is by refraining from kissing any of the contestants until I have selected the one to whom I will propose." Murmurs spread throughout the crowd.

"Prince Liam, why won't you kiss anyone? It is a dating show, after all."

"While this is a dating show, it's my life—and it is also theirs. I would like to respect the privacy of everyone involved. Things may change as relationships naturally progress, but I want my intentions to be clear. I will likely know all the women competing, since they all come from within the royal circuit. I respect them and their families, and I want to maintain good diplomatic connections with them after this competition is over. I hope that sticking to strictly emotional relationships rather than physical ones will aid in hearts not being broken as women are sent home throughout the competition."

Lindsay called everyone's attention back to her. "That is all the questions we have time for today, thank you."

There was another roar of voices begging for more questions and the continuous flash of cameras as Liam's bodyguard, Marcus, came up from his spot on the ground and led him off the stage back to his waiting car through the crowds of people.

"How did it go, Your Highness?" his driver, Dean, asked.

"Much better than I anticipated." Liam slouched in the seat and leaned his head back on the headrest.

Hopefully, I'll be able to handle the competition with the same amount of ease.

CHAPTER FOUR
LIAM

Four days ago

After the big press release, Liam wasn't shocked that there had been a multitude of reactions from the media.

He usually tried to avoid reading news regarding the royal family, but this morning he had taken a deep dive, and he was sinking without a life jacket to save him.

There were a few supportive articles in the *Royal Inquisitor* from writers who believed he would be a good king and shared how excited they were for *Royally Yours*. But the majority of the articles wrote about him in an unfavorable light. The titles of the negative write-ups seemed to be ingrained in his mind, no matter how hard he tried to forget them.

"*Royally Yours* Is Bound to Be a Joke."

"Who Wants to Date the Royal Heartbreaker?"

"Prince or Plotter? Allegations about Liam Run Wild with King Henry Suddenly Dead, Perfect Prince Barrett Abdicating the Throne."

"Rumblings of Displeasure Run Rampant through the Kingdom."

His hopes that the people would accept him had been demolished by each new headline in opposition to him. He could only wish that his father's intentions behind *Royally Yours* would work. He hoped the people would finally see him in a favorable light, getting to know the man behind the crown. And that watching him "fall in love" would help the people fall in love with him, too.

What the people would never know is that love wouldn't be part of this show. Because he never planned on falling in love again—not after Mila. He'd dated Mila for two years, right after he'd turned nineteen, falling hard and fast and fully.

Everything had been perfect with her. That is, until he'd overheard her talking on the phone to her friend about how he was the man who was going to help her "become a princess." He'd confronted her, and she'd attempted to backpedal and talk her way out of what he'd heard, but the damage had already been done. When Liam had broken up with her, she'd admitted everything. How she'd never really loved him. And that all she'd wanted was his title.

He had been crushed.

It was then that he'd made a promise to himself that he would never fall in love again. That his heart would never be up for grabs. He'd stuck to his vow for the past four years, and a televised dating show wasn't going to change that.

But nobody needed to know that. He simply planned to choose someone who understood their relationship was to be a business arrangement rather than a love match. Someone who would never be a threat to his heart.

A knock sounded at his study door, and he called out for them to enter.

"Thank you for meeting with me, Your Highness." Lord Simon Willoughby, the highest member of the King's Council, sat down across the desk from Liam.

"You wanted to brief me on the competition?"

He shuffled the papers in his lap. "Yes, you obviously already know that Lindsay has selected the name *Royally Yours* for the show." Lord Willoughby cleared his throat. "Since we are on the fast track, the King's Council members have selected the twelve women who will be part of the competition."

"I don't get any say in the women I have to date and potentially marry?"

Lord Willoughby's eyes darted around the room. "We had your brother consult in the decision-making process when we were going through the paperwork for abdication. I'm sorry, Your Highness, but there wasn't enough time. I assure you we've selected women of the highest caliber—one princess and the rest from varying degrees of nobility."

Liam preferred to be in control. But the only thing he was controlling right now was his tongue. He physically bit it to keep from saying the things in his head. He nodded tersely, and Lord Willoughby continued.

"The women are all between twenty-two and thirty years old, and they're coming from neighboring kingdoms across Fenimore. I'm confident we have a good mix of candidates and that any of them would make a wonderful queen and partner for you." He looked at the notes in his hands. "The final matter of business is that we have secured the host from *The Perfect Match*, Giovanni Geraldo, for the competition."

"At least that's something to look forward to," Liam muttered. Looking up, he added, "Will I get to see what women will be in the competition before we begin filming in four days?"

"Unfortunately, the production team for the show has decided it would be best that you not know in advance who is coming. That way, they can get more genuine reactions from you at the welcome ball."

"Welcome ball?"

"No one will be in attendance except for you and the women—and the production crew, of course."

Liam nodded, but inside he was tempering his anger. *I should get a say in this. I'm the one who has to marry the winning contestant.* He would need to have Wadsworth set up his paintball equipment so he could release all his pent-up anger and energy after this.

"Is there anything else, Lord Willoughby?"

"There is one final matter. You need a little…royal makeover before the competition begins."

"Dare I ask what a royal makeover is?" Liam pressed his lips together.

"We believe it's best that you get a haircut before the competition. Your appearance needs to read 'future king' not 'playboy prince'."

While getting a haircut may not seem like a big deal to most people, to Liam, his hair symbolized his last ounce of freedom. He'd thought being the future king would mean he'd have all the control he had desired for so long. But in reality, he was surrounded by stifling policies and years' worth of knowledge he was required to learn in a matter of months while also having to court a woman on national television whom he would eventually marry—within the next ninety days.

"Brilliant." Liam stood and ran his hands through his unkempt hair, leaving it mussed. "Do they need me to do anything else for them? Grab the King's Council coffee? Donate one of my kidneys?"

Lord Willoughby's face turned red as he stood, but he held his ground. "The haircut will be all. The royal hairstylist will meet you in the salon room to cut your hair. She's expecting you now."

He pressed his lips together to keep from saying anything he would regret. It wouldn't be wise to start out his time on the King's Council by fighting with its head member. But Liam didn't stop the door to his study from slamming loudly behind him as he left. His brother had been the Perfect Prince, not him.

Arriving in the palace's salon room, he inhaled the fresh scent of shampoo. Liam walked farther into the space and saw his royal hairstylist, Matisse, standing behind one of the chairs. He plopped down into the seat and rubbed his temples.

"Not excited to get your hair cut?" she asked in a voice that was as sweet as sugar.

"Don't take it personally, Matisse." He glanced up at the middle-aged woman in the mirror and couldn't help but smile as he took in her shoulder-length lavender hair. It was a new color every time he saw her, but it was always bright and sunny, just like her personality.

"I'm sorry, Your Highness. I'm under strict orders to make you presentable for the competition. But don't worry, I'll give you the best haircut of your life. I'm sure we can find a happy medium between what the King's Council told me and the grungy style you've got going on." She winked at him in the mirror as she gestured to his mop of light-brown hair. "I won't let you down, Your Highness." She curtsied as much as she could in her hot-pink pencil skirt and then walked him over to the shampoo station to wash his hair.

He closed his eyes as she massaged his temples and lathered shampoo and then conditioner into his hair. After arriving back in the salon chair, he closed his eyes again, not wanting to watch his precious locks of hair fall to the floor.

Listening to the snip-snip of his last bit of freedom being cut from his head was almost too much to bear after the events of the week.

After a few minutes that felt like an eternity, Matisse spoke again. "All done, Your Highness. Are you ready to see your new look?"

He let out a long breath and nodded his head. Matisse spun the chair around. Liam apprehensively opened his eyes and looked at his appearance in the mirror. His stylist had cut off a decent amount of hair but still left it a little bit longer on top. She had styled it with some type of gel that held it in a comb-over with tapered sides. He appreciated that it was still long enough to run his fingers through but professional enough to appease the council members.

His shoulders released, feeling a little more at ease. "I actually like it. Thank you."

"That's what I like to hear." She smiled and began to pack up her things. Matisse pulled something out of her bag and extended it to him. "I know your people already have my information, but here's my card with my personal number if you need my services at all in the future."

"I will be sure to have my people reach out to you if I ever have a hair emergency." Liam laughed lightly. "But seriously, thank you."

She curtsied to him before leaving. He stared at himself in the mirror and sighed, wondering if he would recognize himself by the end of this competition.

CHAPTER FIVE
CHARLOTTE

Three days ago

Charlotte sat in the bay window seat in the living room of her family's estate. She basked in the rays of the afternoon sun through the glass with a romance book in hand, grateful she was inside and protected against the late-winter air.

She had read the same paragraph a dozen times, unable to focus on the words on the page. Ideas ran through her mind as to how she could solve her inheritance situation—how she could find someone to marry her in less than three months.

It had been two days since King Henry's funeral, where Jules had told her she'd found the perfect solution. One that would allow her the opportunity to get married on her short timeline. She said she was waiting on something to be official before she shared details and that she'd be in touch soon.

Charlotte still wondered how she planned to find a man in such a short time. She knew two days wasn't really that long of a wait, but worry was starting to consume her.

If only there was an online dating site for royalty.

Charlotte had once expected to easily find her prince charming, since she had been born into a titled family. The dream had brushed her fingertips, so close for the taking in the privilege of her position. But with the loss of girlhood, so went the lost dreams of fairy tales. It took work to find a partner, and being royal only made things harder.

She wished she could simply ask Jules what she planned, but Charlotte wanted to give her space to grieve and support Barrett through his time of mourning.

Charlotte's phone buzzed, and she set her book down to look at the notification. It was from the *Royal Inquisitor* news app.

Who will be Wistonia's next queen? We can only hope it's someone who can whip Liam into shape.

Of course it was another article about Liam. The news from the Wistonian Royal Press had taken the world by storm. She already knew about Barrett abdicating, because she had been present at the dinner when he had announced his love for Jules and gave up the throne. But she'd never expected Liam would announce he would be hosting a televised dating show to find his bride.

The idea of losing her chance with him—the person she'd been harboring a crush on for the last few years—hurt her heart more than she was willing to let on.

Maybe Jules had been secretly referring to her joining the competition. Or maybe Jules was planning on having her host her own version of the same show.

Those thoughts had nausea swirling in her stomach. Her anxiety was like a train driving full steam ahead, impossible to stop and hard to ignore.

She closed her eyes and took a deep, steadying breath. But nothing could stop her racing heart or wandering thoughts.

I'll just text her. Surely that won't be too bothersome.

Charlotte: Hey Jules! I've been thinking about you and the Wistonian royal family. I hope you're doing okay. I also have a quick question…can you fill me in yet on your idea for my situation?

The weight on Charlotte's chest lightened a smidge when she hit send. She grabbed the book she had been reading and wiggled deeper into the soft cushions as she opened to the page where she had left off. If there was one sure way to cheer her up, it was reading a romantic comedy.

Before she could begin reading again, she saw a notification light up on her phone. She picked it up and saw Jules had already texted back.

Her speedy response reminded her that Jules was a true friend. That they were always there for each other, no matter what the other was going through. That it was always okay to ask for help when you needed it.

Jules: Thank you. It has been a hard few days, but things are getting better!

Jules: Everything is falling into place! I will send over the details to your secretary now.

Charlotte sent back a quick message expressing her gratitude as relief flooded her. She hurried to their secretary's office. When she was about to open the door, her father walked out, making her jump back a step.

He held up a handful of papers and let out an exasperated breath. "You're going back to Wistonia?"

"Yes." She tried to make the word sound like more of a statement than a question, not wanting her father to feel like he had the upper hand.

"I find it shocking that the King's Council suggested you compete for Liam in this dating show."

Charlotte struggled to get her mouth to form any words.

I'm joining the competition to marry Liam?

She attempted to pull herself together—to play it cool and act like she already knew what was going on. "Isn't this what you wanted? For me to find someone to marry by my thirtieth birthday?"

Her father's lips were pressed into a thin line. "Keep in mind that all of this will be televised. I don't want to see anything negative about you in the media."

"You know I can't control what the paparazzi says. It's their job to stir up drama."

"And it's your job to make sure you don't embarrass our family name."

Amaryllis. Buttercup. Chrysanthemum.

Having no energy to argue, she muttered, "Yes, Father."

He handed her the stack of papers and left the room without another word.

She fled out the back door of the house, not bothering to find a coat, and ran to a bench overlooking the land behind their estate. The late-winter breeze brushed along her face, and she shivered, pulling her cardigan more tightly around her.

The crisp, fresh air startled her with the realization that this was her last chance.

I'm going to be a contestant on Royally Yours, *vying for Liam's heart.*

Excitement flooded through her, knowing she was getting a real chance to marry by her thirtieth birthday. But a sinking feeling also settled in her gut as she wondered how she was going to get through this.

Charlotte had already been rejected by one Wistonian prince, and that had been hard, but it had been the best choice for everyone in the end. However, she didn't know how she would get through rejection from the prince who already had a slight hold on her heart.

It had been hard enough seeing images of Liam in the media with other women over the years. *I don't know how I'm going to survive watching him date eleven other women right in front of my face. Liam's only ever treated me as a friend.*

But Charlotte knew she needed to follow through with this. This truly was the only viable option that she had come across in the past week. And the opportunity that Liam *might* choose her at the end of this was worth the risk.

She read over the information on the papers Jules had sent over. The competition would last for a little under three months—the perfect timeline for her to marry by her thirtieth birthday and before Liam's ninety-day period to marry was up. Charlotte would need to arrive at the palace in three days for a welcome ball.

Three days, she gasped, covering her mouth with her hand.

She hurried back inside and packed enough bags for the foreseeable future, her thoughts running a million miles a minute. The biggest risk in joining the competition weighed in Charlotte's mind, settling in as an aching headache.

I only hope I can come out of this competition with my heart still in one piece.

CHAPTER SIX
THE ROGUES

Two days ago

It was always meant to be me.
A mere seven minutes is the only reason it's not.
But I will take the Wistonian throne.
Step one is already complete, with Barrett having abdicated the throne.
Now step two is in motion.

CHAPTER SEVEN
LIAM

Earlier That Day

Liam stood, looking out the front windows of the palace. He leaned his forehead against the window, appreciating the cold feel of it against his skin. A beautiful array of light-pink and purple hues filled the sky as the sun peeked over the mountains without a cloud in sight. The beautiful view felt like a promise of new beginnings was on the horizon.

I need all the new beginnings I can get.

Today was a big day. Today, twelve women would walk into the palace for the competition. And by the time it was over, he would ask one of them to be his wife. And then he would be king.

He wasn't scared of the idea of becoming king. Liam had always *wanted* to be king.

But I don't know how to become king without my father here to train me. Yes, I have Barrett, but he's planning his wedding, and I can't depend on him for everything.

Then his thoughts went to the twelve women who would be arriving at the palace tonight. He shuddered, locking his gaze on the mountains.

These weren't going to be just any women. They were all women of royal standing who were used to fancy things and constant attention. Women who would likely be high maintenance and expect a great deal from him. Women who wanted expensive champagne and to show up on his arm at royal balls in gifted designer gowns. Women who would not see him as more than Prince Liam. He needed a wife to see him as just…Liam.

As the shining sun thawed the winter grounds, palace workers seemed to crawl out of the woodwork like mice. They bustled around, dusting every nook and cranny, mopping the floors, steaming the curtains, and readjusting every vase. He knew that by the time they were done, everything would look absolutely spotless and welcoming for the women who would be staying here for the next few months.

Liam noticed Wadsworth coordinating things across the room, and the butler made his way over after seeing him.

"Good morning, Your Highness. May I get some breakfast prepared for you?"

"Just a small, traditional breakfast, please. I'll take it in the men's sitting room. Thank you, Wadsworth."

Liam demolished his potatoes, eggs, bacon, and biscuit with jam in record time as he reread letters his mother had written him.

His late mother, Queen Margaret, had written letters for him and Barrett, trying to prepare for scenarios they may encounter in life without her guidance, were anything to happen to her. Before she passed away, she had delivered the letters to them herself whenever she saw fit. After she passed, Wadsworth had taken on the responsibility.

Continually receiving her words and advice over the years, even after she was gone, was the best gift she could've given him. Liam hoped he would receive another one from her soon. He could use her advice on how to handle this competition.

After he finished eating, he checked the time on his watch and headed to the palace's salon for the second time that week.

That was two times too many, if you asked him.

He hadn't been in the salon room for more than a minute when Matisse walked in like a woman on a mission.

"Well, come on over, Your Highness. Let's get you ready for one of the biggest days of your life." Her sweet, optimistic voice brought a smile to his lips as she waved him over to the chair in front of her.

She styled his hair the way he liked it and lightly powdered his face so he wouldn't appear shiny on camera.

"Makeup? What are you going to do next, Matisse? Put cucumbers on my eyes?"

"My job is to make you look as handsome as possible on camera." A smirk pulled at the corner of her mouth. "You never know, maybe cucumbers could help your eyes pop more," she quipped.

As she continued to work, he thought about the day's events to come. He wasn't too proud to admit that he was excited for the interview he was about to have with Giovanni Geraldo. As a long-time fan of *The Perfect Match*, he was a little bit in awe to have him host his own dating competition. Yet, the thought of watching that show brought tears to his eyes. His throat strained as he bit them back, trying to shove his emotions down.

But he couldn't shut down the memories that filled his mind. All the evenings he, Barrett, and their parents had spent watching episodes of *The Perfect Match* together played through his head. Having his family watch something frivolous like a reality show had brought a sense of normalcy to his life, and they were some of his most treasured memories. But now that his parents were gone, thinking back on those moments revived the sting of their absence.

"You're all done," Matisse said as Barrett walked into the room.

Liam thanked her and walked over to his brother. "What are you doing here? Getting a hair transplant?" He winked.

"Wadsworth told me you were here. I wanted to check on you before your big day."

Liam's face fell as they walked into the hallway. "I thought you would be busy wedding planning with Jules."

"You know I'll always make time for you. Now, tell me what's wrong."

Liam refrained from running his hands through his camera-ready hair—his usual nervous tic. "I don't know if I can do this, man."

"Do what, exactly?"

Liam waved his hands around. "This whole production. I wish Mom were here. She would have absolutely loved all this, and it feels wrong to do it without her and Dad."

Barrett rubbed a hand along his chin, which was now covered in a light layer of stubble. "I'm sorry. I can't imagine everything you're dealing with. But just think of Mom and Dad sitting on the couch in the men's sitting room, watching you as the lead of the show. I can see it now. Mom would be yelling at the screen in shock or excitement at every turn. Dad would roll his eyes but be just as invested and secretly love her antics."

A small laugh escaped Liam as he imagined that scene playing out, knowing he would store that image away for whenever grief threatened to overtake him.

Barrett dug into his pocket and reached out, dropping two small objects into Liam's palm. "I got you something so they would never be too far from you throughout this process."

Liam looked down at the small, gold objects in his hands. In analyzing them up close, he saw that they were cufflinks. Each cufflink had "I love you" engraved on it, one in his mother's handwriting and the other in his father's. He cleared his throat, trying to bite back the wave of emotion the familiar scripts brought with them and pulled his brother into a tight hug.

"Thank you," Liam managed to get out. Barrett helped him put the new cufflinks on the wrists of the white button-up he wore underneath a charcoal-gray suit.

"I'll be busy with cake tastings today—even though we both already know she will select pumpkin as the flavor." Barrett paused to laugh. "But I'm here for you. And so is Jules. You know she would be thrilled to help with any part of this process."

"I know, man. Thank you." Liam let out a long breath, feeling lighter than he had before. "I should get going. I have my press interview with Giovanni soon."

"Don't blow it," Barrett called after him, falling back into their teasing banter as easily as pulling on an old pair of jeans.

With his new cufflinks and his brother's support, Liam felt more ready than ever to take on the events of the day.

Liam arrived just in the nick of time at a large room typically used for storage. His jaw dropped as he looked around. The room had been transformed into a filming space for *Royally Yours*.

One wall was covered in windows that had been cleaned to such perfection they made it appear as if you could reach out and touch the mountain scenery. Beside each window were sheer, gold, floor-to-ceiling curtains that glittered from the incoming light. The white marble floors had been buffed, and plants had been arranged around the room. A light-gray damask sofa had been brought in and set at the front of the room with an identical armchair beside it. They both sat at an angle, leading Liam to believe this was where the host, Giovanni Geraldo, would interview him and the contestants throughout the season.

Liam heard footsteps approaching and turned around as a group of people came into the room, carrying a hoard of camera gear and microphones. They moved around, setting the equipment up as if he wasn't even there. Lindsay walked in and spotted him. She hurried over, her heels clicking with each step.

"Prince Liam, they have everything prepared for your interview with Giovanni. He will enter and sit down in the single chair, and when you hear him introduce you, you'll take your seat on the couch next to him. You'll answer all his questions, on which I already briefed you, and the interview will conclude when the camera crew says, 'That's a wrap.' Any questions?"

"Sounds simple enough." Liam clasped his hands, wringing them together.

"Let's get moving," Lindsay yelled to the crew.

A cameraman called action, and Giovanni walked in wearing his signature interview attire—a black suit with a hot-pink bow tie. He looked at the camera with a wide, genuine smile on his face that never seemed to age. His presence alone was warm and inviting. Liam could see why everyone was always willing to spill their secrets to him.

"Hello and good day to all. I am your host, Giovanni Geraldo. Thank you for tuning in to this special interview today before our big premiere of *Royally Yours* tonight. I am excited to host the biggest and best season of my career." Giovanni leaned forward, emphasizing each word with both hands. "If you haven't seen the news yet, hold on to your seats, because our bachelor this season is none other than Wistonia's Crown Prince Liam. Please join me in offering him a warm welcome."

Liam took that as his cue and walked toward his seat. He paused to shake Giovanni's outstretched hand and gave a small wave to the camera after he sat down.

"Your Highness, it is an absolute honor to join you on your journey to find love this season."

"Please, call me Liam." He smiled as he leaned back easily in the seat, crossing one leg over the other. "I've been watching *The Perfect Match* since I was young. I'm honored to be meeting you—and a little starstruck, if I'm being honest."

Giovanni reeled back with a large gasp, holding his hand to his chest. "Prince Liam is starstruck by me? You flatter me. Now I know I've hit it big." He shot the camera a wink and laughed boisterously. "Let's get to what the people really want...more information about *Royally Yours*."

"Please, ask away."

"One viewer asked if you already know who will be competing for your hand?"

"They didn't want to spoil anything for me, so I'll be just as surprised as all of Fenimore tonight when I see the ladies walking down the stairs." He thought back to what Lindsay had prepped him to mention. "But let's just say I'm very excited for the women to arrive at the welcome ball tonight." He wiggled his eyebrows, the signature move of the Wistonian royal men and their trademarked "jumping eyebrows."

"Oh, you tease us so. I know I speak for everyone when I say we cannot wait to see who the contestants are." Giovanni clasped his hands around his knee. "Now, Liam, I know you mentioned to the press earlier this week that you understand the gravity of your situation. The woman you select at the end of this will not only be your bride but also the Queen of Wistonia. With that in mind, what qualities are you looking for in a partner?"

"Ah, yes." Liam nodded as he thought through his prepared answer. "I, of course, need someone whom I can trust. A woman who has the welfare of the Wistonian people in mind. Ideally, she will be proper and gracious and kind—all qualities my mother embodied." Liam felt a lump growing in his throat that he swallowed back down. He took a deep breath and continued. "And I am looking for someone who is ready and willing to take on this role quickly. I understand this is an expedited process. It's a lot to date someone publicly. Then throw in the fact that the whole courtship will be broadcasted and we will have to marry immediately? It's a lot. But historically, it has been done before. How many people, kings or queens, have taken chances with a betrothed? In this situation, I still have some agency. I hope to find someone I can grow with. I want to make sure the candidates think through what all of this means and that they know they are free to leave if it's not what they want."

"All of Wistonia would be blessed to have another queen as wonderful as Queen Margaret, may God rest her soul. And I must say, I am impressed with you. It's no secret that the media hasn't painted you in the best light over the years. But before me today, I see a man who has grown up and is ready to take the throne. Not to mention, you're very considerate of the feelings of the women who will be arriving in a few hours." Giovanni gave him a friendly smile.

"You're going to get me all choked up over here, Giovanni," Liam teased, playing to the camera as he'd been trained to do. "I really hope this process will allow everyone to see the real Liam, not the one they believe they know."

"Well said, Your Highness."

Giovanni continued asking him question after question, and Liam thought the interview went smoothly. He answered each question expertly based on his prep with Lindsay, and he hoped he was painting himself in a positive light.

Finally, the cameraman gave them a sign to wrap it up, and Liam practically sighed with relief.

"I know we're out of time, so let's end with this. I wouldn't be a good host if I didn't ask you the question all of Wistonia—really, all of Fenimore—is wondering." Giovanni paused for dramatic effect. "Is 'The Royal Heartbreaker' truly up to the challenge of settling down and becoming king?"

Liam laughed off the question, even though it hurt more than he was willing to let on. "I know my love life can be a hot topic in the media. While the saying is that a picture says a thousand words, what is portrayed in a photo is never the full story. I hope that everyone will watch *Royally Yours* with an open mind and that the women coming to the palace will get to know the real me, not the person they think they know. I said it in my press release earlier this week, but I'll say it again. I know I won't be perfect in this journey, but I will be real and put my all into it." He put both feet on the ground and sat up straight. "In regard to becoming king, I can guarantee you that I am prepared to do whatever is needed to lead this country. I can only hope to gain the love and trust of the people of Wistonia."

Giovanni clapped his hands together excitedly. "Bravo! Bravo, Your Highness." He turned his gaze directly toward the camera. "Who are the lucky women competing for Prince Liam's heart? Make sure you tune in tonight at eight to watch the welcome ball live and find out. From the Wistonian Palace, I am Giovanni Geraldo. Thank you."

The recording light disappeared as the cameraman yelled, "That's a wrap."

Liam let out a long exhale, grateful he had survived another interview unscathed.

"It truly was a pleasure speaking with you, Your Highness. I am thrilled to be part of your journey. I have a feeling good things are coming your way." Giovanni shook his hand and offered him a warm smile before leaving the room.

As Lindsay handed Liam his agenda for the rest of the day, he felt more optimistic than he had throughout the process thus far. He looked down at his cufflinks and smiled, knowing his parents would be cheering him on.

CHAPTER EIGHT

CHARLOTTE

Present Day

"Hello, Charlotte."

With Liam's hands wrapped around hers, Charlotte couldn't remember her own name, let alone get her lips to move and form a response. Remembering this moment was being aired live for all of Fenimore to see, she dipped into a low curtsy.

He rubbed his thumb gently across her knuckles, causing a small gasp to escape from her. She peeked up at him through her eyelashes and saw the corners of his mouth tilt up at the sound.

Charlotte prided herself on being able to maintain a perfect façade, but there was no hiding the fact that she was completely and utterly undone by Prince Liam.

Aster. Begonia. Carnation.

After she finally felt some semblance of composure, she rose and responded, "Hello, Your Highness. I never thought I would return to Wistonia so soon."

"Nor did I. Yet, here we are." Liam's eyes glinted with amusement. "I cannot say I'm disappointed." He gestured toward the group of women waiting off to the side, staring with eyes slit in jealousy at their encounter. "Shall we?"

Charlotte wished she could decipher Liam's feelings about her presence in the competition. He seemed happy enough to see her, but he'd also seemed surprised when he'd first seen her, like she was the last person he'd expected to see.

She took his proffered arm, and whispers amongst the other women hushed as they approached. Charlotte released her hold on Liam's arm as the show's host, Giovanni Geraldo, walked over to the group. She glanced around, trying to find a place to sit, when she made eye contact with a blonde with a kind smile who patted the open space beside her. Charlotte shot her an appreciative look and quickly took a seat next to her.

"Welcome, ladies. And hello to all those watching at home." Giovanni waved directly at the camera and then turned back to face the group of women. "Now that all twelve of you beautiful women have arrived, may I formally present your bachelor, His Royal Highness, Prince Liam of Wistonia."

Charlotte joined in with the other women, politely clapping. She gazed around and noticed a few of the girls sat up straighter as the cameras turned to them, attempting to flaunt their…more feminine assets. Stifling an eye roll, she turned her attention back to the host.

"Tonight, we will have a welcome ball where you'll have the opportunity to dance with Prince Liam and get to know him better. When you're not dancing, I recommend getting to know the other contestants. You never know, you may find your new best friend. Or you may find a competitor you want to keep a close eye on. As the saying goes, *keep your friends close and your enemies closer.*" He looked directly into the camera for dramatic effect.

"To our viewers at home, thank you so much for watching the premiere of *Royally Yours*. You can follow us on social media for fun behind-the-scenes teasers throughout the week. But make sure you tune in every Tuesday at eight to be royally entertained as we watch Prince Liam's journey to find love…and see the dreaded elimination ceremonies. Do you already have a favorite? Let us know who they are, using the hashtag #RoyallyYours on your favorite social media platform. For now, keep watching to see some of these lovely ladies dance with His Royal Highness." Turning back to Liam and the group of women, he proclaimed, "Let the ball commence."

Charlotte watched as Raina—who wore a red dress with a blush-inducing neckline—sauntered over to Liam to ask him to dance. Charlotte faintly remembered her from a horseback outing last fall, and based on that experience, Raina was bound to be trouble of the flirtatious variety.

She had to look away as the music started and they danced so closely that you couldn't fit a sheet of paper between them. Turning to face the woman who had invited her to sit beside her, she introduced herself.

"Hi, I'm Charlotte." She extended her hand, and the woman shook it.

"I'm Bridgette. You're from Findorra, right?"

Charlotte nodded.

"I'm from Westridge, right along the coast."

"That's one of my favorite places to visit," Princess Rosalie said. "Sorry, I didn't mean to interrupt your conversation."

Charlotte pushed herself off the couch and pulled her into a hug. She'd been to countless events with Rosalie since she also lived in Findorra. At least there was one person in the competition she knew she could trust.

"Hi, Rosalie, please join us." Charlotte gestured to their couch, and Bridgette moved over to make room.

"I don't believe I've had the pleasure of meeting you, Your Highness. I'm Bridgette."

"Please, call me Rosalie."

The women continued to talk, and while Charlotte paid attention to what they were saying, her eyes kept being drawn to the dance floor, watching Liam dance with girl after girl.

After about an hour, Liam walked over to their group, and all of them perked up.

"Charlotte, would you like to go talk?"

She stood and accepted his proffered arm. "Of course, Your Highness."

When they were far enough from everyone, he whispered, "Your Highness, huh?"

Charlotte shrugged. "It *is* your title."

"Yes." They sat down on the couch in the corner of the room, secluded from where the other ladies were talking and eating hors d'oeuvres. "I thought that we were good enough friends for you to call me Liam."

"We are. I didn't want the other women to get jealous of our familiarity."

"They'll all be calling me Liam soon enough. I'll marry one of you, after all."

His words brought a blush to her cheeks.

"I wanted to apologize about what happened at my father's funeral. I was coming to speak with you when Lindsay pulled me away for the press release. And life since then has obviously been a little crazy." He motioned around him with a smirk.

"You don't need to apologize, Liam." She set her hand on his arm and gave it a squeeze. "I haven't had the chance to tell you how sorry I am about your father."

"Thank you." He nodded, but he averted his gaze—obviously not ready to talk about it yet.

Before she was able to ask Liam how he was truly doing, the show's producer, Alec, strode back into the room.

"Attention, everyone," he said, waiting for the voices in the room to quiet. "Unfortunately, tonight's ball has come to an end. You are all expected for breakfast at eight tomorrow morning. For the duration of your stay at the Wistonian Palace, you will have a lady's maid to assist you with anything you might need. They are waiting outside of the ballroom to introduce themselves and escort you to your rooms. If you have any issues in your time here, please don't hesitate to speak with a production crew member." Alec nodded and excused himself from the room.

"I'm supposed to meet with Alec to go over some production things." Liam stood and started walking toward the ballroom doors. Stopping just before he reached them, he called back to her, "I'll see you tomorrow. Have a good night."

Charlotte made her way back to her friends and walked out with them.

"We didn't even get to dance with him." Bridgette sighed.

"Next time, I'm sure." Rosalie patted her gently on the shoulder. She stood and ran her fingers through her auburn curls. "Shall we, ladies?"

Charlotte and Bridgette looped their arms through Rosalie's, and together they walked out of the ballroom.

Charlotte's gaze was pulled to the right at the sound of her name being called. Her eyes widened in pleasant surprise as she spotted a familiar face in the crowd. "Maya, are you my lady's maid again?"

"I am." Maya nodded, pulling at the bottoms of her braids and dipping into a curtsy.

They arrived at the guest wing on the second floor, and Maya stopped in front of the room Charlotte had occupied only a few weeks ago.

I can't believe it's only been four weeks since I was last here.

She walked into her room, expecting it to be the same as it had been. What she hadn't anticipated was for the space to have been totally transformed into her dream room. The old, emerald coverlet on the bed had been replaced with a blush-pink pinch-pleat duvet—her favorite color.

A small gasp escaped her lips when Charlotte saw that a built-in bench had been installed beneath the large window with a cozy cushion and a dozen pillows. The base of the bench had been turned into bookshelves. Her fingers grazed over the spines as she read titles written by some of her favorite authors and others she had heard of but hadn't had the chance to read yet.

On her nightstand sat a vase of yellow roses that brightened the entire space.

"How did—" Charlotte's eyes darted around the room again, in awe of how perfectly *her* it was.

"Jules selected everything for you. Is there something you would like for me to change?" Maya asked.

"Please don't change a thing. It's utterly perfect." She pulled her phone out and sent a quick thank-you text to Jules.

Relief flooded Maya's face. "I'm so glad you like it."

She took off her gown while Maya prepared a bath and set out a pair of her pajamas on the bathroom counter.

Charlotte thanked Maya before dismissing her for the evening. She got into the bath and breathed in the calming, lavender aroma. She leaned back and laid her head on the pillow Maya had placed in the tub, letting out a deep breath, trying to let the scent and warm water ease the tension from her shoulders.

Putting on a more polished version of herself all day had been exhausting. But what was more exhausting was her inability to decipher Liam's feelings about her participation in the competition. She couldn't deny that she needed him just as much as he needed a wife.

This might be my only option. My last chance to get my inheritance. Without that, the charities I love could suffer. Maybe we can come to a mutually beneficial arrangement.

She drained the tub and slipped into the pair of silk pajamas Maya had left out for her. Charlotte quickly brushed her teeth before cozying up in bed under the soft, pink sheets that had to be the highest quality thread count.

As she started to drift to sleep, she thought about the children she'd worked with in the orphanage. About how she would do anything for them. She promised herself she would see this competition through—for them. Maybe Liam would agree their relationship could be mutually beneficial for them. But she would have to keep her feelings out of the mix.

I will not let his suave nature, flirtatious comments, athletic physique, or his bright-blue eyes draw me in.

Maybe if she told herself that enough times, she would actually believe it.

Charlotte moved around the setup of cameras to enter the main dining room just before eight o'clock. The grandeur of the room didn't go unnoticed, from the crystal chandelier to a giant handcrafted oak table that had to be at least twenty feet long. Although it was a beautiful room, she honestly missed the smaller family dining room they had used during her and Jules's stay at the palace. It had felt much cozier and intimate than the large table before her.

Her eyes scanned the room, and she noted that most of the women were already there. Although, Liam was noticeably absent. As she was trying to figure out where to sit, Bridgette caught her eye and waved her over to where she and Rosalie were sitting. She sat down in an empty chair beside Rosalie, thankful she might actually have some friends to go through this experience with.

"Have you met Sienna?" Bridgette motioned to the brunette beside her.

"Didn't we meet at one of Rosalie's balls?" Sienna asked.

Charlotte's eyes lit up in recognition. "That's right. You attended with—" Her voice dropped off. "Sorry. It's nice to see you again."

Pink flooded Sienna's cheeks. "No, it's all right. That's when I was still dating Spencer." She sighed as she let her chin fall into her palm.

The woman sitting next to Sienna turned toward her, obviously having been eavesdropping. "Yeah, whatever happened between you and Spencer? I want all the juicy details."

"And you are…?" Bridgette asked.

"Tiffany."

Sienna's eyes darted between the nosy girl and Charlotte, Rosalie, and Bridgette. She sighed and got a far-off look as she said, "Last Christmas, he told me he couldn't date me anymore but didn't really explain why. He stopped responding to my messages shortly after, and I haven't heard from him since. I did see him a few months ago at a charity event, but he avoided me the whole night." She shrugged, taking in a breath. "I've moved on, though."

"I'm so sorry. That's awful, but we're glad you're here." Charlotte gave her what she hoped was a sympathetic smile.

"I'm happy to be here." Sienna looked toward the empty seat at the head of the table. "Where do you think Liam is?"

"That's a good question," Charlotte said as she looked around. Women around the table, whose names she had yet to learn, were starting to complain about his tardiness.

"You're telling me I missed out on an extra thirty minutes of beauty rest for this?"

"Maybe what they say in the media about him is true…"

"Wait until my father hears about this."

The woman said it just like Draco Malfoy in *Harry Potter*. The reference pulled a snort out of Charlotte, which she quickly covered by clearing her throat. She turned her attention back to the group of ladies around her.

"Are your rooms here as dreamy as mine?"

The ladies talked enthusiastically about their living arrangements at the palace. As Charlotte began to speak about hers, Liam finally arrived.

"I apologize for the delay, ladies. Please begin." He clapped, signaling the wait staff to bring out the food.

Plates of egg-white omelets filled with veggies, oatmeal, and turkey bacon were delivered to each person in unison. An overly fake laugh caught Charlotte's attention, and she wasn't at all surprised to see that it came from Lady Raina of Bristol.

Charlotte knew Raina being overly flirty with Liam wasn't much of a reason to dislike her, but there was just something about her she didn't fully trust.

"Your Highness, may I ask if you know what this process will look like? Will we have individual or group dates? How will it all work?" Tiffany asked, batting her eyelashes.

"Our first major group event will be the State Dinner. I know it doesn't allow us much room to talk, but it's a good opportunity for you to see some of the responsibilities of being the queen of Wistonia. There will be plenty of other group dates to come. I know we will have many chances for one-on-one dates as well. In the meantime, I plan to spend as much of my free time with you as my schedule allows."

Tiffany nodded and then whispered with two of the women sitting near her. Many of the other ladies began to talk excitedly about the prospect of spending time with Liam and what dresses they would wear to the State Dinner.

Charlotte ate small bites of her omelet and attempted to pay attention to the ladies sitting next to her, but her eyes kept being drawn back to Liam. Her lower lip throbbed from biting it in frustration as she attempted to push down the twinges of jealousy that she felt whenever Liam shot his signature smile at someone else.

She had no right to be jealous of Liam flirting with other women. He was dating all of them, after all. But her fragile heart found it difficult to watch the man she had adored from afar courting other women right in front of her. It was at that moment she made a promise to herself.

I, Charlotte Elizabeth Croft, will enjoy my time here. I will not let watching Liam courting other women get to me. I will not let his words or actions have control over my happiness.

"Charlotte?" Sienna's sweet voice cut through her thoughts.

"I'm sorry. I didn't quite catch your question."

Bridgette, Sienna, and Rosalie shared a knowing look.

"I asked what you are most looking forward to during our time here?"

"Honestly? Getting to know you all better." Charlotte smiled genuinely at them, but the smile quickly disappeared when she saw their shocked expressions. She quickly added, "And any opportunity I get to spend with Liam, of course."

Her eyes drifted back to him at the opposite end of the table, laughing freely as he engaged in a conversation with a beautiful woman with curly brown hair. As much as she told herself it didn't bother her, the lie tasted bitter in her mouth.

This is going to be more difficult than I thought.

CHAPTER NINE
LIAM

Liam arrived at the women's sitting room door, knowing he needed to start getting to know all the ladies. And times like this, when no cameras would be present, were even more valuable.

He had fewer than three months remaining to find the person he would marry. Even though he was looking for a good partner, not a love match, he needed to pick someone whom he would trust to lead Wistonia alongside him. That was a decision he would not take lightly.

When he entered the room, Liam scrunched up his nose at the overwhelming smell of hairspray and an excessive amount of perfume. He felt the beginning of a headache coming on.

Liam considered trying to escape, unsure if he was ready to handle so many women at once. Before he could leave, there were more women than he could count standing in front of him, all trying to talk at the same time. It was a royal headache in the making.

How am I ever going to juggle this many women at once?

While he did plan on getting to know the women here, he'd also hoped that doing so would help him figure out who he would want to eliminate over time. The first task on his personal agenda was weeding out who was here for the wrong reasons.

Women who simply wanted the crown would *have* to go. He wasn't going to deal with that again. And women who were here looking for true love with him…they would have to go, too. Because he still had no plans to ever fall in love again. Alec had told Liam last night after the welcome ball that he would have an elimination ceremony every other week where he would need to send home at least one woman. He would need to eliminate the women slowly to show his people that he was taking this competition—and the women's feelings—seriously.

But surely, in getting to know all the ladies, there would be a woman in the bunch who would make the perfect partner for him. Someone who understood that love wouldn't be part of the picture and who embodied the qualities of a true queen—just like his mother. He bit back a groan, realizing he sounded exactly like Barrett had when he'd been trying to find a wife.

"Ladies, it will be much easier to get to know you if I talk to each of you separately." He extended his hand to Lady Tiffany and pulled her away to a set of chairs in the corner of the room to speak with her first.

"Now that the cameras aren't here, you can finally tell me how excited you are that I'm here." Tiffany eyed him demurely, her talon-like nails digging into his arm. She got out of her chair and sat on his knee, draping her arm around his shoulders and playing with the collar of his shirt.

His lips twisted to the side. It was going to be more difficult to survive these ladies than he thought.

A new girl cut in during every conversation he had, making it hard to talk about anything beyond pleasantries.

He had a newfound respect for all the leads of *The Perfect Match*.

I have no clue how they keep all the women and conversations separate in their minds.

After he was sure he had spoken with everyone who was in the room, he fled to the hallway. Leaning against the door, he let out a deep sigh and ran his hands through his hair.

"Do you need to escape?"

♛

Liam didn't need to turn around to know the voice was Charlotte's.

He had been completely thrown off by her arrival the night before. Honestly, she had been throwing him off for years.

They had practically grown up together, but the first time Charlotte had caught his eye romantically had been when he was thirteen and she was seventeen. She'd come to the Wistonian Palace for one of their annual balls. She had walked in wearing a beautiful blue dress, looking just like Cinderella arriving at the ball. He hadn't been able to take his eyes off her.

Later in the evening, he had been outside on the balcony, getting some fresh air, when some of the boys in attendance had teased him. He had been a late bloomer and much shorter than all of them, which had led to him being made fun of in his early teenage years. After one of the boys poured a drink on his head, Charlotte came out and quietly scolded them. He never found out what she'd said, but they'd never picked on him again.

Charlotte had told Liam to not let whatever they said get to him, and then she'd asked him to dance. He had been shocked that the stunningly perfect girl would want to dance with him at all but especially in his current state. He motioned to his body covered in liquid, but she didn't seem to mind that he was a mess and still led him to the dance floor. Despite the lemonade dripping down his face and suit jacket, she still held tightly to him as he twirled her around the dance floor. Her laugh was all he heard, and in a room full of people, she was all he saw.

After that night, he couldn't seem to get her out of his mind. His thoughts had constantly wandered to her. His eyes had been drawn to her at every event they'd both attended. But she had been like an unattainable fantasy. He couldn't imagine a girl four years his senior would ever be interested in him in that way.

Later that year, everything had changed after the unexpected loss of his mom in a horseback riding accident. When she had passed, Liam's heart had literally felt like it had been torn out of his body and ripped to shreds. His grief had been raw. Charlotte had been there for him at her funeral, but when she'd continued to show up at the palace to try to cheer him and Barrett up, he had ignored her, avoiding the feelings she always stirred up in him when she was near. Once the traditional mourning period for his mother was over, Liam had still felt the heavy weight of her loss like it was the day she died.

To focus on something else besides his grief, Liam had put all his energy into bettering himself. He had met with a grief counselor and found some new coping techniques. Liam had also had his father hire a personal trainer to help him develop a more muscular physique, run every spare chance he'd gotten, and finally hit his growth spurt at eighteen. Eventually, he was taller than all the boys who had always teased him and had a six-pack of abs to go with it. With his new physique, he hadn't been able to keep women away.

After everything with Mila, he'd dated more casually. By the time he was twenty-two, the media had published photos of him with so many different women that all the magazines wouldn't be able to fit on a bookshelf. That was when the media had officially dubbed him as "The Royal Heartbreaker."

Whenever another negative article was posted about him or a picture of him with another woman surfaced, the same question always came to his mind—one he hated to admit, even to himself.

What does Charlotte think about this?

No matter how hard he tried to guard his heart, Charlotte still seemed to have a grip on it that wouldn't let go. When she'd stayed at the palace the last few months to assist his brother with a local school renovation project, he had tried to avoid her and built up walls through a stand-offish façade. But the longer she'd stayed, the more often she'd seemed to find him and spend time with him, wedging her way back into his life—and right back into his heart.

She probably just looks at me like a little brother. But she did come to the competition knowing I'll choose one of the ladies to marry at the end of this. Maybe she does feel similarly.

He shook his head like it was an *Etch-a-Sketch* board, trying to remove the thought. She was likely oblivious to the hold she had on him. That his heart would be putty in her hands if she wanted it to be. But he couldn't let that happen. He *wouldn't* let that happen. That was why he needed to eliminate her from the competition as soon as humanly possible.

If my heart allows me to let her leave.

Liam cleared his throat and turned around to face Charlotte. "Sorry, what did you say?"

"I asked if you need to escape."

He ruffled his hair as he sighed. "How did you know?"

"I can only imagine how taxing it must be for you to have to talk to everyone in the room."

The exhaustion hit him right after she spoke, as if she could understand him and his needs before they even arose. He shrugged, unsure of what to say.

She waved him over and whispered, "Come on."

His feet followed her of their own accord, like she held an invisible string that pulled him to her. She opened the door to the men's sitting room, and he followed her, quickly shutting the door behind them.

"How are you feeling?" Charlotte asked as she sat down gracefully on the brown leather couch.

"You're coming in with the hard-hitting questions." Liam laughed.

"I think we've known each other long enough to cut the pleasantries."

He nodded. "We're definitely past that point." After he sat down beside her, he kicked his feet up on the table in front of them. "It's an interesting situation to be in."

She nudged his arm with her shoulder. "And?" she prodded.

"I don't need to unload this on you."

"You need someone. Let me be that someone for you," she said, then averted her eyes and quickly added, "during my time here, of course…as your friend."

He pushed down the feelings that threatened to surface. *You need to pick someone safe. Someone whom you could never fall in love with. Someone who is one hundred percent not her.*

Liam knew he should say no. He was rarely vulnerable with anyone, not wanting to show an ounce of weakness. So, opening up to the one person he was trying to steer clear of was like a recipe for disaster. Yet, words were tumbling out of his mouth as if it had a mind of its own. "I would like that."

Maybe eliminating her quickly wasn't the best path. She could be a friend, a confidant throughout the process. And then he would send her home when the time was right. He could only hope this decision wouldn't come back to bite him.

Liam wracked his brain, trying to put into words how he had been feeling the past few weeks. "It's been a lot all at once. On top of trying to learn how to rule the throne, now my dating life will be under further scrutiny as all of Fenimore watches." He leaned back into the couch and sighed. "I just feel like I've lost all control over my life. I absolutely hate feeling powerless. I want the control back. I *need* it back. I want to be able to rule and protect the people of Wistonia. And I feel like I can't do that when who I date is out of my control."

Charlotte leaned over and laid her hand on his forearm. He was thankful he was wearing a long-sleeve shirt to hide the goosebumps that followed her touch.

"First of all, I have to say I am so impressed by you and how well you've held yourself together through the past few weeks. I truly think you're doing a wonderful job. No one has been in this situation before. I mean, who would've thought there would ever be a reality television show where all of Fenimore gets to watch their future king choose his bride? It's wild, when you really think about it. You're paving your own path in all of this. If you feel like you don't have a lot of say in things, then I would say you should make your voice heard. You're the future king, for goodness' sake. It's okay to take back some of the control. It's your life, and you have to live with the outcome of this competition." She squeezed his arm and then settled her hands in her lap.

 Liam's eyes lit up as he gazed into hers. "You're right. I need to remind them that I'm about to be king and that I want a say in how all this plays out." He scooted over and gave her a side hug, immediately regretting it when the divine scent of her floral perfume hit him. In a room full of women, the smell of perfume had been overwhelming. But with Charlotte, it was intoxicating. A literal breath of fresh air to Liam. A reminder of her femininity and beauty that he was trying very hard to forget about.

 He stood abruptly and slowly backed away. "Thank you for speaking with me. I hadn't realized how much I needed to let all of that out." Liam paused. "Also, I know how much you love reading. Jules mentioned she already had books put in your room, but please know you're welcome to borrow any books in the library." He continued walking backward. "I really must go. I have much to do, being the future king and all." Liam backed into a table and hissed under his breath, catching a vase before it hit the floor. He set it back on the table and gave Charlotte a quick bow before rushing out of the room.

After he made it safely to his study, he leaned against the door and breathed heavily.

He didn't know what had come over him. Liam prided himself on his ability to converse with women. He was a flirt, and he was good at it. But all his abilities had gone out the window at the scent of Charlotte's perfume.

I need to be more cautious around her.

Otherwise, the walls he had built up were bound to come crumbling down.

CHAPTER TEN
CHARLOTTE

Charlotte's eyes followed Liam as he left the room. His hasty exit left her wondering if she had said something to upset him, but she shook her head and pushed down the worry.

I'm not concerned about his response. Not anymore. I'm like Ross from that scene in Friends. *It's fine. I'm fine. Totally fine.*

She left and stopped outside the door to the women's sitting room. Charlotte had never been the type of girl to have a ton of female friends. The only true friend she had made was Jules. But she hoped she would form true friendships with some of the ladies here.

Most of her "friends" growing up had really been people she was forced to be around because of her role as the daughter of a duke and duchess. They spoke kindly to her at events but either didn't talk to her otherwise or only talked to her to try to gain something because of her rank. Whether it was publicity or information or an invite to a ball, she never was quite able to trust those around her.

Her dating life wasn't any different. She'd had enough dates with men who were only after her money to know better by now.

She had learned to put on a front—one that was kind and welcoming to those around her but allowed her to guard who she really was so no one would get close enough to hurt her.

So, while she could easily walk around the women's sitting room and converse with ease and look happy while doing it, it was an exhausting endeavor for her. Charlotte took one more moment to mentally prepare herself before entering the women's sitting room.

It looked like just about every woman was there now. Little cliques had formed throughout the space. Her eyes were immediately drawn to Bridgette, Sienna, and Rosalie sitting at a table, drinking tea. They waved her over, and she held up her pointer finger, letting them know she would be there in a little bit.

Charlotte approached the group of women standing nearest to her. They were honestly the women who intimidated her the most, with their flirtatious personalities and bodies they flaunted like they didn't lack an ounce of confidence.

"Hello, ladies. Do you mind if I join?"

Tiffany looked her up and down as if she were a poodle being judged in a dog show. Tiffany slightly raised her chin and whispered to one of the girls next to her before she turned her attention back to Charlotte. "Sure. You're Lady Charlotte of Findorra, right?"

Charlotte raised one eyebrow, impressed. "That's correct. I'm sorry, but I don't know all your names."

"You won't forget them after you know them," Tiffany said like a sly little minx.

She didn't want to know if that was a threat or a promise. "I would be honored to have an introduction."

"I'm Lady Tiffany of Meldovia." She gestured to the brunette woman to her left whom she had whispered to earlier. "This is Lady Piper of Rothwell." Then she waved to the redhead to her right. "And this is The Honorable Olive of Meldovia."

Charlotte curtsied to all of them, though none of the ladies returned it. "It's a pleasure to meet you all." Before she could say another word, Raina sauntered over to their group.

"Hello, Lady Raina," Tiffany hissed through clenched teeth.

"Did you all know my name means 'queen'? What I'm saying is you all should start preparing to bow down to me," Raina said, her hands on her hips.

Charlotte waited for her to laugh, thinking it was a joke, but Raina's eyes darted to the ceiling in an air of superiority as if they were all beneath her.

"So, your name would literally be Queen Queen? Sounds a bit redundant, if you ask me," Tiffany replied with pursed lips.

Charlotte cringed. This whole interaction brought her back to the kind of cruel comments girls would make in high school, and she was *not* here for it. These women were all in their twenties and competing to be queen. They needed to act like it.

Tiffany continued with a hand on her hip. "You should be the one preparing yourself. Because we are Tiffany, Olive, and Piper, and we will end up on T-O-P, top." The three of them did some sort of group handshake that included them hitting their hands together, swiping their hair over their shoulders, and shimmying.

Yeah. Definitely, *Mean Girls* vibes.

"Ugh," Raina moaned as she flipped her own dark hair over her shoulder. She strutted to a different group, likely hoping to tell them the same line about the meaning of her name.

Charlotte had underestimated the conniving nature of some of the women in the competition. It appeared cutthroat alliances were already forming. And this was one of those circumstances when someone might do just about anything to get the crown. She made a mental note to be more conscious of what was going on around her and to watch out for any women who might be the backstabbing kind.

"Excuse me." Charlotte curtsied to Tiffany, Piper, and Olive and walked over to the table where Bridgette, Sienna, and Rosalie sat. She could already tell these three were going to be her ride-or-die people here. They had presented themselves as kind-hearted, trustworthy women who were trying to make friends as they got to know Liam.

Charlotte sat in the linen upholstered chair beside Rosalie and reached for a chocolate tart from the center of the table, eating it in one bite.

"Let me guess, you talked to the 'TOP' crew?" Bridgette asked with a laugh.

Charlotte held her hand over her mouth as she laughed. "I did. It made me even more grateful for the fast friendships I've found with you." She smiled at Rosalie, Bridgette, and Sienna in turn, and they all nodded in agreement.

"Do you think we'll get to spend more time with Liam soon?" Sienna asked. "He seems really busy with all his royal duties."

"I honestly don't really care." Bridgette shrugged. "I'm here for a good time."

"I want to have a good time, too. But I also want to see if there could be anything between Liam and me. I mean, have you seen the man? He's like a Greek god." Sienna fanned her face with her hand.

Charlotte's heart rate increased as a bitter feeling rose within her. *No one else is allowed to think about my man like that.*

Alec walked into the room before she could respond. All the women quieted so he could make his announcement.

"Good afternoon, ladies. I'm excited to announce that tonight you will have your first formal dinner here at the palace. Prince Liam will be there, of course, along with Prince Barrett; his new fiancée, Jules; their cousin, James; and most members of the King's Council. I expect you all will want ample time to get ready before the dinner starts in two hours, so…"

Before he could finish, most of the women were rushing from the room to go prepare for the evening. Charlotte and her friends stood from their table and headed toward the door.

"Thank you, Alec," Charlotte whispered to him as she passed, earning a smile from him.

When she reached her room, Maya was already bustling around, pulling dresses from the wardrobe and holding up different accessories to pair with them.

As she put on a fitted, deep-plum gown for the evening, Charlotte thanked the heavens she didn't have to go through this competition completely alone.

Dinner had assigned seating, and Charlotte hadn't been surrounded by the best company. To her left was Lord

Stephen Howard, who was a member of the King's Council. He had always given her the heebie-jeebies with his sly smirk that seemed to be permanently plastered to his face. One of the other women in the competition—The Honorable Cora—sat on her right, and she wasn't much better company.

All night long, Cora made snide remarks to Charlotte.

"It takes a certain kind of lady to pull off the slicked-back hair look." Cora patted her arm. *"How brave you are to try."*

"What an...interesting perspective to have, Charlotte." Cora *rolled her eyes in an exaggerated manner.*

After each comment, Cora would glance over at Liam, all batty-eyed and demure, hiding her true colors.

Liam was at the opposite end of the table, with Raina on one side and Rosalie on the other. A few of the girls had made excuses throughout the evening to walk to where he was sitting and steal a few words with him. He barely had time to enjoy his filet mignon and potatoes au gratin between the constant interruptions.

Not that she noticed.

When the meal was over, Charlotte pushed her seat back from the table and went to stand when she tripped over something on the floor and fell forward, arms flailing. She braced herself for the impact, but it didn't come.

Instead, she felt warm, muscular arms encircle her from behind. *Very* muscular arms. Ones she could be comfortable in forever.

Charlotte didn't need to look up to know it was Liam who had caught her. He pulled her back to his rock-hard chest and found that the racing beat of his heart matched her own. His hands moved to her waist, leaving a trail of fire everywhere they touched.

Liam steadied Charlotte and looked her over. "Are you all right?" he asked in an even-tempered voice, even though his brows were furrowed, showing his concern for her.

"What a klutz." Cora laughed as she spoke to another girl nearby. "She's bound to be one of the first people to leave. There's no way Liam would want a girl like her as queen."

Charlotte felt her cheeks flush at the comment. She looked up at Liam, briefly nodding that she was okay before hurrying back to her bedroom.

She dismissed Maya for the evening. Charlotte didn't want to talk about tonight or the feelings that had tried to rush to the surface when Liam's arms had been wrapped around her.

It didn't mean anything. He was simply being a gentleman.

But when she showed up to breakfast the next morning, Cora wasn't at the table. Even after they'd begun eating, she didn't turn up.

At the end of the meal, Liam cleared his throat. "Some of you may have noticed that Cora is not present this morning. I sent her home, as I will not tolerate any bullying or disrespectful remarks or actions toward myself or any other person here." His eyes wandered around the table and met every gaze except Charlotte's. "I'm not only looking for a wife but the future queen of Wistonia. Rude behavior is unacceptable and not fitting of someone who is being considered to lead this country." He stood and the room stayed silent with all eyes on him. "I have some meetings to attend today, but I look forward to seeing you at dinner. If you'll excuse me." He bowed and walked toward the door, pausing only to give Charlotte a small smile as he passed her.

The women began whispering as soon as he had left the room. Some people griped about how there was a tattler among them. But Charlotte didn't care what anyone said. All she could think of was how Liam had saved her. He had saved her from falling on her face, but he had also sent home the girl who had picked on her all night long.

It brought her back to a certain memory from what felt like a lifetime ago when she had done the same thing for him—saved him from a group of stupid teenage boys at a ball. Then her mind jumped to the memory of when she had first begun to fall for him.

She had realized her feelings weren't platonic at a ball they'd both attended when she was twenty-six and he was twenty-two. Liam had been announced at the top of the stairs as he entered the ballroom, and when Charlotte had looked up at him, something had clicked inside of her. Like a feelings dial had been turned to the maximum level. He was no longer the young prince who was four years younger than her…he was a *man*. A man she would very much like to get to know better.

Charlotte shook her head, trying to forget about her feelings for him. She stood and hurried to the place that would hopefully help her forget all her worries—the gardens.

The moment she took in the view and smelled the flowers, Charlotte's shoulders lifted. Walking through the greenhouse, she immediately felt at ease.

In the corner, she spotted a new flower that hadn't been there the last time she visited. It was a beautiful pinkish-purple color that drew in her attention, even though the flowers were small. Pulling out her phone, she opened one of her favorite apps, All About that Flora. She snapped a picture of the flower, and the app identified it as clary sage.

After reading all the information she could about it, she put her phone back in her pocket and walked next to a bed of forget-me-nots—her favorite flower—in the greenhouse. When she spotted a few weeds, she knelt and began pulling them.

"What're you doing?" a male voice behind her startled her, causing her to jump to her feet and spin around.

"Liam! I'm sorry. I noticed a few weeds, so I removed them."

"No one is supposed to be in the greenhouse." He looked around, but she still noted the emotion clouding his features.

"I didn't know. I can leave now." She looked back at the flowers behind her, taking in the sky-blue petals and yellow centers, and released a deep breath. "They're my favorite flowers. I hope you know I didn't mean to cause any harm."

Liam moved closer to her, his brow lifted in interest. "I didn't know you were into gardening."

"Really? Queen Margaret taught me everything I know."

His eyes turned quizzical, and his voice softened. "My mom?"

She nodded. "Ever since I was a little girl." And she went on to tell him about the time she'd spent with his mother. As she spoke, the memory of the first time the queen had shown her around the garden when Charlotte was only ten years old played out in her mind.

Charlotte poked her head out from behind a garden statue as Queen Margaret called her name.

"You're not in trouble, sweetie."

She stood and shyly wiped her dirty hands on her dress. Her daddy was going to be mad at the mess. But being in the garden was her favorite, and her own father wouldn't let her grow one at home. Her family visited the Wistonian Palace monthly for business matters, and she always found a way to escape outside to look at the beautiful, lush garden whenever they were there.

The queen knelt to be at her level. "Do you love flowers as much as I do?"

Charlotte nodded with a wide grin on her face, revealing a few missing teeth. "Flowers are my favorite. We don't have any at home, but I've read all the books on them from our library."

The queen wrapped an arm around her, guiding her to the greenhouse. "Well, you're always welcome to come out here and spend time in our garden when you visit. I'll teach you everything I know."

"Over the years, your mother taught me the names of all the flowers on the palace grounds and even instructed me on tending to them." Charlotte followed Liam back out to the gardens, closing the greenhouse door behind her. "Gardens have always been my happy place. My father never let me grow one back home, so your mom told me I was welcome to be among the flowers here anytime I wanted. It felt weird coming back after she was gone, but being here makes me feel like I'm with her."

Liam came up beside her and pressed his shoulder into hers as they both looked at the gardens. "I never knew any of that." He ran a hand through his hair and stepped away. "I'm honestly surprised that someone as prim and proper as you doesn't mind getting dirty in the garden."

"There's a lot about me you don't know," Charlotte teased. "Plus, your mother liked gardening too, and she was the most proper lady I ever met."

"Touché."

"Queen Margaret was really my mother figure growing up. My mom is kind, but she's always been so caught up in her philanthropic endeavors and hobbies that she never really made time for me." Charlotte looked off into the distance with a sad smile. "Your mom always made time for me."

Liam sighed as he shifted, moving a little closer to her. "Mom was always good about that. She always made time for everyone and made them feel seen and loved." His eyes darted around like he was trying to find a different topic of conversation. When he finally landed on a spot near the back of the palace, his face pulled into a large grin. "Do you remember that time we were playing tag in the gardens with Barrett? You and I knocked over the fancy statue of my father and broke the head off?"

"Oh my goodness, yes. We were terrified of getting in trouble and were going to blame it on Barrett."

"But we knew they wouldn't believe us since he's such a rule follower, so we blamed it on a bear that came through and tackled it to the ground."

Charlotte's eyes glistened as she laughed at the memory. "There aren't even bears in Wistonia."

Liam laughed with her. "Yeah, that was probably the worst excuse I've ever come up with. And then as punishment, my father made me attend all his meetings with him for a whole month. I never wanted to break anything again after that."

"And now, here you are, about to be King of Wistonia, and you'll have to attend all those meetings for the rest of your life."

"Thankfully I've gained a longer attention span over the years." He glanced at the watch on his wrist. "I have to run.

I've got a meeting in five minutes." Liam started walking back to the palace when he suddenly stopped and looked at her over his shoulder. "You can go in the greenhouse any time while you're here, if it means so much to you. Forget-me-nots were my mother's favorite, too." He did a quick, two-fingered salute and jogged back to the palace.

Charlotte turned around and gazed at the greenhouse, emotion clouding her throat as she tried to stifle tears. She'd already known forget-me-nots were his mother's favorite flower. And that was exactly why they were hers.

CHAPTER ELEVEN
GIOVANNI GERALDO

Once all the ladies were in their seats, the lights illuminated the interview room. A warm hue shimmered throughout the space, dancing off the sheer gold curtains as the light hit them. Giovanni put on an exuberant smile as the crew counted down to when they were recording.

"Gooood evening, everyone. I'm Giovanni Geraldo, the host of *Royally Yours*. We have a special feature for you tonight. I'll be interviewing each of the ladies in contention to become Queen of Wistonia. We'll answer all your burning questions. Shall we introduce them?" The production crew played the sound of roaring applause, and Giovanni beamed at the sound of it. "Let's get to it."

He introduced each woman in the group, leaving time for the camera to pan to them in turn.

Lady Bridgette and the duchess named Gwyneth appeared confident, with a practiced smile.

The Honorable Mariana, Lady Sienna, and The Honorable Liana all kept shy, closed-lip smiles when they were introduced.

Lady Raina tipped her head down slightly and gave a subtle smile while looking directly into the camera, showing off her flirty persona.

The flirty looks at the camera continued when Lady Tiffany, The Honorable Olive, and Lady Piper were introduced. It was like a weirdly choreographed medley of shoulder shimmies and winks as they were all introduced one after the other.

Lady Charlotte and Princess Rosalie stood out to Giovanni as the most polished women. They both nailed the 'royal wave' and shared genuine smiles with the camera without overdoing it.

"Aren't they fabulous?" Giovanni beamed as he gestured to the ladies seated on two long couches opposite him. "As you might have noticed, Prince Liam has already sent home one lady in the competition, The Honorable Cora. You'll learn more about that on the episode." He clapped his hands together in excitement. "Now, let's jump right into the hard-hitting questions." He turned to face Rosalie. "Princess Rosalie, viewers at home are wondering what it's like being the only princess here. Does it give you a leg up on the competition?"

"Definitely not." Rosalie laughed lightly. "While I might understand his role as a prince on a deeper level, I have as much of a shot with Prince Liam as any of the other lovely women here do."

"Might I add something?" Olive rose her hand.

Giovanni nodded. "Of course."

"I do think Rosalie has a bit of an…advantage. I mean, how are the rest of us supposed to compete with a princess?"

Rosalie's face turned a shade of red close to her hair color.

Charlotte jumped in to defend her. "A position doesn't make a person. It's one's qualities and personality that reveal who they truly are. I think anyone who is an honorable and honest person, regardless of their rank or title, would be able to step into the role of queen with grace."

Giovanni watched as Rosalie turned to Charlotte and mouthed, "Thank you."

"Well said, Lady Charlotte. That's the perfect segue into this next viewer question." He glanced at all the ladies. "How are you getting along as a group? Have any friendships or rivalries formed?"

Tiffany jumped in, sharing about the "TOP" crew, and they went on to do their group handshake on national television.

"Splendid." He clapped and smiled through gritted teeth. Giovanni bit back a laugh at what looked like amateur cheerleading choreography. He couldn't show any bias, but times like this made it more difficult.

Raina stood, drawing attention to herself. "I, for one, have made *so* many friends. I guess I'm just easy for them all to love. Hopefully, I'll get some alone time with Liam soon and he'll fall for me just as quickly." She pressed her shoulder to her cheek as she smiled before sitting back on the couch.

Giovanni gave her a tight smile. "Anyone else? What about you, Lady Sienna?"

"I have been lucky to form some fast friendships with a few of the women here, which I hope to maintain after this experience is over." Sienna crossed her legs at the ankle. "But isn't Prince Liam the real reason we're all here?"

"Right you are." He grinned widely, glad they were back on track with this interview. "What events with Liam are you ladies looking most forward to?"

"I'm excited for the upcoming State Dinner. It will be wonderful to be part of such an impactful event where we'll get to interact with him and leaders of the other kingdoms in Fenimore. Whomever Liam selects will have close working relationships with those leaders," Bridgette said.

Liana nodded along with her. "I'm also looking forward to the State Dinner—and any other group events we get to have with His Highness."

Piper scoffed. "Why look forward to group dates when you can look forward to one-on-one time with him?"

"I'm also looking forward to that alone time." Raina waggled her eyebrows.

Giovanni cleared his throat. "Unfortunately, that's all the time we have for this interview. But make sure to continue tuning in to learn more about the women in the competition and send in your questions with the hashtag #RoyallyYours."

CHAPTER TWELVE
THE ROGUES

"I already have all the arrangements made for tomorrow evening," the blond man whispered. His eyes darted toward the door. Although it was locked from the inside and they hadn't turned on any lights, he was paranoid that someone might find them.

That someone might *hear* them.

That someone might discover their plans.

"What is our next step?"

A sliver of light shone through the curtains covering the lone window in the room, allowing him to see the sneer on the other man's face.

"We need to make sure our backup plan is in place. We must achieve our ultimate goal—keeping Liam from ascending the throne," the dark-haired man said.

"I already have our backup plan in place," he growled. "We need to focus on making sure our pawn continues to sabotage the competition and stay under the radar. If you keep an eye on her, I'll take care of the rest."

With every second that passed, he felt more confident about their plan. Nothing would go wrong.

CHAPTER THIRTEEN
LIAM

Liam made it to the meeting room in the nick of time. It wouldn't be a good look to be late for his first Fenimore Kingdoms Alliance meeting—a yearly meeting with all the kings from the countries in Fenimore—especially when he was the one hosting.

In about an hour, they would all be heading to the dining room for the State Dinner. Barrett had started all the early plans, but Liam had taken the reins a month ago after Barrett had abdicated the throne. This was his first big event that he was really doing on his own, and he wanted—*needed*—everything to go perfectly.

But for now, he needed to get through this meeting.

He was already concerned with gaining the love and loyalty of his people. *I also need to gain the respect of the other rulers in Fenimore.*

"Prince Liam, it's not a secret that you aren't as popular with the public as your father or brother. How are you planning to remedy that?" King Maxwell asked.

All eyes in the room fell on Liam. He pushed aside the sting, putting on his diplomatic front. "I hope to gain the trust and respect of our people as they see more of who I am. If that isn't enough, I'll do whatever it takes to earn the love of my people." He met the eyes of all the kings in turn as they sat around the large oak table in the council chamber.

Looking at the faces of those who were in attendance didn't do much to calm Liam's nerves. Most of the rulers throughout the kingdoms in Fenimore had been friends for longer than Liam had been alive.

The only king who wasn't in attendance was King Colin of Edgemont. He had sent a trusted duke in his place. King Colin was known to be somewhat of a recluse. After his wife had passed away a few years prior, leaving him alone with a newborn baby, he'd gone off the map. He hadn't attended an event or even appeared in the media since losing his wife.

Liam would never admit it to anyone, but he was struggling with how to connect to the leaders of the other kingdoms. All of them were in their mid-to-late fifties, most with children close to his age. The exception was King Colin, who was only a few years his senior.

He felt like he had something to prove in a room full of people who were probably already judging him. Liam shifted in his seat before meeting the eyes of Duke Wesley Hughes. "Any news or updates from Edgemont?"

"The royal board in Edgemont is pushing for King Colin to remarry. He wanted you all to know before news reached the media. Feel free to send any eligible prospects my way. Other than that, we have nothing much to report."

Why is everyone so interested in royals getting married? I could lead the country just fine on my own, and so can Colin.

Some of the kings began offering their opinions on who they thought should become the new queen of Edgemont.

"Order," Liam called out, but it did nothing to quiet them.

"Gentlemen," King Edgar of Bristol chided in a deep, powerful voice, and everyone immediately quieted.

Liam took advantage of the silent room to regain control of the conversation, asking the other kingdoms for any updates. Once everyone at the table had the opportunity to speak, he stood.

"It is time we join your wives and our other guests for dinner. If you will follow me, gentlemen." Liam led the group of men to the formal dining room for the State Dinner. All the queens who had traveled with their husbands, the women in the competition, and the members of his council rose from their seats as they entered.

Liam approached the head of the table and was surprised by the sudden tears he felt welling up at the thought of sitting where his father had always sat. When he noticed Charlotte had been placed beside him in this evening's seating arrangements, he gulped.

"Would you like to switch seats?" Charlotte whispered once he'd sat down, her eyes searching his own. Like she could see the pain he tried so hard to hide. Like she could truly see *him*.

"I'm just fine here," he said more harshly than he meant to. Liam tried to ignore the way she winced at his words. He turned to Wadsworth, who had appeared at his side out of nowhere, always present and swift in his duties.

"Shall I have the first course brought out, Your Highness?"

"Yes. Right away, please."

"As you wish," Wadsworth said.

Liam turned back to their head butler and smiled at him. "Thank you very much, Wadsworth."

"Of course, Your Highness."

"Please do call me Liam."

The butler held a wrinkled hand up to cover the smile that had formed on his lips, but only after Liam had seen a glimpse of it. He simply nodded at the prince before motioning at the line of servers on the wall, sending them on their way to retrieve the opening course.

The conversation around the table flowed nicely as they ate the hors d'oeuvres course of goat cheese crostini with a fig-olive tapenade. As those around him dug in and conversed, Liam simply sat and observed.

He primarily watched how the women in the competition interacted with the visiting royalty. Duchess Gwyneth and The Honorable Liana appeared timid, hardly touching their food and not speaking with anyone at all. Lady Piper and Lady Raina seemed to be doing a bit too much *talking*. He watched as Raina placed her hand on Lord Howard's and then leaned in close to him, whispering in his ear. Maybe it was actually a bit too much *flirting*.

He quickly ate his serving, and the wait staff cleared all the plates from the first course. As quickly as they'd left, they reappeared with silver dome-covered plates. In a synchronized motion, they lifted the domes to reveal the main course of herb-crusted venison medallions served with roasted potatoes and asparagus.

As the attendees enjoyed the entrée course, a loud gasp from the other side of the table made Liam stop cutting his meat.

"Something scurried across my foot." Queen Alexandra of Meldovia pulled her legs up off the floor.

"It just touched me, too." King Nicholas of Rothwell's eyes darted beneath the table.

"It's a mouse," the Honorable Olive squealed, pointing under the table by her feet.

Most of the women—and some of the men—let out small gasps, pulling their knees to their chins. A few of them went as far as to stand on their chairs.

Before he could react, Charlotte's voice called out from beside him. "Wadsworth, please alert the grounds staff to handle this immediately."

Wadsworth got to work, and within a few minutes, the staff had cornered and caught the mouse, removing it from the room.

Everyone at the table laughed about the situation as they got back in their seats and started enjoying their meals again.

Liam glanced at Charlotte out of the corner of his eye. He was in awe of her ability to smooth over the situation. But he couldn't think about it for long because she wasn't a realistic option for him. She couldn't be since she was the greatest threat to his heart.

Surely there was another woman at this table who could have done the same thing. Someone who wasn't a beautiful, flashing hazard sign.

He tuned out the rest of the conversation around him as he ate his venison, focusing instead on the rhythmic motion of his fork and knife as he cut each bite.

"Your Highness?" the butler whispered in a louder tone than usual.

"I'm sorry, Wadsworth. What were you asking?" Liam looked around to see the whole table looking at him.

"Everyone is done eating the main course. Shall I have the plates cleared and the desserts brought out?"

"Yes, of course." Liam willed the blush he felt to not cover his cheeks and further embarrass himself. He needed to get his head back in the game.

I'm the future king of Wistonia. I am powerful. I am in control.
Maybe if he kept telling himself he was in control of all this, he would start believing it.

After the plates had been cleared, the staff brought out mini pedestal bowls with his favorite dessert—English trifle. He was about to take a bite when he noticed strawberries—instead of blueberries—in his bowl.

Liam gestured for Wadsworth to come over and pointed out the error.

The butler's face turned a dark shade of red when he saw the issue. "I'm so sorry, Your Highness. This won't happen again. I'll have another one prepared for you right away."

His father had traditionally asked that English trifle be served with strawberries, but Liam had developed a severe allergy to them as an adult.

"Are you still allergic to them?" Charlotte asked, digging into her bowl and taking a large bite.

"I am." Liam nodded. He had requested a chocolate sponge cake with a strawberry filling for his twentieth birthday. While eating it, his tongue had suddenly swelled, and he'd struggled to breathe as his throat began to close. Luckily, Barrett had been there and quickly rung for the doctor, who had arrived just in time to deliver epinephrine and keep him from going into anaphylactic shock. Ever since then, he'd carried an EpiPen with him, but he had never needed to use it again.

Wadsworth returned with a fresh dessert, this one topped with blueberries instead of strawberries, and he dug in. Liam bit back a moan as he took a perfect bite of the sponge cake, custard, blueberries, jam, and whipped cream.

After dessert was finished and all their guests had retired to their rooms for the night, Liam walked out to the balcony overlooking the palace gardens. He inhaled the sweet scent of blooming flowers, signaling that spring was finally upon them.

"Your Highness, may I have a word?" Lord Harrison Ackerley, the youngest member of the King's Council, aside from himself, joined him on the balcony.

Liam nodded with a sigh. "What is it now? Does the council want me to shave my head entirely this time?" He leaned against the balcony railing, running his hand over his face.

"Not this time, Your Highness. I apologize for waiting until everyone had gone to bed, but I didn't want any prying ears. I have some important information I believe you need to hear."

Liam's brow lifted, his attention caught. "Go on."

"I beg your pardon in advance if this is overstepping my bounds, but I heard some unsettling questions at dinner tonight that I believe should be brought to your attention."

"By all means, then."

"I was seated beside your cousin, Prince James, at dinner. He was speaking to Lord Willoughby nearly the whole evening. After dessert was served, their conversation took a turn." Harrison took in a deep breath and let it out in a sigh before continuing. "Prince James began asking questions about the ninety-day period within which you must marry to ascend the throne. They spoke about what would happen if you were without a wife by the end of that time and what that would mean for Prince James since he would be next in line for the throne."

"I can't imagine my cousin would do anything to sabotage this process for me," Liam said.

"Nor can I. I simply wanted to warn you that these conversations are happening. If I were in your position, I would want that kind of information shared with me."

Liam softened. "Thank you for having my back, Harrison. Everything is fine, though. I don't think we have anything to worry about."

Harrison nodded. "It's what any friend would do, Your Highness. I'll keep my eyes open for anything suspicious and fill you in on anything noteworthy."

Friend. It seemed like it had been forever since Liam had one of those.

"I appreciate it." Liam clapped him on the back. "And you don't need to be so formal around me. You can call me Liam."

Harrison shook his hand. "I'll see you at the next council meeting."

Liam thanked him and turned, looking back out at the garden.

Forget any worries about his cousin being up to no good. Tomorrow he would have his first elimination ceremony. That was what he really needed to be concerned about.

CHAPTER FOURTEEN
CHARLOTTE

"Can you believe she's wearing that?" Tiffany didn't attempt to hide her loudly whispered remarks as she spoke to Olive and Piper. "Even I wouldn't dare to wear a dress that low cut."

Charlotte, who stood a few steps behind the trio, followed Tiffany's gaze to find Raina wearing a bright-orange dress with a plunging neckline that left very little to the imagination.

After spotting Bridgette, Rosalie, and Sienna on the other side of the ballroom, Charlotte walked over to join them. Bridgette pulled her into a side hug when she arrived.

"You are a vision in purple, Charlotte."

She looked down at her lilac dress, running her hands over the crepe material. "Thank you. All of you look great, too." Charlotte smiled brightly at each of her friends, feeling lucky to have met such wonderful people through this surreal experience.

Sienna smiled at her as she looped an arm through hers. "Come on. Alec is here. They're going to start recording any minute." The four ladies joined the other women gathered at the bottom of the grand staircase.

The producer quieted all the women and then said, "And we're rolling in five, four, three, two…" He spun his pointer finger in a circle to show that they were now rolling as the camera aimed at the host, Giovanni, at the top of the staircase. Tonight, he was dressed in a sky-blue suit covered in glitter that danced in the chandelier lights.

"Hello, all! Thank you so much for tuning in to *Royally Yours*. I am your host, Giovanni Geraldo. I hope you have enjoyed the wonderful footage you already saw this evening of Prince Liam interacting with our beautiful group of ladies over the past two weeks. To conclude tonight's episode, we have the dreaded first elimination ceremony," he said in a somber tone, then his voice crescendoed back to its normal enthusiasm. "Prepare to be royally entertained, Fenimore! You may be wondering how Prince Liam will deliver the news of who will stay and who will go."

He flashed a large grin before proclaiming, "With a royal ball, of course! If His Royal Highness asks a lady to dance during one of the ten songs tonight, that is his invitation for them to remain in the competition. Sadly, the one woman he doesn't ask to dance will be leaving the palace, along with anyone who does not accept his offer to dance. But have you looked at him?" Giovanni flashed sultry eyes at the camera. "Who wouldn't want to date our handsome prince?" His gaze turned to the group of women. "What do you think, ladies? Should we bring him out?"

Charlotte politely clapped along with the group of women around her. A few of them even let out a little shout of excitement. But Charlotte wasn't excited. She shifted her weight on her heels, trying to contain her nerves.

I don't know if Liam will ask me to dance tonight. If he does, does that mean he's genuinely interested, or does he pity me and only see me as a friend? She shook her head, trying to clear the questions that flooded her thoughts.

Before she had a chance to gain control, Liam appeared at the top of the staircase, looking dapper in a navy-blue suit, a white button-down shirt, and a burgundy tie.

"Ah-ha! Here he is, ladies and gentlemen. His Royal Highness and our bachelor, Prince Liam," Giovanni declared, sweeping his arm toward Liam as if all eyes in the room weren't already on him. All the women continued to clap as Charlotte looked up at him, trying to get her racing heart to slow. Giovanni's eyes found the camera again. "We'll be back shortly with the elimination ball. Don't go anywhere."

"Aaaand, we're out," Alec said, pulling his headphones off. "Great job, everyone. If anyone needs to go to the restroom, do it now. You won't have another moment for quite a while during the filming of the ball." At his words, a few of the women scurried off to the nearest ladies' room.

Bridgette pulled Charlotte, Rosalie, and Sienna in closer and whispered, "Who do you think he's going to send home?"

"I have no clue, but I hope all of us stay." Rosalie's smile didn't fade, always the optimist.

"Can you believe if we survive the night, we'll already be in the top ten?" Sienna's eyes went wide.

"There were only twelve of us to start." Bridgette giggled.

"True." Sienna's eyes moved around the ballroom, and she sighed dreamily. "I could get used to a life of evenings like this."

All her friends nodded in agreement, and Charlotte mirrored the motion right along with them, though she remained quiet. It was taking everything in her to merely keep up the appearance that she was perfectly fine. That she wasn't a bundle of nerves at the thought that Liam may not see her in a romantic light. That he might send her home broken-hearted and with no way to gain her inheritance.

Rosalie wrapped her arms around them, pulling them all into a group hug. "Can we agree that we'll be happy for each other, no matter what happens in this competition? I know it's hard to be here competing for the same man, but I love all of you already and don't want our friendship to be hurt by this process."

"One hundred percent," Bridgette said.

"Definitely." Sienna smiled.

"Sisters before misters until the end," Charlotte added, and they all laughed.

They went back to stand with the other ladies just as Alec started counting down again.

When the camera light turned red, Giovanni smiled wide. "Welcome back, Fenimore. Let the elimination ball commence."

Liam walked down the grand staircase with a smirk on his face. When he made it to the bottom, you could hear a pin drop in the large ballroom. Finally, Liam approached Sienna. "May I have this dance?" She nodded and accepted his extended hand. He led her to the middle of the ballroom as the camera crew followed them, and a string quartet began to play from the corner of the room along the wall of floor-to-ceiling windows.

Liam danced to a song with her before he bowed and walked back to the group of women, this time offering a dance to Piper from the "TOP" girls. He twirled woman after woman around the ballroom as Charlotte stood on the sidelines, keeping up her façade with a dazzling smile. Though she might fool others, there was no fooling herself.

She had made the promise to herself last week that she would enjoy her time here, that she wouldn't let it get to her, watching him with the other women. But as she watched him dance with a horde of other women, she couldn't deny how much it killed her inside. There was no disguising the fact that her heart was barely held together by a thread, which he pulled more and more undone with each woman he asked to dance who wasn't her.

Unraveled and vulnerable, she stood and waited…and continued to wait, trying to maintain the pleasant front her father had trained her to have since she was a little girl.

Giovanni's voice startled her as it rang clearly throughout the room again. But the words he spoke were what really sent her heart racing. "Royal viewers, this will be the last dance of the night. Unfortunately, whoever is not asked to dance will leave the competition this evening. Let's see who His Royal Highness chooses for the final dance."

Charlotte could feel her heartbeat in her throat as Liam walked over. Only she and a duchess named Gwyneth remained, waiting to see if they would remain in the competition.

She prepared herself for heartbreak. *I'm going home. Why would he choose to keep me over an actual duchess? He only sees me as a friend. Maybe it's for the best… I'll be okay.* But a tiny bit of her heart held on to hope. *Please, please choose me.*

After a minute that felt like an eternity, Liam stopped in front of her and extended a hand. "May I have this dance, Lady Charlotte?"

She was certain her heart had stopped beating. While she had tried to convince herself that she would be okay if he didn't ask her to stay, she knew there wasn't any truth to that.

She would have been shattered—completely unraveled—if he had sent her home.

But he hadn't.

Charlotte avoided Liam's gaze while she composed herself. She curtsied to him, and her nerves heightened at her sudden awareness of the camera crew circling them as she placed her hand in his. "Of course, Your Highness." She hoped her words sounded sure and that her nerves wouldn't betray her for all of Fenimore to see.

Liam guided her onto the dance floor and pulled her close to him for a waltz. Her breath hitched as her eyes finally met his. Up close, she could see how the navy suit brought out his eyes. His blue irises called to her like the invitation of the ocean's lapping waves. Two beautiful pools of sea blue that she could get lost in forever, if she wasn't careful.

He led her through the dance, holding her close to him, as was traditional in the waltz. Yet she couldn't help but wonder if he had chosen her specifically for this dance for that very reason.

No, stop reading into things, Charlotte. She repeated those words to herself over and over as she followed him through the steps, trying—and failing—to ignore the feel of his chiseled abs and forearms as they pressed into her.

"I'm sorry you had to stand around waiting for so long. I knew you'd understand I was saving the best for last." She was drawn back into the moment as Liam's warm, minty breath came out in a whisper over her ear, making the hair on her neck stand and sending goosebumps over her whole body.

Charlotte tried to think of warm-colored flowers to rid her body of the goosebumps, not wanting Liam to see the effect his nearness had on her.

Red roses. Sunflowers. Orange zinnias. Poinsettias. French Marigolds.

"Mmm-hmm," was the only response she could manage without laying all her feelings on the table for him to plainly see.

He pulled his head back to look at her, his eyes earnestly searching hers. "You knew I was going to ask you to stay, right?"

Thankfully, the next step in the dance was a spin, so she was able to avert her eyes for a moment and regain her composure.

"Charlotte?" Liam said her name in a quiet question.

She released a deep breath through her nose. "I couldn't be sure," she said with a slight shake of her head.

He grimaced. "I'm sorry. I'm making a mess of all this already."

"No, you're not. I, for one, think you're doing great."

He grunted in response, causing her to laugh lightly as he twirled her out and then pulled her back into him so closely that they could hold a sheet of paper between their bodies.

"I didn't get to thank you yet. For what you did after dinner the other night with Cora. You didn't have to do that, but thank you," she said.

"We stand up for each other. It's what you and I do."

His words yet again took her right back to the night many years ago when she had been the one to stand up for him and then danced with him—a much younger Liam, drenched in lemonade—in this very ballroom.

"I guess it is." She beamed at him, and his lips pulled up at the corners into a hint of a smile.

The song came to a close as he dipped her. Liam drew her back to him, their faces nearly touching, both slightly out of breath—and it wasn't because of the dancing.

"Brava! They look like naturals out there together, don't they?" Giovanni asked as he walked back out onto the ballroom floor. He headed over to the remaining lady who hadn't been asked to dance. "Since that was the final dance, that means we must bid goodnight to Her Grace, Duchess Gwyneth."

The cameras panned to Gwyneth, zooming in to capture her expression. Any glimpse of tears or anger would make for more compelling television.

Liam walked over and escorted her out of the ballroom.

"That's all we have for you tonight on this episode of *Royally Yours*. Please follow us on social media and use the hashtag #RoyallyYours to let us know which was your favorite dance of the night and whom you think our beloved prince will choose to be Wistonia's next queen. Join us again Tuesday night at eight to see what happens next and continue to be royally entertained. Goodnight." Giovanni kept a wide smile on his face until Alec gave the all-clear that they were no longer live.

A couple of ladies let out sighs as they speed-walked to the nearest restrooms. Charlotte turned to leave the ballroom, but she was bombarded by her friends surrounding her, so she couldn't escape.

"Girl, what did he say to you during your dance?"

"He was giving you total come-hither eyes."

"All the other ladies were practically seething as they watched you."

Charlotte held up her hands as they all talked at once.

"Okay, first of all, what are 'come-hither eyes'?" Charlotte asked.

"You know…something more than ogling but less than a look I'm too much of a lady to speak of." Sienna winked at her, and all of her friends laughed conspiratorially.

"You're so bad." Charlotte swatted at her friend's arm, but she couldn't hide her smile. "He really didn't say much." She shrugged. "Why were people angry watching us dance?"

"Well, for starters," Bridgette said, holding up a finger before continuing, "he danced the only waltz with you." She held up a second finger. "He also looked at you with those 'come-here' eyes or whatever Sienna called them." Bridgette held up a third finger. "Last, but certainly not least, I could feel your chemistry from the other side of the room. Sparks were totally flying."

Rosalie fanned her face with her hand. "We could all feel the heat between you two."

Charlotte looked among all her friends as if they were going to say "gotcha" at any moment. But they didn't. And nothing could stop the thoughts from flooding her mind that maybe—just maybe—her feelings weren't one-sided. That maybe there was the slightest chance Liam could feel the same things for her that she felt for him.

She tried to force that idea out of her mind, not wanting to get her hopes up. Because if she got her hopes up and then he didn't choose her at the end of this, she wasn't sure her heart would recover.

"We've just known each other a long time. And waltzes are supposed to be romantic." Charlotte attempted to shrug off their observations with simple answers.

Her friends all looked at each other with glints of mischief in their eyes. They definitely weren't buying it.

And honestly, she was having a difficult time believing her own words.

※

The next morning, after breakfast, Charlotte cozied up in a chair in the library with her current read, a romantic comedy that was the perfect mix of humor and romance. She was lost in the world the author had created when Rosalie barged into the room, waving her over.

"Did you forget about the announcement?"

Charlotte glanced at the time on her phone and remembered the contestants were supposed to be meeting in front of the gardens in two minutes. "Shoot. We can still make it if we hurry. Thanks for coming to find me."

They hurried outside and found the camera crew waiting for them, already filming. After they arrived, Giovanni read what was written on the teleprompter.

"Welcome, ladies. I have exciting news to share today. The Wistonian Palace is going to be throwing a garden party." He paused for dramatic effect. "And you will each be hosting one or two royal women from somewhere in Fenimore."

The women around Charlotte began to whisper in hushed tones about who they thought would attend from other kingdoms.

"As a host, you will each oversee the duties typically held by the Queen of Wistonia. You will need to have a welcome gift prepared for each of your guests, tailored specifically for them. You will also work with the kitchen staff to select dishes and drink options appropriate for your guests. Finally, you will each decorate your table in a way designed to honor those whom you will host."

Giovanni gestured to his side. "Now, let's give a warm welcome to Prince Liam, who will assign the women you'll be hosting."

The women clapped politely as Liam walked out from the gardens to join Giovanni on camera. "The King's Council and I have personally selected the royal ladies who will be visiting the palace and whom each of you will be hosting. A few of you may have family members attending the garden party, since we're all titled. But no one will be assigned someone of their relation. Any questions?" Liam asked and looked around, smiling at them.

Charlotte could've sworn his eyes brightened as they met hers. But clearly, she was seeing things. *It was just the sun hitting his eyes. Or maybe he was looking at someone behind me. He could've randomly thought of English trifle, too. He loves English trifle. Liam was absolutely, positively not smiling brighter because of me.*

"Great. Now as I call out your name, please come forward to receive your assignment," Liam said. He went through a stack of envelopes in his hand, handing them out. About halfway through the pile, he called Charlotte's name, and she approached him. She gave him a small curtsy before taking her envelope from his hand, her fingers lightly brushing his.

The small touch sent a shiver up her spine, just like the kind she read about in all her favorite romantic-comedy novels. Charlotte always thought the reactions characters in books had to a small pinky touch or the grazing of an elbow were unrealistic. But now she finally understood what the smallest of touches could do, because she was completely undone from just their fingers brushing against each other.

Objectively speaking, fingers aren't usually seen as an attractive attribute of the body. *But his fingers? Ten out of ten, would recommend.*

His hands were warm despite the still brisk spring air. And even though his hands had a few callouses from his workout regimen, they still felt soft and gentle as they met hers.

STOP THINKING ABOUT HIS FINGERS, she yelled at herself.

Pulled back into the moment by Liam clearing his throat, she found his eyes again.

"Everything all right?" His voice was low enough that the cameras likely wouldn't pick it up.

She straightened her shoulders and put back on her polished smile. "Everything's great. Thank you." Charlotte clasped the envelope more tightly and strolled back to her friends.

"Sparks," Rosalie whispered before her name was called, and she walked toward Liam.

"Chemistry," Bridgette added.

"Burning attraction." Sienna winked at her.

Charlotte searched for any reason—any reason at all—that her friends were wrong. But what she found instead was a glimmer of hope. That maybe what her friends were seeing was actually there. Tangible. Her heart raced, and her head spun at the thought that maybe Liam could have feelings for her, too.

If there was even the slightest chance he felt for her as strongly as she did for him, she might not ever have to leave the Wistonian Palace.

I might actually find my happily-ever-after. And keep both my heart and my inheritance intact.

CHAPTER FIFTEEN
LIAM

"I'm enacting the Secret Prince Society for this conversation," Liam said with a sigh as he fell backward onto the brown leather couch in the men's sitting room, immediately rubbing his temples after he was solidly planted on the cushion.

"Oh, boy, this will be good. What secret information do you not want me to sell to the media?" Barrett raised an eyebrow and smirked at him while undoing the wrist buttons of his dress shirt and rolling the sleeves up to his elbows.

When they were children, Barrett and Liam created the Secret Prince Society. They were sworn to secrecy regarding anything either of them said within the confines of their society. As children, they'd used it for silly things like when Liam had broken a priceless vase that had been gifted from the king of another country. But the conversations they had in secret had grown more serious over the years.

Most recently, Barrett had enacted the Secret Prince Society to—in not-so-subtle terms—tell Liam he was in love with Jules. Since she wasn't of royal standing, Barrett couldn't have both her and the throne. So, Barrett asked him if he would be okay with leading Wistonia in his place so he could marry his dream girl. Now Liam needed to ask him a question of his own.

"I need…" Liam swallowed hard, choking on the next words—ones he'd never thought he would say. "I need dating advice." Liam said the words so quickly they were almost indistinguishable.

Barrett leaned toward him, a saccharine grin growing across his face. "What? I couldn't quite catch that?"

Liam shoved his brother's arm. "Don't make me say it again. It was painful enough to utter those words once."

"So, my baby brother—*The Royal Heartbreaker*—needs my assistance when it comes to women." Barrett held it together for only a second before laughter erupted out of him.

Liam pulled his brother into a headlock. "I take it back. I don't need to talk to you." He loosened his hold and started to stand.

"Stop your whining. I won't make fun of you anymore. I swear. I just couldn't resist." Barrett ran a hand over his mouth, like he was trying to wipe the smile off his face.

"Fine." He sat back down on the couch with a huff. "Lindsay told me earlier this morning that Alec wants me to come up with ideas for some of the dates. They apparently want things to seem more personal—as if my whole dating life being put on display for everyone to see isn't personal enough," Liam scoffed. "Anyway, I want your input on date ideas."

"Hmm…what about a little trip into town? They'll have the Founding Day Celebration soon," Barrett suggested.

"It's already on the calendar for the women to go into town for the celebration. Group dates are also already planned for your wedding and a charity event."

Barrett continued to ponder the question. "I have just the thing." He hit his hand on his knee. "What about a baking date?"

"A baking date?" Liam asked, not fully on board with the idea.

Barrett shrugged. "It worked for Jules and me. We ended up baking together in the kitchen, and look at us now."

"I guess I could use that as an idea." Liam tapped his bottom lip with a pointer finger. "I need a few other ideas that are related to things I enjoy doing."

"What about paintball?"

Liam laughed at the idea. "You think these women would be okay getting hit with paintballs?"

"It would show you who in the group is a good sport, and who's willing to jump into the trenches with you. Plus, that's one of your favorite hobbies, so how much more personal could you get?"

"Valid argument. If they hate the idea, I'm totally blaming you, though." Liam winked. "What about archery or ceramics as another group date?"

"Ceramics? When have you ever taken up pottery making?"

"Never…I've just seen it in the movies, and they always make it look so romantic."

Barrett shook his head. "I think one date where the women might get dirty is plenty, so I would go with archery. You could always wrap your arms around the lady of your choosing and show her how to shoot an arrow if you want to make it 'romantic.'" Barrett held up air quotes with the final word.

"You're the worst." Liam shoved Barrett's arm. "I know how to be romantic."

"Says the man who came to his older brother—who could barely talk to a woman until the end of last year—for dating advice."

Liam slumped back down onto the couch. He ran his hands over his eyes as he let himself sink further into the worn cushions.

"How're you really doing?" Barrett set a hand on his shoulder.

"This whole situation is weird. It's exhausting trying to be like you—putting on my best front so the people of Wistonia will like me. And then trying to balance that with dating and getting to know these women. Don't get me wrong, I'm thrilled that I'm going to be king. But it's overwhelming. There's a lot of pressure, learning the ropes and trying to find a bride on such a tight deadline. Not to mention that it's all being filmed for everyone to see."

"You know you don't have to be like me, right? You're going about it all wrong. You need to be yourself. Let our people and these women see the real you."

"But what if they don't like the real me? They don't want to see the hot mess who has no clue what he's doing." Liam's chin started to quiver. He clenched his jaw, reining in his emotion. "What if I'm not good enough to be king?"

"You're more than enough. You're strong-willed and a natural-born leader. You're well-spoken, and people listen to you. I know you can be sassy and goofy, but when you're serious, you can take complete control of a room. Just look at how you've handled the interviews you've done so far. When we announced my abdication and the dating competition, the people could've revolted, but they didn't. And I think it's largely due to how you composed yourself and answered questions during the press conference and your interview with Giovanni. If the people can't see that you would make a wonderful king, that's on them. I love this country too much to have passed the throne on to you if I didn't think you would be a good ruler. I know you'll make a good king, Liam. But you need to believe that yourself."

Liam nodded with his eyes closed, taking in his encouraging words.

Barrett rose and pulled him into a tight, brotherly hug. "Let me know how the dates go. And text me if you ever want to meet to discuss Wistonian policy and procedure. I'm happy to help."

"I appreciate that. Thank you…for everything."

Liam left the room to find Lindsay and share the date ideas, feeling a little lighter from his brother's words with each step.

If Barrett believed in him, surely he could find the strength to believe in himself.

Liam headed to the palace kitchen with his stomach in knots. He hoped Barrett was right about this baking date being a good idea. He had never baked anything before, but a single recipe couldn't be that hard to follow. Surely the lady they selected for the date had experience baking. Unless their family had a baker like his family had. Shoot. *I can't believe I let Barrett convince me this was a good idea.*

"Oh, Prince Liam," a feminine voice called from behind him. He turned around and saw that it was Olive. "I was wondering if you could talk?" She batted her eyelashes at him.

Liam glanced at his watch. "I only have a few minutes until my date."

"Date?" She pouted. "I guess we'll have to make the best of those minutes, then." Olive moved closer to him, rubbing her finger up and down his arm.

He gave her a forced smile. "What would you like to talk about?"

"Well, there's this question that only just came to me. How often would a queen actually get to wear her crown? And would she have access to all the royal jewels?"

He felt his heart in his throat. *This is like Mila all over again. Was I too optimistic that people would actually be here for something other than gaining the crown? Olive does have strong political connections. However, I can't keep women who clearly convey they're only here for the crown. This will make my decision at the next elimination ball much easier.*

"The crown isn't worn often to events in Wistonia. However, the *royal* jewels are worn for various *royal* occasions. Now, if you'll excuse me, I must go to my date." He pulled his arm from her hand and walked the rest of the way to the kitchen.

"Your Highness, perfect timing." A female production assistant ran toward him as fast as her heels would let her. "We're going to have you set up in the kitchen, and then we'll have your date walk in so we can film your reaction. Then the two of you can bake your hearts out."

"Will you be filming the whole time?"

"Yes," she said as she intently looked at her clipboard.

"How am I supposed to talk to her about anything real—anything personal—with cameras in our faces?"

"You'll get used to it. Just pretend they aren't there." She stopped when they arrived at the kitchen entrance.

Easier said than done. Liam already felt like his whole life was a breach of privacy. His every accomplishment and failure had always been printed by the media for the world to see. Now he had to talk about things—real, personal things—the media didn't know. No one knew.

His thoughts drifted back to Barrett's advice. *Let our people and these women see the real you.* He would try to be himself and ignore the cameras—for the sake of whoever had been chosen as his date and all those who would be watching at home.

"Any final questions, Your Highness?"

He met the production assistant's gaze. "Do you have a recipe for us to follow?"

"Of course. We selected a foolproof one. Easy-peasy," she said as she pushed him through the entrance toward the waiting cameras.

Easy-peasy. Right.

The main producer, Alec, appeared from behind one of the cameras and showed Liam his mark. "Giovanni is going to introduce the date on the back end, so we won't need you to do that. We just need to film the whole date so we get enough footage." He walked away before Liam had a chance to respond. Suddenly, Alec was spinning his finger in the air and pointing at him, letting him know the cameras were rolling.

Liam's gaze turned to the doorway as Sienna walked through it, wearing a maroon sweater and a pair of fitted jeans. Her long brunette hair was curled and down, framing her face. She was beautiful and definitely a contender in his mind. From his knowledge, she had been dumped by her long-term boyfriend a year ago. *Maybe she's looking for a loveless relationship just like me.*

"You look lovely, Lady Sienna."

"Thank you, Your Highness. And please, call me Sienna."

"Only if you'll call me Liam." He smiled at her.

"Deal," she said, pulling him in for a side hug after she arrived at her mark.

"Let's see what we're baking today, shall we?"

"Yes," she exclaimed, bouncing a little. "I love baking. This is the perfect date."

"That makes one of us," he muttered. She turned and looked at him with a puzzled and slightly hurt expression.

"No. I didn't mean I'm not excited for this date. I only meant I've never baked before." He attempted to backpedal. "I'm glad I have a baking pro in my midst."

"Oh, I wouldn't call myself a pro."

"I'll be the judge of that by the end of today." He winked at her.

She blushed at his words and pressed a hand to her cheek. He flipped over the paper recipe that was on the large quartz-topped island in the middle of the kitchen. Even though the room was big, it currently felt small with the two of them and all the camera crew and producers squeezed in with all their equipment.

"Vanilla cupcakes," he said, attempting to show some semblance of enthusiasm for the very plain dessert they would be making.

It seemed Sienna could sense his disappointment. "I'm sure we can find a way to spice up the frosting."

He smiled at her. "Sounds great. Let's get started."

She pushed her sweater up to her elbows and pulled her hair back into a ponytail before grabbing the recipe from his hands and reading off the steps. "Do you want to get the oven preheating for us? And then you can fill the muffin pan with cupcake papers."

Liam set the oven to the temperature she indicated and got to work on the tasks she gave him. They worked well together. She measured the ingredients to make sure they were exact, while he was the designated mixer. Once all the ingredients had been combined, he let her fill the little cupcake liners with the batter.

After they put the cupcakes in the oven, Liam leaned against the counter, casually crossing his legs. It felt weird to talk with all the cameras there, but this was what he'd signed up for. "Tell me a little bit about yourself. What is something I should know about Sienna?"

She bit her lip as she searched for an answer. "I'm obsessed with the *Clue* game app on my phone. I love puzzles and games that challenge my mind."

"I used to play *Clue* with my mom all the time when I was younger." He smiled at the memory.

"She was as smart as she was beautiful and graceful, then." Sienna set her hand lightly on Liam's, but he felt nothing. She was beautiful and kind, but there was no spark. It was exactly what he needed. Yet he felt a yearning in his heart for something more.

No, he told his stubborn heart. This is what you need. Love only complicates things and leads to hurt and loss.

"What about you? What's something I need to know about Liam?" she asked.

"I love being active. I run in the gardens and back by our pond when I want to clear my mind. I also like things like paintball, riding dirt bikes, archery…you know, manly activities. But I'll let you in on a secret." He leaned in closer to her. "Growing up, I watched *The Perfect Match* every week with my family. My mother loved the show and roped us into watching it. But after she passed, my father, brother, and I continued the tradition...and I actually grew to like the show."

"Were you excited to meet Giovanni Geraldo, then?" She giggled.

"Ecstatic. He's just as genuine and exuberant in person as he is on television." He shifted his feet. "If you don't mind talking about it, I wanted to ask about your past relationship. I know you were together for a long time."

Sienna's smile faded, and her gaze dropped to the countertop. "I don't mind. Spencer and I dated for four years before he ended things last Christmas." She shook her head softly and sighed. "I thought he was my forever person, but I was wrong."

"I'm sorry." Liam reached over and took her hand in his, squeezing it gently. "I was hurt by someone in the past as well and know how difficult it can be to put yourself back out there. Do you think you'll find love again?"

"I can't say for sure. I'm scared to put my heart on the line again, but I'd like to think I'll find love again someday." Sienna rubbed her thumb across his and gave him a sad smile. "What about you? Do you think you'll find love through this competition?"

"I think I'll end up with exactly what I need at the end of all this."

She opened her mouth to respond but was interrupted by the oven timer beeping. Sienna walked over to it and removed the muffin pan, her face falling when she saw the cupcakes.

Liam ambled over to see what was wrong. It took only a moment to see why her face fell. The cupcakes were dark on top—basically black. "Did I do something wrong?" he asked.

"The oven was set to 450°. The recipe called for it to be set to 350°."

"It's what's on the inside that matters, right?" Liam chuckled, playing things off for the camera, even though he felt like a failure yet again. *How can I lead a country if I can't even turn the oven on correctly?*

"Exactly." She set her hand on his forearm, rubbing gently. "Maybe we can cut the tops off? We still have to make the buttercream frosting. That should help bring some moisture back into them."

Liam got to work cutting the top from each cupcake while Sienna added all the frosting ingredients into a mixer. After he was finished cutting as much of the burnt cupcake tops off as he could, he joined her on the other side of the counter. He swiped his finger through the mixing bowl. And before she could stop him, he licked the frosting off his finger.

His eyes lit up as the bright flavor danced on his tastebuds. "What did you put in it? That's amazing."

"Thanks. I followed the recipe but added some lemon zest to spice it up. A little bit of citrus can go a long way." She smiled at his praise.

Once every cupcake was topped with an ample amount of frosting, they each picked up a cupcake and clinked them together.

"Cheers," he said.

"Bon appétit."

They pulled the paper wrapping off and dug in. As soon as the cupcake hit Liam's tongue, he gagged. "Why is it so salty?" he said, even though his mouth was full, running to the sink to rinse the excessive sodium taste off his tongue.

Right after Sienna took a bite, Liam could see she was attempting to keep a pleasant expression, but when she could no longer stand the awful taste, she spat it into a paper towel. He grabbed a glass of water for her that she guzzled down.

They made eye contact and burst into laughter.

A few tears escaped her eyes from laughing so hard. "I don't understand. I followed the recipe exactly." She went back over to their ingredients. "Do you think the sugar bowl somehow got mixed up with the salt?"

"That must've been what happened." He nudged her shoulder with his. "It's not your fault. You're still a baking pro in my eyes."

The corners of her mouth turned up into a hint of a smile as she said, "Thank you."

"What do you say we get out of here?" He held out his arm to her. She pulled her hair out of her ponytail and gave it a little shake before accepting his proffered arm.

Liam led her out of the room, with the camera crew following them, and headed to the palace entrance. He pivoted when he noticed the rain falling steadily outside and took her on a mini tour of the palace. Even with her hand on his bicep and her close proximity, he didn't feel any romantic chemistry between them their entire date.

That was exactly what he'd been looking for—a loveless relationship with someone he could respect and who would also make a wonderful queen. Sienna fit that to a tee.

But after he dropped her off at her room and walked to his study, he couldn't help but wonder what a life without love would look like and if that was truly what he wanted after all.

CHAPTER SIXTEEN
GIOVANNI GERALDO

Giovanni's eyes were bright, and his smile was wide as Rosalie and Charlotte sat down on the gray couch opposite him.

"I'm in for a treat today as I meet with Princess Rosalie and Lady Charlotte to learn behind-the-scenes information about the planning process for the garden party." He turned toward them. "Thank you both for joining me this afternoon. Now, for the viewers at home, what can you share about the process for planning a garden party?"

"Planning a royal event is a big undertaking. Then imagine having only a week and a half to execute every aspect perfectly." Rosalie laughed.

"It's preparing us for what the duties of a queen would look like," Charlotte added.

"Precisely. As for the details, we've been working on things like selecting décor for the table settings that will honor the countries the guests are from. We've also researched and hand-crafted menus in honor of our guests."

"Not to mention the welcome baskets we're creating for each of their rooms, tailored specifically for them."

Giovanni's eyes grew wide. "It sounds like there's a lot more to it than putting up a few streamers and ordering a pizza. That's usually the extent of my party planning." He chuckled.

"Maybe just a little bit more." Charlotte giggled.

"You heard it here first, viewers. Tune into next week's episode to see the garden party for yourselves." Giovanni did a two-finger salute to the camera.

CHAPTER SEVENTEEN
CHARLOTTE

Charlotte let out a slow breath, attempting to ease her nerves. She couldn't believe they were almost one month into the competition. That meant the second elimination ceremony would be happening at the beginning of next week. It also meant only about eight weeks remained until Liam would make his final decision.

She rid her mind of those thoughts, grabbing a new book from her end table. With a sigh, she put it back down. *No, I need to focus on what's happening today.*

The royal guests for the garden party would be arriving soon, and she wanted everything to run smoothly. She would be hosting a royal mother-daughter duo, Queen Caroline of Westridge and her daughter, Princess Brielle. Charlotte knew them both to be extremely kind and genuine from her brief interactions with them.

The ten remaining women in the competition had only been given a week and a half to arrange everything for the garden party. While that seemed like a short amount of time, Charlotte knew the duties of a queen often required making preparations for guests on much shorter notice than that.

She checked her appearance in the full-length mirror one final time to make sure nothing was out of place. She wore a pale-blue, long-sleeved, floral-patterned dress, and her hair was pulled into a low bun with decorative braids. When she believed herself to look satisfactory, Charlotte made her way to her guests' rooms. She wanted to double-check that the welcome baskets on their beds contained everything she'd requested.

Looking through Queen Caroline's basket, it appeared everything was in order. The lavender-scented bath salts had been placed next to some of Her Majesty's favorite snacks. She went next door to Princess Brielle's accommodations and examined the contents of her welcome gift on the bed. Most of the basket was filled with an assortment of different kinds of chocolate-covered pretzels, which were Brielle's favorite.

But...what's that smell?

Charlotte dug through the contents until she found the culprit. She wrinkled her nose as she pulled out a decent-sized chunk of blue cheese from the bottom of the basket. That had *definitely* not been on her list of things to include. She sprayed some air freshener in the room and took the stinky cheese with her, asking a servant she passed to throw it away in the kitchen.

Let's hope nothing else goes wrong today.

When she arrived back in the contestants' guest wing, she saw her friends were waiting outside her door.

"Sorry if you were waiting on me," Charlotte called out, hurrying to join them.

"We just got here." Rosalie smiled at her. "Let's go, ladies."

"Before we see everyone else, I've been dying to know how your one-on-one date with Liam was, Sienna. Tell us everything," Bridgette said as they started walking. Charlotte bit back a wince, unsure if her heart could handle hearing how their date had been, even though Sienna was her friend.

"We had a baking date that went horribly wrong." Sienna laughed.

"What happened?" Rosalie asked.

"Somehow the salt and sugar bowls must've been switched. It tasted like our cupcakes had a cup of salt in them." Sienna grimaced while they laughed lightly. "Liam also turned the oven on too high, so the tops were burned. It was a royal disaster."

"Sounds like the cupcakes didn't turn out, but how was your time with him? Surely you got to know one another a bit better?" Bridgette said.

"We did. We chatted while baking, and he also took me on a palace tour afterward." Sienna looked around as if searching for what to say next. "Jury's still out if there's something romantic there. I guess only time will tell."

Her answer had Charlotte biting back a smile. She wanted the best for her friend. But she also wanted Liam to be hers at the end of this.

"There's still a lot of time to figure that out." Rosalie wrapped an arm around Sienna's waist. "I think the only one of us who knows where their feelings truly lie is this one." She nodded her head toward Charlotte.

Charlotte's mouth fell ajar. "But I—"

"Don't even try to argue it," Sienna replied, and they all laughed.

A slight blush covered Charlotte's cheeks as she looked at the floor to hide her smile.

Bridgette patted her shoulder. "I'm glad you're finally accepting the feelings that are so clearly there. Everyone can see them."

Charlotte looked between all her friends. "Is it really that obvious?" Her eyes widened. "Do you think Liam knows?"

"Oh, no," Sienna said.

"By everyone, I mean all the women in the world. Men are oblivious," Bridgette added with a shoo of her hand.

"Did you see the recent news headlines, though?" Rosalie asked.

"I make it a habit of not reading things posted in the media, especially when they're about me." Charlotte sighed.

"I think you'll want to hear this one." Rosalie handed her phone over to her. "Just read it."

Charlotte took the phone from her and bit back a gasp when she saw the header photo. It was the moment at the elimination ball after Liam had dipped her and pulled her back into him. Their faces were so close they were nearly touching, and the way they were looking at each other brought a shiver up her spine and made her breath catch.

There was a saying about how a picture doesn't lie. And if this one wasn't lying, she would say the two people in the photo definitely had feelings for each other. *I can't get my hopes up. It could be nothing.*

To avoid her thoughts, she read the headline. *Lady Charlotte the Frontrunner in Prince Liam's Search for a Bride?* She read more of the article and found a poll where readers could vote on whom they thought Liam would choose. She was the clear winner by far with Rosalie, Sienna, and Tiffany getting a decent number of votes as well.

"What if Liam sees this?" she asked.

"Don't worry about it." Rosalie wrapped her arm through hers, pulling her to a stop near the palace's back doors. "As Bridgette said, men are oblivious."

Charlotte hoped that was the truth. She pushed down any concerns and smiled at her friends, putting back on the façade of the duke's perfect daughter. Lightly tugging on Rosalie's arm and glancing back at Bridgette and Sienna, she said, "Let's go greet our guests."

Charlotte walked into the palace gardens and took in the beautiful setup with wide eyes.

Long tables covered in elegant white linens with a delicate white lace overlay were set up in the grass near the gardens. Each section of the tables had a different centerpiece, selected by the ladies in the competition to honor their guests. Charlotte had chosen a beautiful arrangement of cornflowers, hydrangeas, white roses, and baby's breath as the centerpiece where the royal women of Westridge would be seated. She had carefully selected each flower to represent the Westridge flag colors of light blue and white.

Walking down the length of the table, she admired all the beautiful flowers that had been selected by the other women. At the end of the table, she drew in a sharp breath when she saw a flower she didn't recognize. It appeared similar to a thistle and was a brilliant shade of blue. She quickly grabbed her phone from her clutch on the table and raced back to the arrangement, taking a picture of it in her All About That Flora app. It came back with a result showing that they were globe thistles. A beautiful name for a beautiful flower.

Charlotte waved Bridgette over and showed her. "I've never seen this one before. Isn't it brilliant?"

Bridgette covered her mouth with her hand. "You have an app to track the flowers you know?"

"And to learn the names of new flowers I discover."

"You're such a nerd." Bridgette grinned, pulling her in for a side hug.

"I'm a plant nerd, and I'm proud of it." Charlotte grinned at her over her shoulder, walking back to put her phone away.

Across from the tables, farther from the gardens, the staff had arranged round tables covered with foods one would typically find at a high tea. Like the centerpiece decor, each contestant had worked with the kitchen staff to select a few items specifically for the guests they were hosting.

Charlotte went to check on the food she had selected, wanting to make sure everything was perfect. She walked past the large array of food options, her mouth instantly watering at the sight of mini chocolate mousse pies, until she came upon the table marked *In Honor of Her Royal Majesty Queen Caroline of Westridge and Her Royal Highness Princess Brielle of Westridge.*

She ran through the list in her head as she observed the offerings on the three-tiered stands.

Peach tarts. *Check.*

Almond-and-grape chicken salad on mini croissants. *Check.*

Cranberry-orange scones. *Check.*

Spinach-and-cheese mini quiches. *What. No.*

The sign in front of her that should have read *spinach and cheese* instead said *spinach and shrimp*. Crustaceans were not allowed. One, that was not what she had requested. Two, the queen of Westridge was allergic to shellfish.

Charlotte speed-walked with as much decorum as she could to the nearest member of the kitchen staff. "Excuse me," she called out.

"Is there an issue, miss?"

"Yes. I requested spinach-and-cheese mini quiches for my table, and it appears that the spinach-and-shrimp ones were put out by mistake."

The staff member read down the list in her hands. "It shows you requested a last-minute change this morning."

"The queen of Westridge is allergic to shellfish. I didn't request any changes to my menu." Charlotte's worries heightened. Was someone trying to personally sabotage her? Her heart started to race, and she struggled to catch her breath.

Alyssum. Bachelor's Button. Candytuft. Dahlia.

Charlotte blew out a long breath, feeling only slightly more at ease. She was reading into things. Surely someone wouldn't be so cruel as to request a change to a food a guest was allergic to. It had to have been an honest mistake.

"I'm so sorry, Lady Charlotte." The staff member looked skittish. "What would you like me to do?"

She laid a hand on the girl's arm. "It's not your fault. Mistakes happen. We need to have the spinach-and-shrimp mini quiches removed immediately from my table." She bit the inside of her lip, trying to think of a solution to replace the missing dish. "Is there enough time for the chefs to whip up anything additional?"

"The quiches would take too long to prepare." The girl's eyes fell to the ground.

"What about a smoked salmon canapé? That shouldn't take long for them to put together," Charlotte suggested.

The light returned to the girl's expression as she looked up at her. "That should work perfectly, miss. I will have the change made right away. I apologize again for the mistake."

Charlotte nodded at the girl and walked over to Rosalie, who was standing at her own table of food.

"Is everything okay?"

Rosalie continued staring at her table as she shook her head. "I specifically requested blueberry galettes and these are blackberry." Her face fell as she turned to Charlotte. "My guest doesn't eat anything with seeds in it."

Charlotte reached out and took Rosalie's hand in hers. "There was an issue with one of my dishes as well." Maybe someone *was* trying to sabotage other women in the competition. "My guests enjoy blackberries. Why don't we swap out my stand of peach tarts with your stand of blackberry galettes?"

"You would do that?" Rosalie's eyes brightened, and her words were filled with hope.

"Anything for a friend." Charlotte smiled and grabbed the stand from Rosalie's table, carrying it over to hers and swapping it with her tarts. She carried the tart stand back to Rosalie, who pulled her into a tight hug. Looking over her shoulder, it appeared most of the women had arrived. Women of royal standing ranging from queens to the daughters of barons were in attendance. There were around thirty guests in total, including the women in the competition.

"The garden party is about to begin. We should join our guests."

"Let's get this party started," Charlotte said, straightening her back and trying to muster every ounce of confidence she could as she walked around the camera setup.

Charlotte approached her table, dipping into a low curtsy and bowing her head in deference. "Your Majesty. Your Highness. It's truly a pleasure to see you again."

"The pleasure is all mine, Lady Charlotte." Queen Caroline of Westridge smiled at her in return, extending her hand for Charlotte to shake.

The queen's daughter, Princess Brielle, stood and gave Charlotte a small hug. Her blonde curls bounced against her sky-blue dress as she moved.

"Great minds think alike." Brielle motioned between their similarly colored dresses.

"They do." Charlotte smiled, sitting in the open seat next to her. "Your dress is lovely."

After the queen rose to get a plate of food, Brielle leaned her head closer to Charlotte's. "I apologize if this is too forward a question, but I have to know. How is the competition going for you?"

"Did you read the media articles?" She grimaced.

Brielle waved off her comment. "I know more than to believe what they say. I've had my fair share of fake news spread about me as well. But...between what they say about you and what I've seen with my own eyes on the show"—she fanned herself with her hand—"I could feel the chemistry through the television when you danced with Prince Liam."

"I—" Charlotte stopped, unsure what to say in response to that. "I think the competition is going well so far. I'm honored to be here. When it comes to how I feel about Liam, it's like the saying goes...*a picture is worth a thousand words*." She looked at Brielle, her feelings on display for all to see.

"If he doesn't pick you, it will be his loss. But from woman to woman, I don't think what you're feeling is one-sided," Princess Brielle said.

"Only time will tell, I suppose." Charlotte wrung her hands together.

Brielle eyed all the food behind them. "What do you say we visit the tea table?"

"I'd say that's a fabulous idea." Charlotte gestured for her to go first and followed behind her, loading a plethora of appetizers and sweets onto her plate.

After their guests finished the repast, Charlotte finally felt like she could breathe again.

"The selection you arranged for us was exquisite, Lady Charlotte. I've never had a blackberry galette before, but I believe it may be a new favorite sweet of mine." Queen Caroline dabbed the corners of her mouth lightly with a white linen napkin.

"I'm glad you enjoyed it."

Brielle turned to her mother. "I think it's time we rest before our meeting with Prince Liam and the King's Council tomorrow to renew our trade contracts. Can I escort you back to your room, Mother?"

"Yes, dear, that sounds lovely." Turning to Charlotte, the queen added, "Thank you for the lovely time, Lady Charlotte. You were a wonderful host."

"Of course, Your Majesty." Charlotte dropped into another low curtsy.

Brielle gently patted her shoulder before she stood and accompanied her mother inside. With her guests gone, Charlotte was left alone with her thoughts.

What if Princess Brielle was right? What if her long-time crush could turn into something more—something deeper? What if Liam felt the same way for her that she did for him?

Maybe Liam didn't even know his feelings himself. But she was determined to help him realize that what he was looking for had been right in front of him all along.

CHAPTER EIGHTEEN
LIAM

Liam watched from his desk as his brother tried to cover a yawn with his hand.

"You really should get some sleep, old man. We can go over trade agreements another day before your early bedtime strikes again."

"Ha-ha, very funny. I didn't know we had a comedian in the family." Barrett stood, stretching his back. "I *am* getting a bit tired. Promise you won't stay up too late, darling?" he teased.

"Don't wait up for me, dear," Liam quipped.

"In your dreams." Barrett looked back and winked at him before leaving the room.

Liam chuckled. It was strange to think they hadn't been close for most of their lives. But he was thankful for his brother's friendship and guidance, especially now when he needed his brother's crash course on how to be king with only two months left before he would ascend the throne.

It's not nearly enough time, he told himself as his face fell into his hands. There was too much to learn. Too much he didn't know. And he was exhausted. He rubbed the dark circles that were starting to form under his eyes from countless sleepless nights. He stayed up most nights studying and spent every day trying to find a wife on a ticking timeline. It wasn't a sustainable schedule.

Is all of this useless?

There was no use questioning anything now. He didn't have a choice. So, he got back to reading.

A knock on the door had Liam chuckling as he walked over to open it. "Back so soon, darling? Did you forget your sleepy-time tea in here?" He jumped when the open door revealed Piper standing there, not his brother.

"I apologize." He rubbed his hand across his face to hide his embarrassment. "I thought you were someone else."

"I didn't realize you were expecting someone." She slowly started to back away.

"I thought you were my brother," he called out after her, letting his face fall into his hand. "He was just here, and we make fun of each other." *Crap. I'm not good at explaining things.* "Please, feel free to come in."

Piper turned back around with a smirk on her face. "I thought you'd never ask." She sauntered into the room, brushing her side against him as she passed. She sat on the armrest of the chair in his study and patted the chair, wanting him to sit next to her.

He purposely left the door to his study open before sitting beside her. "How was your day?"

"It's been wonderful. I slept in and spent most of the day with my 'TOP' girls. The only thing that would've made it better was if I had gotten to see more of you." She tapped his chest with one finger.

"I wish I had more free time to spend with all of you." *I need to change the course of this conversation.* "Tell me about your life in Rothwell."

Liam listened to her talk about her childhood, her go-to hangout places, and her family for the good part of an hour. *Do women even breathe when they talk? Or did they find a way to live on words instead of oxygen?*

"Thank you for sharing that." Liam gently patted her arm as he stood. "Unfortunately, I should be getting to bed, but thank you for stopping by." He smiled at her, and Liam could see she was putty in his hands.

"No, thank *you*, Prince Liam." Piper glided to the door and blew a kiss at him over her shoulder before leaving, closing the door behind her.

Liam walked over to his desk and fell into his chair, rubbing his temples. He started reading his book again. If there was anything that could put him to sleep, it was policy.

In the early hours of the morning, he was awakened by a hand gently shaking his shoulder. Liam slowly rubbed the sleep from his eyes.

"You fell asleep in your study again, Your Highness," Wadsworth said, his eyes filled with concern. "I'm...worried for your well-being, Liam. You need sleep. And not the kind you're getting at your desk. You need to take care of yourself. Otherwise, you can't care for your people or have the energy to find the best wife for you—someone who loves every part of you."

"Whoa, tell me how you really feel." Liam raised an eyebrow as he laughed. "You don't have to worry about me. I'll sleep once I'm king."

"You know I only say all this because I care about you."

Liam nodded. "You've always been part of our family."

"There's another family member I think you need to hear from. I'll be back shortly." Wadsworth paused, looking over his shoulder. "I'll also bring a pot of coffee while I'm at it. It looks like you could use it."

Liam grunted a response as he rested his head on his hand. Finally, their head butler returned with a large, steaming mug of exactly what he needed. Caffeine. He took a few sips, ignoring the burning sensation in his throat from the lava java. Setting the cup down, he looked back up at Wadsworth. "What are you going to have Barrett say to me? He's already been telling me to sleep more—" Liam's words halted when he noticed Wadsworth reaching into his jacket.

"I think it's time you hear from her again. And this letter seems relevant to your current situation."

Liam reached out and grasped the letter from Wadsworth's extended hand. His mother's script on the envelope almost undid him. But he held it together, craving her words more than anything. *For my dearest Liam, when you are searching for love.*

"I'll give you your space to read it, but please ring for me if you need anything."

Liam simply nodded, unable to form any words as he leaned back in his chair. He pulled the slightly yellowed piece of paper from the envelope and started reading.

My Dearest Liam,

My sweet, sassy, strong-willed, second-born son. I don't know if I've ever told you this before, but I've always related to you more than you know. You may not know it by looking at me now, but I won over your father with my own sass and stubborn nature. I've been able to use those qualities as Queen of Wistonia to stand my ground. To fight hard for what I believe in. And I still have my moments in private with your father when I fall back into my headstrong tendencies and unleash my sassy side.

I honestly think that's why you and your father don't get along as well as I wished you did. He likely sees the sassy, control-seeking parts of me in you that drive him to the brink of insanity, even though he loves you as unconditionally as I do.

I've never shared with you the story of when your father and I first met, but it's a doozy. I was the only child of an earl and was so excited when my name was included on an invitation to a ball held at the Wistonian Palace. I put on my best dress and had a maid fix my hair in the most gorgeous updo. But when I arrived at the ball, it was as if I was invisible. After no one asked me to dance all night, I retreated to the gardens for a breath of fresh air.

That was where I found your father, hiding from the ball. (You know he never really enjoyed dancing.) I walked up behind him and asked if he was enjoying the view. He spun around so quickly that he tripped over his feet and fell toward me. I reached my hands out to try to catch him, but instead, my hand connected with his nose, and I gave him a nosebleed. His momentum carried him forward, and he got blood all over my favorite dress when his body collided with mine.

I was so distraught, knowing my dad would make a scene if he saw my best dress looking like that. Not to mention the fact that I had given a prince a nosebleed. Your father told me he knew just the trick for getting blood out of things and took me back inside the palace. He left me in the kitchen and came back with a soft shirt and shorts I had to tighten with a hair tie so they would stay on my waist. He had me change, and then he himself worked to get the stain out of my dress.

We stayed in the kitchen, eating sweets and talking away the entire evening. By the end of the night, my dress was as good as new, and I knew I would never be the same again—my heart was lost to him. We were so entirely different. I was decisive, obstinate, and assertive, while your father was charming, diplomatic, and driven. But we made sense together. We made it work not only because we loved each other, but because we continued to choose to love each other. Day after day. Even when things got hard.

I tell you this story because not every relationship starts out perfectly. Some start out messy. Some relationships seem to have all the odds against them. Some even start without love. But each relationship has its own path—its own journey. I know that you are a lot like me and that you want to control every situation. That you will likely hate dating because of the unknowns, the things over which you have no power.

First, you must know that you don't need to change yourself for anyone—including our country. Use who you are to your advantage. Let everyone see you for who you truly are.

And my biggest piece of advice for you today, my dear boy, is to listen to your heart. Don't overthink every little thing when it comes to dating. Just enjoy the time you spend with that special woman you will one day choose to be my daughter-in-law. Simply just be with her. Be yourself and the rest will follow. Love will follow.

I love you always,
Mom

Liam took in a deep breath and let it out slowly. Emotion clouded his throat from his mother's words. He had always been close to his mom when he was growing up, but he'd never realized how similar they were, that so many of the characteristics he'd thought would make him a bad ruler had also been held by his mother, who was one of the best rulers he'd ever seen.

He also couldn't believe he'd never heard the story of how his parents met. They'd made him a believer in true love. He had long since abandoned the idea of ever finding love for himself because loving someone meant that he had someone to lose. And he wasn't sure his heart could manage another loss like that.

But what if it is worth it? His mother seemed to believe it was. And he knew she would want that for him.

If he was honest with himself, there was only one girl he believed had the possibility to take hold of his heart.

A certain woman with dark-blonde hair that shone in the sunlight.

A woman who stood up for others she thought were being wronged.

A woman whose eyes were the perfect light-brown color, like pools of coffee with the perfect amount of cream he could get lost in forever.

A woman who was his opposite in many regards, which just might make her the perfect match for him.

A woman with whom he felt like he could be his whole self.

A woman whom his mother already loved and would've been proud to call her own daughter.

A woman named Charlotte.

"Good evening, all! Thank you for tuning in to *Royally Yours*. I am your host, Giovanni Geraldo. I hope you enjoyed watching the fantastic baking date and that splendid garden party. Can you believe it's already been two weeks since the last elimination ceremony and one month since these ladies arrived at the palace?" He held a hand to his heart in feigned shock. "Unfortunately, that means it is time for another elimination ball to occur," he said somberly with a pout on his face.

Giovanni turned to face a different camera with his usual enthusiasm. "But the show must go on, and women must be eliminated for our beloved prince to find the one lady that will walk this life beside him as Queen of Wistonia."

He swept his arm wide across the ballroom as he spun to face yet another camera. "Prepare to be royally entertained, Fenimore! Let the ball commence."

The string quartet started playing a song Liam was sure was popular with teenagers these days—his cue that it was time for him to enter the ballroom. He walked in and down the grand staircase with confidence to the waiting group of women.

"As a reminder to our ladies and the viewers at home, the one woman who is not asked to dance will be leaving the competition." Giovanni gestured to Liam. "Prince Liam, it is time for the first dance."

Liam sent a two-finger salute to Giovanni. Walking in front of the group of women, he extended a hand to Rosalie. "Your Highness, may I have this dance?"

"Of course, Your Highness." She curtsied to him, and he escorted her to the dance floor. He danced a song with her before bowing and leading her over to the area where production had brought couches in.

He danced song after song, asking a different lady to dance when a new song began. The women whom he was asking to stay stood out for one reason or another. Each of the ladies he had danced with so far either had qualities that would make them a good queen or powerful connections that would be beneficial for Wistonia.

After a few dances, they all were starting to blend together, though. There was only one woman who really stood out. Liam pushed she-who-must-not-be-named from his thoughts, trying to focus on the woman currently in his arms.

What's her name again? Lia? No, that's not right. Liana. That's it.

When their dance ended, he walked back to the group of waiting women. As he walked in front of them, deciding whom he would pick for the next dance, his mother's words came back to him. *Listen to your heart.* So, he didn't think. He just did what his heart was telling him.

"Lady Charlotte, may I have this dance?" She wore a form-fitting, plum-colored gown with a soft, flowy skirt that moved with her as she walked toward him to take his hand. His heart pounded in his chest as her fingers lightly grasped his. He led her to the dance floor as a new song started. Another waltz.

Liam pulled her close to him as he led her through the beginning steps.

"I'm starting to think you're purposely choosing me for waltzes so you can hold me close, Liam." She smirked at him as his mouth fell open, startled by such an honest admission from her.

He quickly recovered and quirked an eyebrow at her. Leaning closer, he whispered, "What would you do if I said you were right?"

Now it was her turn to be speechless.

He let out a low laugh. "I'm joking. I don't have a choice in the song selections. But I can't say I'm minding the way things have turned out so far."

"Has anyone ever told you that you're a shameless flirt, Your Highness?"

"Only the media, every day of my adult life. I am 'The Royal Heartbreaker,' after all." He winked.

Her expression grew serious as her eyes found his. "They're wrong about you." A playful glint returned to her eye. "Though the flirty part has always been accurate."

"Thank you for always seeing me. The real me." He rubbed his thumb over hers as their song came to an end. "Allow me to escort you over to the couches."

Charlotte shook her head as a flirtatious grin covered her face. "I'd rather you watch me as I go."

"Who's the shameless flirt now?" he teased as a blush covered his cheeks.

"Still you." She smirked and sashayed away, and Liam couldn't help but watch. He was a gentleman and—*mostly*—kept his eyes above her waist. But even just the way she walked was attractive.

He returned to the group of women still waiting to see if they would be chosen to continue in the competition. He danced with another two ladies before Giovanni appeared back in the ballroom, earning the attention of the cameras.

"Royal viewers, this will be the last dance of the night. Unfortunately, whoever is not asked to dance will leave the competition this evening. Let's see who His Royal Highness chooses for the final dance."

Liam approached the two waiting women, pleased that this was an easy decision after Olive questioned him about the royal jewels. He paced in front of the ladies before stopping in front of The Honorable Mariana.

"May I have this dance?"

"Oh, of course, Your Highness," she exclaimed excitedly.

They danced to the final song of the evening, and then he escorted Mariana over to the other ladies that would be staying while the cameras panned back to Giovanni.

"Since that was the final dance, that means we must, unfortunately, bid goodnight to The Honorable Olive."

Liam approached her, offering his arm before escorting her up the grand staircase. She stifled tears, letting out little squeaks with each step.

When they reached the doors, he awkwardly patted her back. "I'm sorry, Olive. I wish you nothing but the best. I've enjoyed my time here with you." He looked back at the ballroom, where Giovanni was beckoning him to return. "I have to film a bit longer, but if you would like to chat, I'm happy to talk after." He turned and hurried back inside.

Liam stood next to Giovanni as he delivered the typical send-off for the episode.

"And we're clear. Great show tonight, everyone," Alec said.

Liam headed back out into the hallway to find that Olive hadn't waited to talk. He was honestly thankful for that, and it confirmed he made the right choice in sending her home.

As he lay down to go to bed that night, his thoughts roamed back to his mother's letter. Liam wished his mother were here to help him through this process. She had always known exactly what to say.

CHAPTER NINETEEN
CHARLOTTE

Charlotte enjoyed the feel of the wind whipping through her hair as she pushed Artemis—the horse she was riding—to a gallop on the final straightaway back to the stables. She couldn't remember a time when she'd ridden this fast. It made her feel free.

Free of all obligations.

Free of her father's expectations.

Free of everything that had held her back in the past.

She slowed Artemis as the stables came into view through the trees that backed the Wistonian Palace's gardens. A stable boy helped her dismount when she arrived. Charlotte thanked him before turning around and patting Artemis's side. "Good ride, girl."

It was ironic that the horse she rode was named after the goddess of the hunt. Because Charlotte was also on the hunt...for ways to show Liam the depth and truth of her feelings for him. In a competition to not only become his wife but also *queen*, she could imagine he had some reservations about finding a woman who would be there for *him*, not just the throne.

She was on the hunt for ways to prove to Liam that she was here for him—that she wouldn't be here if the royal bachelor wasn't him. Charlotte didn't care about her inheritance anymore. She was one hundred percent here for Liam, and she wanted to make sure he knew that.

The angle of the late-afternoon sun signaled to Charlotte that she needed to start walking back to the palace soon if she wanted enough time to change before dinner. Before she could walk away, a voice behind her stopped Charlotte in her tracks.

"Are you going out for a ride?" Liam gestured toward the stables behind her.

"I actually just got back from one."

"How—" Liam swallowed hard. "How was it?"

"It was just what I needed. The wind in my hair. The sun shining on my face. What more could a girl ask for?"

"I'm glad you enjoyed it." He kicked pebbles with his shoe as he looked at the ground. "What horse did you take?"

"I asked your stable hand for the fastest mare."

"Ah, so you took my mother's horse."

She nodded. "Do you want to join me next time?"

He ran a hand through his hair, his eyes still on the ground.

Charlotte took a step closer to him. "Is everything okay, Liam?"

"I—I haven't ridden a horse since my mother passed away."

Charlotte's eyes glistened with empathy and recognition. "That's why you didn't want to ride with us when I was at the palace in the fall. Oh, Liam, I'm so sorry. It must be so difficult to get back up on the horse, as the saying goes, when you have such traumatic memories connected with riding. Please forgive me for bringing it up."

"You don't need to apologize. It's okay. I know I should be over her being gone by now. It's been years."

"There isn't a time limit for grief." Charlotte set her hand on Liam's arm, hoping to provide even an ounce of comfort.

"It's times like this when I wish she were here the most. When I want to ask for her advice." He walked over to a bench along the outside of the gardens, and Charlotte joined him.

"She's still here with you. I know it isn't the same and nothing could compare to her physically being here, but I still feel her, don't you? Whenever I walk through these gardens or when I catch a whiff of someone wearing floral perfume."

"You're right." He gave her a sad smile. "I think of her whenever I see a forget-me-not flower or when I see someone do a random act of kindness. I also can feel her when I watch an episode of *The Perfect Match*." He laughed. "She would've absolutely loved watching me star on this show."

"She would be so proud of you." Charlotte wrapped her fingers through his.

"Thanks. I really want to do her memory justice by being the best king I can be. I'm just not sure I'm ready. Barrett had his whole life to prepare. I have ninety days that are mostly dedicated to improving my image and this competition. I don't want to let her down. I don't want to let my people down. I just don't know how to make them listen to my words and trust what I'm saying."

"The goal isn't to make the people listen, Liam. The goal is to make them *believe*. The fact that you're worried about letting your people down is exactly why I believe you won't. You care, Liam—more than maybe even you realize. But I can see it." She rubbed his palm with her thumb. "I've always seen it. You'll make a great king. You need to believe that yourself if you want the people to believe it. Show them you care. Show them you love them and this country. Not only with your words but with your actions."

Liam gently squeezed her fingers. "Thank you. I hadn't realized how much I needed this." He stood, pulling her with him. "Also, a bit of insider information since I know you like adventures…I have the perfect date for you coming up tomorrow."

Her eyes filled with hope as they collided with his.

"Err, sorry, poor wording choice. It's more of a group activity. But I think you'll enjoy it."

"Will you be there?" she asked.

"Yes, of course."

"Then that's all I'll need to enjoy it." She smiled up at him, even though her insides twisted at her forward words.

A slight blush climbed up his neck. "I need to go speak with production, but I'll see you at dinner?"

She nodded, and he lifted her hand to his mouth, kissing her knuckles before he left her. The action made a shiver crawl up her spine. Charlotte had never thought it was possible for part of her body to be jealous of another part…but here she was, her lips jealous of her knuckles because they'd been graced by Liam's lips.

As he walked away, she imagined what it would be like to feel the soft touch of his lips on hers.

Charlotte finished the final page of the chapter she was on as Maya walked into her room. She got up and looked at the contents of her closet with Maya, trying to decide what to wear for today's group activity. It would be recorded and televised—not to mention Liam would be there—so she wanted to look cute. But the note about the activity from the production crew was that they should dress in activewear they didn't mind getting dirty.

Because of all her time gardening, Charlotte didn't mind getting a little dirty. But she laughed at the thought of how some of the women in the competition might respond to this date. Things could get interesting today.

"I think you should wear this, miss." Maya pulled out a long-sleeved, charcoal-gray quarter-zip in an athletic material. "You could pair it with some long black leggings and your color-block tennis shoes to bring a little bit of color to your outfit."

"That should work well. It's a bit chilly today. Thanks, Maya." Charlotte grabbed a sports bra from her dresser and took the stack of clothes from her. She changed and then sat on her couch, pulling on socks and shoes. Charlotte stood, wiping her hands on her leggings. "How does it look?" She spun in a circle to show off her outfit.

"Prince Liam won't be able to keep his eyes off you," Maya said.

"That's what I like to hear." Charlotte smiled. "I've gotta get going. Thank you again." Charlotte jogged from her room down to the palace entrance and joined the group of waiting women. All the front curtains were closed so they couldn't see what activity had been set up on the front lawn.

"What do you think we're doing?" Rosalie asked as she sidled up beside her.

"Hmm…something active?" she teased.

"Wow, I never would've guessed that, Nancy Drew." Rosalie nudged her shoulder with a giggle.

"Did we miss it?" Sienna asked as she arrived with Bridgette, both a little out of breath.

"You're just in time." Rosalie gestured to the front door as it opened, and Giovanni walked into the area.

"Ladies, I bet all of you are excited to discover the group date Prince Liam has planned for today. That's right. Prince Liam selected today's date himself. It is an activity he enjoys doing in his spare time, and he would love to include you in it." He looked around the room. "Are you ready?" he asked, his booming voice echoing off the palace walls.

"Yes," a few ladies called back.

"I didn't hear you." Giovanni held a hand to his ear. "I said, are you ready?"

"Yes!" Their shouts filled the room.

"That's more like it. Let's go see what our bachelor has in store." Giovanni opened the double doors at the palace entrance, and the group of women barreled through them. Charlotte and her friends were in the back of the group, but she could immediately tell the activity wasn't what the ladies in front of them expected by their shocked faces and gasps.

She moved to the side so she could see, and her lips pulled up into a smile when she saw what activity had been set up on the palace's front lawn.

Paintball.

Since playing paintball had been her previous means of dealing with anxiety, this was right up her alley. When someone played as many paintball games as she did, they were bound to get good at it—and she was an excellent shot. These ladies definitely wouldn't see her coming.

Liam came out from behind one of the inflatable barricades on the lawn in an all-black outfit and a mask. He removed the face covering as he approached the ladies. His smile was wide, and Charlotte could tell he was completely in his element.

He grabbed a microphone from one of the tech crew and faced the group of women. "If you couldn't tell by the set-up behind me, we're going to be playing paintball today." He gestured to a table next to him. "Each of you will be given protective gear as well as a paintball gun." Liam held up one of the guns and walked everyone through a tutorial on how to shoot it.

Charlotte tuned him out, already having a good understanding of the basics, and instead watched the expressions of the ladies around her. They ranged from shocked to repulsed to terrified.

"So, come on up and grab your mask, and we can then draw for teams," Liam said, pulling her attention back to him. She stepped toward him and grabbed her facemask. Charlotte turned around, and her mouth dropped open in surprise when she saw that only her three friends had joined her. "Does no one else want to play?" Liam asked as his brows furrowed.

"We're happy to watch," Tiffany called back.

Liam nodded, but Charlotte could see the apprehension in his expression.

She walked over to him and ran her hand down his arm. "You're trying to show everyone another side of you. Plus, paintball is a true test of strategy. Not to mention, there are often times you have to do things because of royal obligations that you don't want to. It's their loss if they don't want to participate and show off all those things for you. I surely plan to." She mustered every ounce of bravery within her to wink at him, laying more of her cards on the table.

Before he could respond, he was pulled aside by the head producer, Alec. When he returned, he smiled at the camera. "Since most of the lovely ladies here would prefer to observe today's activity, we've decided to bring in some reinforcements." He gestured to the palace doors.

Charlotte watched as Barrett, Jules, and some royal staff members exited the palace, dressed and ready for battle. Jules immediately walked over to Charlotte, giving her a tight hug.

"I just arrived this morning and have been dying to see you." Jules continued to hold on to her.

"I'm happy to see you too! You've been staying with your parents far too long. But that doesn't mean I won't kick your butt in paintball." Charlotte pulled back and smirked at her.

"I'm officially terrified." Jules laughed before walking back to Barrett.

"It's now time to draw for teams. Ladies first." Liam motioned for Charlotte, Bridgette, Rosalie, Sienna, and Jules to go pull a team color out of a basket.

After everyone had drawn for teams, Charlotte was confident hers would win. She had Liam on her side, along with a few of the stable hands she recognized, some male servers, and Rosalie. They were going up against Barrett, Jules, Bridgette, Sienna, and some other members of the staff.

"It's your dream come true, Barrett. You're surrounded by a bunch of women," Liam whispered loud enough that Charlotte could overhear.

"Oh, you're going down, brother. I can't wait for the day you finally lose," Barrett said, pulling down his goggles and face protection. He turned around and pulled his team into a huddle.

Liam moved closer to Charlotte, pulling their team into a huddle.

"All right, who has experience playing paintball?" he asked, and everyone except Rosalie raised their hand. Liam's expression grew from astonished to one of admiration as he looked at Charlotte's raised hand. She moved her hand to the side of her face, trying to hide her growing blush. Liam turned to Rosalie, showing her the trigger on his gun. "This is how you shoot. But just have fun." Turning back to everyone he said, "We should split up into pairs to help watch each other's backs. So, grab the person nearest you when it starts."

A whistle blew behind them. "It's go-time. Dream Team on three," Liam said, putting his hand in the middle of their huddle. Charlotte put her hand in with everyone else. "One, two, three."

"Dream Team!" they shouted in unison.

Charlotte grabbed her paintball gun and put on her mask. After moving into position, Liam slung his arm around her shoulder.

"It looks like it's you and me, angel." Liam pressed into her side as they hid behind an inflatable barricade.

Her heart skipped a beat, hearing the nickname he'd called her when he was a young teenager. She hadn't heard him call her that in years. What used to be an innocent nickname hit her a lot differently now that they were both grown adults.

"I've got your back if you've got mine," Charlotte whispered as she peeked over the top of the barrier.

"Let's take them down." Liam winked at her and gestured for her to follow him.

They raced for the barrier to the right of them, ducking as they ran. Liam was looking behind her when she noticed someone creeping up behind him.

She grabbed his arm, spinning with him so she had a clear shot of the palace staff member who was trying to sneak up on them. Tapping the trigger of her gun, she got him out in one shot.

Liam whipped his head around, and his eyes grew in admiration, looking genuinely impressed with her. "Nice shot. Thanks for having my back."

"Anytime." She smirked at him behind her mask. Her gaze moved behind him to the other women on the sideline who hadn't wanted to participate. Though many of them tried to hide it, she could see the jealousy oozing from them by their tightly clenched jaws and pinched expressions.

"I see another duo," Liam whispered to her, pulling her attention back to the match.

She followed him around the barricade, and they went back-to-back, both taking out one of the other opponents before they even had a chance to shoot at them.

Maybe we truly are the dream team.

They continued working together to take out the opposing team. At the end of the battle, the only players remaining were her and Liam against Barrett.

"If we get Barrett out, we win." Liam smiled at her through the mask.

"Let's do this." Charlotte looked around the side of the barricade and signaled that the coast was clear. They ran to another barrier, and as she looked over the top, she saw a flash of movement to the right. She pointed out Barrett's location to Liam, and they split up, setting up an attack from both sides so he wouldn't have anywhere to go.

As she rounded the corner, Charlotte rapidly tapped the trigger of her gun with her pointer and middle finger. She heard the paintballs come out in rapid succession.

Pop. Pop. Pop.

They made contact with their target, hitting Barrett squarely in the chest.

Liam picked her up and spun her in a circle. She slid down his front as he set her down, allowing her to feel every contour of his rock-hard chest and abs. They walked hand-in-hand over to Giovanni who declared their team the winner.

Barrett joined them and pulled off his mask, his face covered in shock. "That was some sharp shooting, Charlotte. You might even be a better shot than Liam."

"It can't be that hard," Raina whined as she walked over from the group of watching women and grabbed one of the loaded guns. "How do you work this thing?" She turned toward them just as the gun went off, aimed right at Charlotte.

Charlotte pinched her eyes shut and blocked her face with her arms, bracing for the impact of the paintball…but it never came. She opened her eyes when she heard a grunt in front of her to find Liam leaning over and breathing heavily.

"Liam, did you get hit? Are you hurt?" She turned him around, looking for any evidence he had been shot. Her eyes dropped to his waist where she finally spotted the paintball splatter…right in the one area a man never wants to be hit.

"Are you…are the…" Charlotte pondered how to word her question.

Liam remained hunched over in pain for a few minutes, breathing deeply. As she was about to step closer to check on him, he finally looked up.

"If you're asking me if my Crown Jewels will be okay, the answer is still unknown at this point," Liam rasped, still leaning over with his hands on his knees.

Barrett erupted into laughter. "Please tell me someone got that on video." He looked to the camera crew, who shook their heads. "What a missed opportunity. That could've gone viral." He wiped a tear from his eye and clapped Liam on the back. "Better you than me, though. My wedding is in a week, and I need everything…"

Liam finally stood upright and held up a hand to stop his brother. "Please don't finish that sentence."

Charlotte attempted to hide her amusement as the crowd dispersed. Walking over to Liam, she rubbed his arm. "Are you sure you're all right?"

He smiled at her. "I'll survive. Thanks for the concern, angel."

"Sure thing, hot shot." She lightly punched Liam in the arm, trying to play off the way she was feeling.

"Hot shot. I guess I could get used to that. But I think I might prefer Hot Stuff or Hottie McHot Pants." Liam nudged her arm with his as they slowly walked back to the palace.

"I think Mister Arrogant is more fitting." Her laugh turned into a squeal as Liam's hands grasped her waist, tickling her sides.

She tugged free of his hold and ran back toward the palace with him chasing after her.

"Admit it. I know you think I'm a beautiful specimen," he yelled after her, his voice drawing closer with each word.

She slowed the smallest bit, and his arms wrapped around her again. At his touch, Charlotte's grin pulled so wide her cheeks hurt. It was moments like this when she wished she could take a mental screenshot and replay the scene in her mind over and over again. Because this was a moment she didn't ever want to forget.

The moment she knew her crush had developed into something much deeper.

The moment she knew she had fallen madly in love with Liam.

CHAPTER TWENTY

LIAM

"This is your last chance to back out. Any final words before you're officially a married man?" Liam teased as he walked into Barrett's bedroom, where his brother was getting ready for his wedding.

"I can't wait." Barrett's smile was so big it looked goofy on his face. "There's nothing that could keep me from marrying my beautiful bride. If anything, I'm worried about her backing out. I don't know how I got so lucky."

Liam snorted. "Would you believe she actually said the same thing to me this morning when I warned her it was *her* final opportunity to back out?"

"Really?" Barrett looked at him with a starry-eyed expression.

"Yeah, so you'd better hurry up before she discovers how much of a nincompoop you are." He pulled Barrett into a headlock, and the two wrestled for a moment, like they were children again. Barrett tousled Liam's hair when they were done, and Liam smiled at his older brother. "I'm happy you found each other. Jules is perfect for you."

Barrett took off his shirt and put on a white button-up. "She really is. Now we have to find the perfect girl for you—unless you already know who it is." He waggled his eyebrows.

I know who my heart would choose if I allowed it to make the decision. But I don't know who my head—my logic—will allow me to choose in the end.

"That pause says it all." Barrett's eyes widened. "Talk. Who's the perfect girl for you?"

"It's your big day. We can talk about my love life after you get back from your honeymoon." Liam would avoid his brother's question like a matador side-stepping a bull.

Barrett looked at him for a moment before he continued putting on his white ceremonial suit. "Fine, but I'm not going to forget this conversation." A sly smile pulled at his lips. "Well, I might forget it on my honeymoon because I will have plenty of other things on my mind then." He winked at Liam. "But when I get back, I will immediately be coming to you for the details regarding who has caught The Royal Heartbreaker's fancy."

"I'll see you out there." He started walking toward the door when he suddenly remembered what he'd brought for his brother. "Oh, I almost forgot." Liam reached into his coat pocket and pulled out the cufflinks Barrett had given him with his parents' handwritten "I love you" on them. "I wanted you to borrow these for the day. To have Mom and Dad close to you."

Liam reached out for a handshake, but Barrett pulled him in for a hug with tears in his eyes.

"Thank you." When Barrett let go, his dopey, lovesick smile had returned.

Liam slipped out of the room and had his driver, Dean, take him to the large chapel where the wedding would be held. He braced himself before he entered the building. Inside, he would join the nine women still remaining in the competition. And he was trying not to freak out that he would be celebrating his own wedding day with one of them before he knew it.

♛

Liam walked through crowds of people—his people—waving and smiling at them as he walked from the car to the church. He could sense his bodyguard, Marcus, walking at the same pace as him along the edge of the crowd.

Liam brushed the shoulders of his ceremonial suit as he approached the group of women waiting for him inside the chapel. They were dressed to the nines in their fancy gowns and matching fascinators. Each of them looked like they were playing the part of his wife, attending a royal wedding with him. Even Raina had dressed conservatively, which was definitely a change.

Scanning the lobby of the chapel, he saw several people whom he should probably greet. His cousin James was standing in a corner next to a large stained-glass window, deep in conversation with Lord Howard and Lord Willoughby, both members of the King's Council. Liam also made a point to speak with the rulers that were attending from neighboring nations.

Liam couldn't help but think how different this royal wedding was from others. Royal weddings were typically filled with formality and tradition. If Barrett hadn't abdicated the throne, they would've had a more traditional royal wedding as well. But because of the events that had transpired, they had chosen a more relaxed setup for their big day.

As he neared the women in the competition, he could overhear them dreaming about their own weddings.

"I'll have peacocks imported to be released outside after we say I do," the Honorable Liana said.

"Only the finest of dress designers will do for my wedding. I want something couture. A dress no one has ever seen before. One made for a queen," Lady Piper added.

"The food at my wedding will be top-notch. Caviar. Truffles. Wagyu beef. Only the finest quality products will do," Lady Tiffany said.

Red flags were raised left and right in Liam's mind at their extravagant tastes.

"What do you dream of having at your wedding, Prince Liam?" the Honorable Mariana asked him.

"I've never really thought about it." He mulled over the question. "Maybe I would incorporate a fun new tradition, like paintball." He shrugged, and most of the women around him gasped. Liam walked over to Charlotte and leaned down toward her. "And Raina's definitely not invited," he whispered in her ear and stepped back, winking at her. Honestly, if it weren't for Raina's political ties, he would've already sent her home.

Charlotte attempted to cover her laugh with her hand, but many of the other girls turned to face them with sharp glares. Turning her back to the other women, she looked up at him. "I wish we could be standing up there with Barrett and Jules today."

His brother and future sister-in-law had asked him to be the best man and Charlotte to be the maid of honor. However, after Charlotte's addition to the competition, they'd decided to keep those titles in spirit only and not have anyone stand up at the altar with them. There was no need to cause more jealousy or tension among the group of women vying for his hand.

"I do too. But on the bright side, at least now we can enjoy watching the whole wedding without fear of passing out, standing up there for all of the world to see." He motioned to the camera crew walking into the sanctuary.

"Maybe you would've passed out, but I'm the very picture of grace." Charlotte winked at him.

He feigned a gasp, holding his hand to his chest. "You wound me."

She swatted her hand playfully at him just as the doors to the sanctuary were propped open. Liam ushered the women two at a time to their seats in the second row.

The first row on Barrett's side remained empty in memory of his parents and grandparents who couldn't be with them physically that day. The empty seats for his mother and father brought a heaviness to Liam's chest. He wished they could be there to see this moment, but he knew they were present in their own way.

Finally, he ushered Rosalie and Charlotte into the sanctuary. Rosalie scurried down the row first, leaving Charlotte to take the open seat beside Liam.

A string quartet started playing, and the room of guests fell silent, rising to their feet. Liam stood, watching as his older brother walked down the aisle toward the altar. As his brother neared the row he sat in, he could see the unshed tears brimming in his eyes. Barrett stopped and pulled Liam into another hug before going to stand in place with the priest at the altar.

The song changed to the one that had been playing the first time Barrett and Jules danced together. The only reason he knew that was because Barrett had been talking about it dreamily for weeks. Liam didn't have a habit of remembering songs that were played at balls.

Except for every song I dance to with Charlotte.

Liam turned his head to watch his new sister walk down the aisle. She wore the widest grin, and tears already streamed down her face. Her arm was threaded through her father's, and he looked like he was doing everything in his power to hold himself together. Jules looked beautiful in her A-line wedding gown with a lace overlay. The skirt held just enough volume that it didn't cling to her body, but not enough to overpower her dainty frame. Jules's lady's maid from her time at the palace, Rory, held her long train as she walked down the aisle.

Liam had been told the details of the dress by Jules. He didn't fully understand what all the fashion terms meant, but apparently, that kind of stuff was important to women, so he did his best to remember it and compliment her later.

When Jules arrived at the altar, Rory delicately laid the train behind her and received the bouquet of white roses from her, taking a seat beside Jules's mom.

"Who gives this woman to be married?" the priest asked.

"Her mother and I." Jules's father kissed her on the cheek and set her hand in Barrett's after giving him an embrace so giant it could only be described as a bear hug.

Liam attempted to pay attention to the wedding—he really did. But it was difficult to listen to what the priest was saying with Charlotte sitting next to him, their shoulders touching. The light contact shouldn't have had any effect on him. Shoulders weren't a part of the body people found attractive, right? But here he was, feelings fluttering in his stomach, his heartbeat going haywire because of the pressure of her fully clothed shoulder on his.

"Our bride and groom have chosen to write their own vows as a proclamation of their love for one another. Prince Barrett, you'll go first. Whenever you are ready." The priest motioned to him, positioning a microphone in front of Barrett.

Liam's attention was pulled back to the altar as Barrett's voice came through the speakers, his words laced with emotion.

"Jules, I didn't know what love truly was until I found you. You opened my eyes to what it means to truly live. To do something wild." Barrett smiled at his bride as she laughed freely. "I'm a better man for knowing you. And I promise to continue to grow each day because that's what you deserve. You deserve the best the world has to offer. And I will continue to work every day to be that for you. I'm not perfect, so sometimes I might fail. But I promise that I will choose to love you every single day. Until my dying breath, I will choose you. Over and over." Barrett paused as his voice broke. Chin quivering with emotion, he continued, "Today, I give all of myself to you. My heart, my being, my everything. I love you, Jules."

Liam watched as his brother wiped Jules's tears away with the pad of his thumb. Her gaze was filled with so much love Liam could feel it. Their love for each other wasn't empty words. It was tangible. It was real.

A stifled sob from his right caught his attention. Liam glanced to the side and noticed Charlotte attempting to discreetly wipe tears from her face. He reached inside his pocket, pulling out his handkerchief, and conspicuously pressed it into her hand.

"Thank you," she whispered to him, dabbing her eyes with it.

Liam continued to look forward, trying to focus on what was happening in front of him, ignoring what was happening in his brain and heart, ignoring his desire to wrap his fingers around hers.

The priest moved the microphone in front of Jules and nodded to her.

Jules took in a deep breath before she began. "Barrett, I've dreamed of marrying my very own Prince Charming since I was a little girl. At that point, I thought it would be my daddy." She paused as everyone in attendance laughed. "But from the moment I met you, I knew I wanted that man to be you—before I even knew you were an actual prince. Those were the days I thought you were a long-lost Hemsworth brother." She giggled, and Barrett let out a loud chuckle, his eyes glued on her. "Our story wasn't a conventional one, and things haven't always gone the way either of us expected, but it's still perfect because it's ours." Tears flowed freely down her face as she continued. "You are my happily-ever-after. My dream come true. My Prince Charming. I promise to love you more every day. I promise to hold your hand and wipe your tears whenever life gets hard. I promise to make you laugh every moment I can. And I promise to always throw my purse at you so we never forget the moment we met. I love every part of you, Barrett Phillip Louis Alden, and I cannot wait to officially be your wife." She smiled at him, and he kissed the trail of tears falling down her cheek.

Barrett and Jules exchanged their rings, and then the priest spoke again. "I now pronounce you husband and wife. Prince Barrett, you may now kiss your bride." As their lips met, the wedding guests erupted in applause. Liam even heard a few cheers and whistles ring through the room.

He clapped for his brother and sister-in-law as Barrett dipped her. Liam tried to keep his thoughts away from kissing, but trying to do so was like when someone tells you not to think about something and then that's literally the only thought your brain can produce.

Kissing. Kissing. Kissing.

As his mind focused on the one thing he didn't want it to, he turned to Charlotte, taking in her plump rose lips. Ones that were begging to be kissed. And his own lips were particularly lonely and un-kissed as of late.

Stop it, he scolded himself.

Liam stood with everyone around him as Barrett and Jules walked down the aisle, holding hands and gazing into each other's eyes as if they could only see each other. Jules's parents followed behind them, and Liam fell in line next. It was customary at royal weddings for their immediate family members to see off the happy couple. He followed them in slow steps. Outside the chapel, a horse-drawn carriage waited for them.

He smiled as he watched Barrett assist Jules into the carriage, then climb in next to her. They sat down beside each other, and Jules wrapped her arm through Barrett's. As the carriage started moving, they both looked up and waved goodbye. Liam waved before returning to the chapel to make sure all the ladies made it safely to their cars.

Barrett and Jules had decided to wait to leave for their honeymoon until the morning so they could host a dinner reception at the Wistonian Palace.

As he assisted the nine remaining women in the competition to their waiting vehicles, Liam couldn't help but think that, in less than two months, all of this would be for him. He would be escorting one of the ladies to a horse-drawn carriage after their wedding. He would be married on television for the whole world to see. And then…he would be king.

His insides twisted at the realization. *I want to make the right choice. Am I really ready for a wedding? Am I ready to take a wife?*

He shoved the questions deep, deep down. *It doesn't matter if I'm ready. This is happening, whether I'm ready or not.*

CHAPTER TWENTY-ONE
THE ROGUES

"Let's be quick about this," the blond man sneered, looking at the wedding guests standing all around them after Barrett and Jules's wedding ceremony. "Being seen speaking with each other in public isn't smart."

"Agreed." The man with dark hair turned toward their female pawn. "What updates do you have?"

She flipped her dark hair over her shoulder. "Well, let's see. At the garden party we threw, I sabotaged some of the women who are audience favorites. I also poured a ton of salt in with the sugar for Liam's baking date with Sienna, so that was a catastrophe."

"Very well." The dark-haired man turned back to face him. "Have you thought of any details that could be key to taking down Liam?"

He nodded, a maniacal grin stretching across his face. "There is one thing…Liam is deathly allergic to strawberries."

The other man's mouth turned up at the corners as he leaned closer to the woman. "Do you think you could use your skills of persuasion to have someone make Liam a dessert with strawberries hidden in it?"

"His birthday is next week. I'm sure I could convince one of the girls that strawberries are his favorite since his allergy isn't public knowledge." Her eyes darted back and forth between the men. "But is the goal really to kill him?"

The blond man—the one in charge—waved a hand in the air. "Someone will likely have an EpiPen on hand. Either way, the girl who gives him the strawberry-filled treat will be sent home. And you'll be one step closer to being the woman he selects."

"And one step closer to being queen." She smiled.

The dark-haired man snapped his fingers, their signal to switch the conversation because someone was approaching.

"It was the most beautiful ceremony. Prince Barrett looked so happy with his new bride."

Not a moment later, Prince Liam approached them, smiling at the woman. "Excuse my interruption, but I am here to escort you to the car."

"Of course." The men bowed to the prince before he led their pawn away, back to the palace and the competition.

After they were out of earshot, the blond man spoke in a low voice. "I want you to keep a close eye on her and make sure she holds up her end of the bargain. I can't afford for anything to go wrong."

The other man gave him a curt nod and left the chapel.

He waited a few minutes before leaving, walking to his car with an arrogant strut. *Who am I kidding? Nothing will go wrong. And soon enough, I'll be the most powerful man in Wistonia.*

CHAPTER TWENTY-TWO

CHARLOTTE

"Checkmate." Rosalie slid her rook into place.

Charlotte looked around the board and sighed. "You got me again. How are you so good at chess?"

"When I was younger, my parents traveled a lot. Our butler taught me everything he knew about chess. He would play with me every night before I went to bed."

"That's so sweet—except for the fact that you beat me every time."

"Maybe I'll teach you my tricks one day, if you're lucky."

Charlotte leaned back in her seat, stretching her arms. "What do you say about a different game? There's nothing on our agenda tonight. We could see if the other girls are interested in a game night."

"I love that idea. I'll have my lady's maid gather any of the other women who want to join if you'll start putting together some game ideas?" Rosalie asked.

Charlotte nodded in agreement and got to work. Taking mini slips of paper, she wrote down fun activities for people to guess in a battle of charades. She also set up a truth-or-dare-themed *Jenga* on one of the tables. Shortly after Rosalie returned, ladies began arriving in the women's sitting room.

"This is a great idea, ladies," Tiffany said, walking toward them.

Charlotte forced herself to keep her jaw from dropping. *Is Tiffany actually being…nice?* She quickly recovered and smiled at Tiffany.

"I love any opportunity to win."

Whomp, there it is.

Rosalie and Charlotte shared a knowing look as Tiffany sat down with the "TOP" girls. Well, they were only the "TP" girls since Olive had been sent home at the last elimination ceremony. Turns out those three wouldn't end up on top in the competition after all.

After all the ladies had arrived, Charlotte and Rosalie led them all over to the table where *Jenga* was set up.

"These are truth-or-dare-themed *Jenga* pieces. When you remove a piece you either have to do what that piece says or answer the question on it. Does anyone want to go first?" Charlotte said.

"I will." Raina walked up and pushed a piece through before anyone else even had a chance to respond. A big grin covered her face as she read the wood block she pulled out of the stack. "It's a dare. Read the last text you received." Raina pulled her phone out of her pants pocket and smiled. "He would be an idiot not to choose you. You're the prettiest girl there." She raised one shoulder and smirked, placing the piece she had pulled on the top of the stack and sitting back down.

Charlotte pressed her lips together as some of the ladies in the room began whispering. If Lady Raina lacked anything, it surely wasn't confidence.

Rosalie approached the *Jenga* stack to go next. She slowly pushed out a piece from the middle and read it aloud.

"Truth. Share your greatest fear." Her face turned a deep shade of red, matching her auburn hair. "My biggest fear is public speaking."

"Really?" Wrinkles appeared on Charlotte's forehead as her eyebrows lifted in surprise. "I never would've guessed that."

"I know it sounds a bit silly since I'm a princess and have to do a lot of press conferences, but public speaking has always been hard for me." Rosalie shrugged, placing the piece on top of the stack before sitting back down.

"I'll go next." Sienna popped up and quickly took a piece off the side. Her lips pressed together as she looked at the piece. "Dare. Walk around on all fours like a dog through the next player's turn." She laughed. "Good thing I'm wearing pants instead of a dress tonight." Sienna put the piece on top before dropping to her hands and knees and walking around on the floor as Liana took a turn.

"I pulled a truth piece." Liana held up a wood block in her hand. "Share the thing you spend the most money on." She didn't miss a beat as she said, "Clothes. Definitely clothes." She placed the piece on the stack, and Mariana rose from the couch to go. Sienna sat back down, no longer having to pretend she was a dog.

Mariana pushed a piece through the bottom of the stack, slowing her movements as it nearly fell over. She slid it out the rest of the way, releasing a breath as she held it up in front of her. "It's a dare. Speak in a foreign accent the rest of the evening." She smirked. "That should be easy," Mariana said in a flawless Australian accent. Everyone looked at her with wide eyes, and she only shrugged in response. "I spent a year in Australia when I was growing up."

"I'll go next," Bridgette called out. She approached the *Jenga* stack, evaluating it from all sides before selecting which block to remove. She swiftly removed a piece, making it look easy. "Truth. Share a bad habit you have." Bridgette bit her lip as she thought. "I think one of my worst habits is that I'm always late for everything. Having a lady's maid has definitely helped in this competition. If I didn't have her, I wouldn't be on time for anything."

Tiffany, Raina, and Liana nodded in agreement, sharing how they would be late all the time without the help of their lady's maids too.

Charlotte approached the game and was about to attempt to pull her own wood block from the stack when a throat clearing at the door stopped her. All attention turned to the sound as Liam poked his head into the room.

"What are you ladies up to in here?" he asked.

"We're having a game night," Charlotte responded.

"Do you have room for one more?"

Charlotte looked at all the women, who each, in turn, nodded at her. "Of course. Please join us."

Liam smiled at her as he walked their way. "What game are we playing?"

"We're finishing up some truth-or-dare *Jenga*. Charlotte is going, but then we can play charades," Rosalie said.

"I can get behind some charades. After you, Charlotte." He gestured toward the stack that was leaning slightly to the right.

She walked up, scoping out what piece would be the best to try to remove. Not finding any that looked promising, she started pushing the one closest to her, hoping for the best. Charlotte almost had the piece out when she saw what was written on top of it.

Dare: Kiss the person to your right.

Charlotte slowly turned her head to the side. She spotted Liam standing next to her. On her right. Then all she could think about were his lips. She gulped so loud she was sure it could be heard throughout the room. Yanking as hard as she could on the piece, the whole *Jenga* stack went tumbling to the ground, including the block of wood with the dare she would rather forget about.

"Darn," she said, though a smile covered her face. "Let's head over to the couches for charades." Everyone made their way to sit down when Liam came up beside her.

"What was the truth or dare on the piece you were pulling?" he asked, his tone flirtatious.

She looked up at him with a sassy smile. "Wouldn't you like to know." When they arrived at the couches with everyone else, Charlotte turned to him again. "Why don't you go first, Your Highness?"

"It would be my honor." He bowed to her in a teasing manner.

They drew for teams, and each group sat on a separate couch. Charlotte sat at the end of one couch, near the fireplace, and Liam sat opposite her. He narrowed his eyes at her, one eyebrow raised, and pointed at her then at the ground. It was a motion he used to do in games as a child to say *you're going down.*

"In your dreams," she mouthed back.

They decided one person would go at a time, and they would have one minute to get their team to correctly guess as many clues as possible. The team who had the most points at the end would win.

Liam stood up to go first, and Charlotte flipped a timer for him to begin.

He pulled a piece of paper from the bowl and held one palm out flat, patting his other hand on it and then dabbing gently at his face.

"Applying powder?" Tiffany guessed. Liam shook his head no, then pretended he was holding something between his thumb and pointer finger and did upward motions on his eye, keeping his mouth open.

"Ohhh, doing makeup." Sienna shouted in excitement, pulling a smile from Liam as he dropped the piece of paper and picked up another.

He laughed after reading the next slip of paper, and he clapped his hands together, taking a wide stance and shaking his hips. Liam moved into a little shimmy as he stepped forward and backward.

"Dancing?" Liana guessed tentatively.

Liam pointed at her with his eyes wide and waved his hand asking for a little more.

"Salsa dancing," Piper guessed.

"Yes," he exclaimed, pulling another paper out of the bowl. He quickly pretended like he was climbing up a ladder and then twisting something above his head.

"Changing a lightbulb," Sienna said.

He nodded and headed back to the bowl.

"You have fifteen seconds left," Bridgette called out from beside Charlotte.

Liam picked up another slip of paper, and his face turned a deep shade of red as he turned toward Charlotte. He dropped to one knee, grabbed Charlotte's hands, and looked into her eyes earnestly. His blush migrated to her face, evident by the rush of heat flooding her cheeks.

No one guessed. Everyone just stared at the two of them, mouths either dropped open in surprise or pressed firmly together in jealousy.

Charlotte stared into Liam's sea-blue eyes, knowing in her head this was a game—knowing that he wasn't actually proposing to her. But the knowledge in her head couldn't seem to slow the aching in her heart, longing for this to be real.

"Time's up," Bridgette whispered.

Liam stood and slowly released Charlotte's hand. Turning back to his team, he asked, "How could none of you guess that? That was the most obvious one."

"Guess what?" Tiffany said with an attitude.

Liam held up the slip of paper in his hand. "Proposing. I was acting out a proposal."

"Oh, right." Tiffany sank back into her seat. "Sorry, I thought the time was up."

Everyone else mumbled their agreement.

Liam sat back down across from her on the opposite couch, but she avoided eye contact with him for the rest of the evening.

She feared if she looked into his eyes again, her heart might betray her and cause her to say something stupid. Like how real this was for her. And how she wished Liam would be offering her a real proposal at the end of this.

The sound of ringing church bells floated in the air as Charlotte stood with the other women in downtown Brookside. Every town square in the kingdom was likely bustling with families celebrating Wistonia's Founding Day. Brookside was the closest city to the Wistonian Palace, and it seemed they'd pulled out all the stops to celebrate their country. This was the first time the ladies in the competition were leaving the palace together aside from Barrett and Jules's wedding, and Charlotte couldn't wait to celebrate.

The Honorable Mariana was the only remaining woman from Wistonia in the competition. She pulled them all into a circle to share what they could expect the day to look like.

"It's a national holiday, so almost everyone has the day off and celebrates from morning until late into the night." Mariana pointed to the street next to them. "Brookside has a large parade in the afternoon down Main Street. And in the evening, citizens of Wistonia host large feasts throughout the country. There are always plenty of desserts featuring the Wistonian apple. If you can find any food trucks that haven't sold out of them yet, you'll want to make sure you try one."

"What about Liam? What's he doing that's so important he can't join us today?" Raina asked with a pinched expression.

"Founding Day is the one day a year that the Wistonian royal family opens the doors for people to tour the palace and the gardens. The reigning king sits in the throne room and welcomes people to the palace, hearing their joys and grievances and accepting a bounty of gifts. Since they're currently in between reigning monarchs, Liam is sitting on the throne today."

Raina rolled her eyes as she crossed her arms. "I still think he should be here. It's selfish. We've given up a lot to be in this competition."

Charlotte stood taller. "I'm proud of Liam. He's stepping up and taking on the role of reigning monarch and caring for his people. There's nothing selfish about that."

Her friends, even Tiffany, nodded in agreement. Raina walked off in a huff.

"We'll meet at the parade in a little bit, but have fun, everyone." Mariana smiled and headed off.

Walking down Main Street, Charlotte couldn't help but smile. Loud merriment ensued all around her. Children danced in the closed streets with emerald-green and gold ribbons, flooding the town with Wistonia's colors. Adults kept an eye on their children while enjoying food and drinks from all the food trucks surrounding the square.

"I wish Findorra had a big Founding Day celebration like this," Rosalie said, sidling up next to Charlotte. "We don't even get the day off."

"Does a princess ever truly get a day off?"

Rosalie smirked. "Good point." She held her finger in the air as if she had the most brilliant idea. "That shall be my first decree when I am queen one day—declaring a national holiday so our people get the day off."

"That's a decree I can get behind." Charlotte smiled at her friend.

As they continued walking down the street, they came across a collection of booths offering everything from face-painting to mini Wistonian flags to wave during the upcoming parade.

Charlotte stopped and grabbed a fried-fish sandwich from a food truck as they awaited the start of the parade. Each bite was superb, from the perfectly seasoned, crispy fish to the tangy tartar sauce and the hint of lemon juice. She threw away her empty plate, and the women made their way to the area blocked off by palace guards for them to stand and observe the parade.

A line of fans stood near the guards, waiting to take pictures with all the women still in the competition to be their future queen. Charlotte's cheeks were sore by the time she smiled for one last photo.

The parade went off without a hitch. It was about an hour long and filled with a plethora of floats. Charlotte's favorite float had been decorated by the Wistonian Orphanage. They'd covered their mobile float in brightly colored streamers that fluttered in the wind. Some children rode on the float, waving at the crowd and wearing construction paper crowns. Seeing them pulled at her heart, the way it always had when she'd worked with children in Findorra.

She briefly spoke with the orphanage director, Lila, at the end of the parade. Charlotte could hardly wait to get back to the palace since Lila had told her she would be bringing the children there for a tour of the palace at the direct request of Prince Liam.

Charlotte followed the rest of the ladies back into the palace as guards led them through the crowds of people touring it. Most women went back to their rooms to freshen up, but she wanted to see it all—to get the full experience of a Wistonian Founding Day. She walked down the halls, greeting each person she passed. Many of them did double-takes, looking back at her, wondering if they'd truly seen someone from their television in the real world.

When she came upon the throne room, Charlotte slipped in quietly, hoping to go unnoticed. She didn't want to interrupt Liam's meetings with his people. Hiding in the background near the wall of windows, Charlotte took in the scene before her. The room was grand in every sense of the word. It was nearly as large as the ballroom and had a similar wall of floor-to-ceiling windows. Everything was gold—so much that it would be tacky if it were anything but a throne room, showing off the splendor of their kingdom.

But to her, the thing that shined most in the room wasn't the gold or the many chandeliers. It was Liam sitting on the king's throne at the head of the room, looking like the perfect image of a king. He wore his white ceremonial suit along with his crown, which she had rarely seen him don over the years. She thought he looked handsome in everything he wore, but there was something about a man in formal wear that made a girl's heart pitter-patter.

Charlotte stood in the shadows as Liam met with family after family. He spent an ample amount of time with each of them. She noticed he spent most of his time quiet, really listening to what they were saying. He was going to make a wonderful king, and she hoped the people were able to see that, too.

She slipped out of the throne room and walked to the women's sitting room, hoping to find some of her friends.

"Oh, yay, you're here." Charlotte clapped at the sight of Rosalie and Sienna in the room. "I was hoping to find you. Let's find something fun to do together."

Her friends nodded in agreement, and they played card games while chatting about the day's events.

Suddenly, the door to the room burst open, and Bridgette came hurrying in.

"You have to come and see," Bridgette said through deep breaths. "On the front lawn. Sooo cute." She fell onto the couch like her mission of relaying news was accomplished.

"You don't have to tell me twice," Rosalie said, standing from her seat.

Charlotte and Sienna stood and followed her out of the room, heading to the front lawn to see what was so cute that it couldn't be missed. When they walked outside, Charlotte immediately realized what all the fuss was about.

Every heartstring in her chest tugged at the sight of Liam playing soccer with the orphanage children on the palace's front lawn. Charlotte knew how athletic Liam was. She'd had the great honor of seeing him run shirtless through the palace gardens during her last visit to Wistonia. Seriously, he could make a living charging people to see his abs. Or they should, at the very least, be photographed and hung in some ab hall of fame for everyone to see for the rest of eternity. But looking at him now, one would never guess that he had a chiseled runner's body beneath his joggers and long-sleeve tee.

He fumbled down the field, intentionally running slower than the kids, but pumping his arms quickly to make it look like he was really trying. He went to kick the ball into the goal and missed, sending his leg high into the air and landing him on his bum, making all the children laugh. It was so adorably silly she couldn't help but laugh with them.

Seeing Liam interact so well with kids made her heart melt. If the entire Wistonian population could see this, surely they would all fall in love with their future king as much as she had.

Liam picked up a young boy, threw him over his shoulder, and spun around in a circle. The child's laughter could be heard from a football field away. Charlotte's heart fluttered at the sight.

I don't know how anyone could watch a handsome man do that and not fall madly in love with him.

After seeing the softer side of Liam today with the children and his people, there was no turning back. She knew, without a shadow of a doubt, that her heart was one hundred percent in this. Charlotte could only hope that by the time the competition came to an end, Liam would have fallen as wildly in love with her as she had with him.

CHAPTER TWENTY-THREE

GIOVANNI GERALDO

Giovanni walked into the interview room with swagger, adjusting his hot-pink bow tie before sitting down in his chair. Tiffany walked in shortly after, taking a seat opposite him.

"Lady Tiffany, it's a pleasure to be meeting with you today."

"I'm happy to be here." Tiffany sat up straighter in her chair.

He leaned forward in his seat. "There's a question that viewers at home have been dying for me to ask. Everyone saw the images of you and the other ladies watching the parade on Founding Day. What else did you all do to celebrate?"

"Obviously His Highness was busy acting as reigning monarch throughout the day. However, we all went downtown and experienced Founding Day like true Wistonians. We tried local cuisine from the food trucks and watched the parade, as you mentioned. Oh!" Her eyes lit up. "We also watched Prince Liam playing soccer with children from a local orphanage." She fanned her face with her hand. "I don't think I've ever seen a more attractive sight."

"He will make such a fabulous king, am I right?" Giovanni waggled his eyebrows.

"He most definitely will." Her gaze turned playful. "Do you want a little insider secret before the next episode?"

"When do I ever *not* want a secret?" He chuckled.

"I had a one-on-one date with Liam between his brother's wedding and the Founding Day celebration."

"Stop it right now." He reached over and grabbed her hand. "Give us all the details."

"We had a high tea together in the middle of the ballroom. The set-up was absolutely gorgeous, and I really enjoyed the sunshine beaming through those beautiful windows. The ballroom looks very different in the daylight."

"How magnificent." He crossed one leg over the other, clasping his hands behind his knee. "Can you tell us anything else?"

"You'll have to tune in just like everyone else for the details." She winked at him.

"Oh, you tease." He stood and gave her a small hug. "Thank you very much for your time today."

♛

Giovanni readjusted in his seat before Sienna walked in to join him. His wide grin reappeared as she approached him, and she shook his hand before taking a seat.

"Lady Sienna, I've been looking forward to speaking with you since your baking date with Prince Liam aired."

A slight blush covered her cheeks. "That afternoon was amazing. The whole competition feels more real once you have alone time with him. It feels like you're really dating then."

"Tell me everything." Giovanni emphasized every word.

"Obviously you saw the disaster of the baking portion of the date." She giggled. "But I think situations where things don't work out according to plan help draw people even closer together. I really appreciated how Liam was able to laugh about it—that he didn't take himself too seriously." Sienna sighed and looked off to the side, a dreamy look in her eyes. "Our walk around the palace afterward was what truly stood out to me. We talked more seriously with each other, and it felt like a normal thing, just taking a stroll with your significant other. I honestly haven't been able to stop thinking about him since our date."

"Ooooh." He wiggled his fingers in front of his mouth. "Do you think there's the potential you'll fall in love with our dashing prince?"

"It's too soon to make any sort of declaration, but I can see the potential there for sure." She smiled sweetly at him.

"I, for one, cannot wait to see your journey play out." Giovanni reached over, giving her hand a soft squeeze.

CHAPTER TWENTY-FOUR

LIAM

Liam was always confident going into a first date. He had already been on one-on-one dates with Sienna, Tiffany, and Piper. Even though he had known the dates were being filmed and would be aired, Liam had hardly been nervous about any of them.

Until today.

The instant Liam was told that today's one-on-one date would be a picnic in the gardens, he let Alec know he wanted it to be with Charlotte. Even if he didn't fully know what he wanted anymore at the end of this, he knew he wanted to make Charlotte happy. And she would appreciate a date in the gardens more than anyone.

But as he headed to the gardens for his date with her, his suave, confident manner was nowhere to be found. Liam's stomach was in knots, and it was definitely not a sensation he was familiar with.

Once he reached the camera crew, he noticed an emerald-green and gold checkered picnic blanket had already been set up with a full picnic spread. He grabbed a fresh roll, happy to find it was still warm. Liam shoved it in his mouth and chewed quickly, hoping the bread would help calm the butterflies swarming inside. Instead, the bread felt like a heavy weight in the pit of his stomach.

"We'll have you stand here, Your Highness, so we can get the best angles of you and Lady Charlotte when she arrives," a member of the camera crew said, gesturing to a spot a few feet away. Liam moved over and clasped his hands behind his back, restraining himself from running his hands through his hair. He didn't need anyone else to see his tell-tale sign of nerves.

But the instant he saw Charlotte approaching, his hand was instantly in his hair. She looked like a vision in her long, sage-green dress and a sand-colored boater hat. She looked like a *queen*. One as poised and proper as his mom. The reminder of his mother made the roll turn over in his stomach.

Thoughts of her always filled him with a range of emotions. He wanted his mom to be remembered by him and all the Wistonian people. But he had a hard time finding healing in his memories of her and anything that he connected with her—like the gardens and horses.

The fact that Charlotte reminded him so much of his mother brought a lot of pain with it. Seeing her in the gardens and knowing that was a connection they shared together was beautiful, but seeing Charlotte walk toward him amongst all the flowers still stabbed at his heart. He swallowed down his emotions and the pain.

Maybe one day I'll be able to see connections to my mother in a positive light.

Liam forced a tight smile on his face as Charlotte reached him. He took her hand and kissed her knuckles. "A pleasure to see you, as always, Charlotte."

She smiled at him as they both sat down on the picnic blanket.

"They set up quite the spread for us." Her eyes darted around, hungrily taking in all the food.

He handed her a plate. "Please eat anything you want."

Charlotte started packing sweets onto her plate. She paused to lick her fingers when her eyes found his again. "Are you going to eat anything?"

He hadn't planned on it after the roll had rebelled against his stomach, but he didn't want her to feel awkward being the only one eating, so Liam grabbed a plate and started adding a few finger sandwiches and desserts to it.

"I was trying to be a gentleman and let you pick what you wanted first."

His answer seemed to satisfy her, and she began eating. Her eyes closed in satisfaction after she took a bite of a mini chocolate croissant.

"Charlotte, may I ask a bit of a prying question?"

"Depends on the question," she responded with a smirk.

"Why did you enter the competition? Don't get me wrong, I'm happy to have you here. I've had brief encounters with most of the women here my entire life, but we've basically grown up together."

Charlotte stopped eating, and her eyes darted around as if she was trying to figure out if she was going to tell him the truth or come up with a lie. "I actually didn't find out about the competition until the last minute. I don't know if you're aware, but Jules actually recommended me for a spot. She knew I was in a bit of a…sticky situation and thought this was the perfect solution."

His heart stopped at her words. He knew from Barrett that she had to get married by her thirtieth birthday—which was coming up very soon—to receive her inheritance.

Is that the only reason she's here? To get married and receive her inheritance? I can't handle another Mila situation—someone tricking me into believing they have feelings for me when all they want is money or the throne.

He was still fighting his own heart on whether he would change his ways and allow himself to love again, and of the women left in the competition, the only real threat to his heart was Charlotte. But he didn't know if he could allow himself to fall in love with her if she didn't feel the same way about him—if this was about convenience rather than love for her.

Charlotte eased his thoughts with the wave of her hand as if she could read his mind. "That's not really why I came, though."

"What is your reason?" Liam's voice was husky, his heart in his throat as he hung on to every word she said.

"If you have to ask, I don't think you need to know yet." She slowly bit her lower lip, and he was a goner. "A girl's gotta keep some air of mystery about her."

"Then you can call me Sherlock Holmes, on the case." He winked at her and dipped an imaginary top hat. Liam played along, even though he was dying to know the real reason she had come to vie for his hand.

She shook her head at him, though he saw the laugh she tried to hide behind her hand.

Out of nowhere, drops of water landed on Liam's face. "What the…" He looked around as he wiped the water off with his sleeve. He spotted the sprinklers in the ground as the culprit and quickly grabbed Charlotte's hand, pulling her to her feet. "We have to go before they all turn—" His words were cut off as the other sprinkler next to them turned on, now showering them from all sides. He pulled her behind him, moving as fast as he could out of the gardens. When they reached the edge of the pond on the outskirts of the gardens, Liam finally turned around to face Charlotte.

Laughter from deep within sprang forth before he could stop it from escaping. Charlotte's dress was soaked completely through, appearing a dark-green color instead of the light green it had been moments ago. He tried not to notice how the fabric clung to her body, further accentuating her feminine curves. Liam instead kept his eyes on hers, which looked like a raccoon's from all the mascara she had dripping down. Her hat must have flown off in the run, leaving her hair looking like she had just come out of the shower.

Liam shook off his linen jacket, happy to find that his shirt underneath was nearly unscathed from the surprise shower. Charlotte's lips turned down in a pout, and he wanted to kiss it right off her face. She looked like an adorable, soaking-wet puppy who'd just had its favorite bone taken away.

"How?" she sputtered. "You're not wet at all."

He shrugged, and his lips pulled up at one corner in a sly smirk. "Do you want my shirt?" Liam started to lift the hem of his shirt, watching her gaze take in the abs that he worked so hard for.

"You're incorrigible," she huffed, crossing her arms over her chest.

"Now, this is the Charlotte I've been waiting to see," he said. She raised an eyebrow at him. "The real one beneath that mask you try so hard to keep up." He started laughing again as she walked to stand beside him.

"I've got plenty more where that came from, Liam Charles Frederick Alden."

She leaned over and shoved his arm. He didn't have a chance to brace himself, caught off guard by the push. He knew he was going to fall into the pond, so he grabbed her arm, pulling her with him.

Charlotte let out a little yelp as they both fell into the water, his hand still wrapped around her arm. When his head surfaced, he continued laughing. Charlotte grazed her hands across the water, splashing him in the face.

He smiled his most flirtatious smile before swimming closer to her. Wrapping his arms around her while treading water, he whispered, "I would love to see more of that, Charlotte Elizabeth Croft." Pulling his head back, he laughed freely.

He was about to let go of her when she wrapped her arms around his back, hugging him to herself. Liam watched as her eyes fell to his lips, and he slowly inched his face closer and closer to hers. Their mouths were close enough that he could feel her breath intermingling with his. Her hands moved up to his neck, playing with his hair at the nape of his neck.

Liam hadn't known this kind of feeling existed. That someone could have such a hold over his emotions. That he could tangibly feel the romantic tension in the air between them. He had always vowed to never love again. But if this was what love felt like, maybe it was a feeling he wanted. If this was merely the lead up to a kiss, he could only imagine what it would feel like to have Charlotte's lips on his.

Before he could brush her lips with his, she let out a mischievous giggle. Charlotte moved her hands to his shoulders and shoved him under the water.

He came up coughing out pond water. Liam shook his head at her, though his eyes shone with amusement. "You're gonna pay for that."

"What?" she asked innocently with a playful tilt of her head. "You said you wanted to see more of that side of me, Your Highness. I was only honoring your wish." She did a weird curtsy in the water.

He laughed and turned to better face her, only then noticing the cameras that had followed them. Pushing down his embarrassment that all this was being filmed, he cleared his throat and jerked his head to the right.

Her eyes widened as she took in the camera crew. Happiness swirled inside him that she had been so caught up in their interaction that she'd momentarily forgotten the cameras were there, too.

Maybe this feeling between us is mutual.

Luckily, he didn't have to have the answer to that question today. He got out of the water and turned back to help Charlotte. She grasped his forearms, and he easily pulled her out. Liam walked over and grabbed his linen jacket from the ground. Crossing back to her, he draped it over her shoulders.

"Sorry it's a little wet, but it's the best I can do at the moment."

"I appreciate the gesture." She smiled at him.

Liam motioned back to the palace. "I should really get you back inside before you catch a cold. I'm sorry our date took such a wild turn." He offered his arm to her, which she accepted. Her touch felt as natural as breathing air.

"I'm not," she whispered for only him to hear.

Feelings started swirling in his belly, and this time, it wasn't because of the roll.

♛

Liam sat at the dining room table, pushing green beans around on his otherwise empty plate. His appetite may have recovered from his picnic date with Charlotte, but his mind hadn't stopped running a million miles a minute.

He'd tried to maintain a polite conversation with some of the women at dinner, but it was like his brain wasn't connecting with his mouth.

"Your Highness, this meal reminds me of our museum date," Piper said.

"Why would lettuce wraps remind you of a date to an old museum?" Raina wrinkled her nose.

"I don't know…" Piper sputtered. "It just did."

Liam knew he should defuse the tension between the women, but he didn't have the energy. His mind was otherwise occupied with thoughts of Charlotte.

What did she mean that if he had to ask why she'd joined the competition, he didn't need to know yet? After their pond escapade, he couldn't help but think that meant she had real, deep feelings for him. But if that was the case, why hadn't she said anything over the years?

He set his chin in his palm. *This isn't me. I'm not the guy who obsesses over whether a girl likes me. What is Charlotte doing to me?*

Once the meal concluded, Liam was ready to retire to his room for the evening. He'd had enough of the cameras today.

Before he went to bed, he stood on the balcony attached to his room, overlooking the gardens. Everything that happened with Charlotte today had made him realize his heart was softening. That the vow he'd made to himself to never love again after Mila had broken his heart may not be what he wanted anymore. That maybe—just maybe—he was open to the idea of having a love match at the end of this competition.

♛

Liam couldn't get Charlotte out of his mind all week. A few days prior, all the women had accompanied him to a charity event for the seventy-fifth anniversary celebration of Feed Wistonia, an organization that provided food to those in need. But no matter how hard Liam tried to focus during the event, his eyes kept searching for Charlotte in the room, wondering to whom she was talking and wanting to watch her do what she did best—enchant everyone with her charming, kind personality.

He had missed questions people asked him and had to be poked countless times by his brother and Lindsay throughout the evening to draw his attention back to what he was supposed to be doing.

This evening, he sat waiting for Raina, who was running forty minutes late for their candlelit dinner date. His eyes roamed around the small room, taking in the romantic décor the production crew had set up. Liam sat at a small round table, where the chairs had been placed close enough together that their legs would touch. Gold chargers sat on the white tablecloth, along with a centerpiece of red roses. Candles were lit all throughout the room, providing a warm glow, and rose petals were scattered over the white marble flooring.

It would be a dreamy setting for a date...if his date would ever arrive.

Charlotte would never be late. His head fell into his palm, and he corrected his thought. *A queen would never be late.*

"Hello, darling," Raina purred, strutting into the room in a skin-tight red dress with a slit up to her mid-thigh.

I don't think she owns any clothes in a color other than red.

"Raina, you look lovely tonight." Liam stood and helped her into her seat. What he really wanted to do was take off his suit jacket and help her cover up more.

"I know." She leaned in toward him, pressing her leg against his and twirling her dark hair around her finger. "It takes time to look this good."

He nodded, biting his tongue. Liam didn't want to say something stupid in front of the cameras. He motioned toward the staff that they could bring out their meals.

Dinner plates were placed before them, and the domes were lifted in a synchronous motion to reveal filet mignon, lobster tails, smashed potatoes, and broccolini. He thanked the wait staff and started cutting into his filet.

"How are you enjoying your time at the palace?" Liam asked after finishing his first bite.

"I would be having an even better time if I got more alone time with you." Raina bit her lip and slid her hand onto his thigh. He placed his hand on top of hers and took it, giving it a gentle squeeze and discreetly removing it from his leg.

"I wish I had more time to spend with everyone, but the duties of a future king wait for no one." He continued eating his dinner while she merely pushed her food around the plate, nibbling on one piece of broccolini.

Her lips turned pouty as she moved her fingers in circles on his forearm where it rested on the table. "Not even me?"

Liam shot her a forced smile. "Unfortunately, no. But you do have me all to yourself this evening."

"We'll have to make the best of it, then," she said, tilting her head.

The rest of the meal passed by slowly as Liam tried to evade Raina's forward advances and flirty comments. He mostly kept his gaze locked on his plate as he devoured the rest of his filet and lobster.

Her efforts were all for naught with him. Nothing about her fakeness was attractive to him. Her political connections were the only reason she was still here. That, and the fact that Raina wasn't someone he would ever fall in love with. She wasn't a threat to his heart.

CHAPTER TWENTY-FIVE
LIAM

Liam was honestly starting to worry for his sanity. He was becoming lackadaisical in his duties, unable to be present in his studies when his mind was elsewhere—on *someone* else.

But Liam was determined to make this day different. Because today was his birthday. His twenty-sixth birthday, to be exact. He needed to get out of his own head and celebrate his last birthday before he became king. Nothing grand was on the schedule, but he wanted to enjoy the day with a clear mind.

Wadsworth had given him a note with his morning coffee, informing him of a new meeting scheduled in the men's sitting room at nine. Liam put on a maroon sweater over his white button-up, a nice complement to his gray dress pants. He walked to his sitting area and took a large, final gulp of his coffee to prepare for whatever the meeting was.

Liam was in such a rush to get to the men's sitting room that he'd forgotten to grab his EpiPen, but he hadn't needed to use one since he was twenty, so he brushed it off. He heard voices coming from behind the door to the room before he opened it. Liam pushed it slowly, confused that the room appeared to be empty. Suddenly, all the women in the competition burst out from under tables and behind the couches.

"Surprise!" they yelled in practiced unison.

"What's all this?" Liam looked around at his final nine women.

They all smiled before Bridgette stepped forward shyly. "We thought we'd throw you a small birthday party. We know you have a lot going on in your life right now, but you still deserve to be celebrated, so we put this together for you."

"All of us." Tiffany stepped forward, making sure her part in this was known.

Liam took it all in. The effort these women had put in to make his day special hit him right in the heart. Emotion swelled inside him at their thoughtfulness.

He cleared his throat, hoping his words would come out devoid of the emotion he felt. "I'm honored. Thanks for planning this for me."

"Let's get this party started." Piper cranked up old hip-hop music on the Bluetooth speakers.

He ate a plate full of his favorite breakfast foods—cinnamon sugar donuts, breakfast sandwiches on croissants, and English trifle. That last one wasn't technically a breakfast food...but it had blueberry jam in it, so that counted, right?

Once they were done eating, Sienna pulled out the card game *Uno*.

"I thought we could play this game but with a twist...we'd make it *Spicy Uno*," Sienna explained as everyone sat around a table.

"You know I'm down for that." Raina giggled.

"It's not spicy in that way." Sienna blushed. "There's an added layer to the game. There are certain numbers that cause something to happen when played. For example, if anyone plays a six, everyone slaps the table, and the last person to do that has to pick up a card. When a seven is played, everyone has to be silent until another seven is played. If you talk, then you have to take a card."

"Ooh, this is going to be fun." Piper scooted her chair a little closer to him.

Sienna explained the rest of the rules as she shuffled the deck and passed out the cards.

"I could totally get behind this. Let's play." Tiffany picked up the cards Sienna had dealt her.

Liam took his own hand and started rearranging them by color and number. Once he finished, he looked up, and his eyes connected with Charlotte's across the table. She gave him a small smile and a little wave, and he could've sworn his heart skipped a beat from the simple motion. He shoved his heart far, far down. *I said I was going to have a clear mind today.*

Her smile fell when he didn't respond, but he wouldn't let it impact him. Not today.

Throughout the game, she kept trying to catch his gaze, but he avoided it like the plague. If he looked at her for too long, he would catch something far more dangerous than that—feelings.

"Uno," Liana called out, holding her final card close to her chest.

When it was his turn again, Charlotte started to open her mouth to say something, and he slapped a seven in a matching color down on the pile. Silence. Perfect. That was exactly what he needed.

Liana played her final card a few people later, ending the game.

"Good job, Liana." He turned to face Sienna. "That was really fun."

Liam glanced at his watch and noticed it was lunchtime. He stretched his arms and stood. "I have a King's Council meeting, so I, unfortunately, must get going. Thank you all for planning this special morning for me. It truly means the world." Liam quickly hugged each of the women before leaving with a genuine smile on his face.

"What's on the agenda for today, gentlemen?" Liam plopped down in his seat at the head of the table just in time. Not a minute early or late.

"You," Lord Willoughby replied.

"That sounds ominous," he teased.

"We need to talk about your progress in the competition and how the Wistonian people are responding to the show."

"Okay." Liam gulped. He had been avoiding reading any articles about him. Better to live in ignorant bliss and hope for the best than to see his name smeared across the media. "What would you like to know about the competition?"

"How many women are you down to now?" Marquess Richard Dunmore asked.

"Nine. I have sent three women home, between the elimination ceremonies and individual conversations."

"That's decent progress." The councilman nodded, seemingly pleased with his answer.

"And what are the prospects looking like? You have a little over a month remaining until your ninety days are up. That means you have to propose and have the wedding before then so we can fit in your coronation as well," His Grace, Duke George Knowlton, said.

Liam knew how much time he had left. It was like an internal clock constantly counting down inside him.

Tick.

Tick.

Tick.

Thirty-four days.

Tick.

That was all that remained. And he knew it. But hearing someone else say it out loud made it feel more real—that he would be married by the end of May.

He shoved his anxieties down and calmly answered the question. "The prospects are looking bright."

"That sounds like the inside of a fortune cookie." Lord Howard chuckled.

Liam clenched his fists under the table. "I have multiple women here who would make an excellent queen, and I am certain I will be able to choose the best fit for me and the throne before my time is up." He looked back to Lord Willoughby. "Dare I ask how the people are responding to the show?"

"You're winning over the people, Your Highness." Lord Ackerley smiled at him.

"The latest polls show your support has grown by twenty-six percent in the last month alone. It appears the people like what they are seeing on the show. They comment about how they like seeing the 'real you' and 'the man behind the curtain.' I would say keep doing what you're doing because it's working so far." Viscount Clive Eston straightened a stack of papers in front of him on the table.

Liam exhaled a sigh of relief. He was gaining the trust of his people. The show was working. *Maybe I can do this after all.*

"I will have Wadsworth hire the best wedding planner in the country to begin preparations for the last Saturday of May. Then we can have the coronation ceremony that Sunday," Liam said.

"You're cutting it close, having your coronation ceremony on the ninetieth day. Isn't that a bit risky?" Lord Howard narrowed his eyes at him, a smug expression on his face.

"What's life without a little risk?"

"Let us know what we can do to support you, Your Highness." Lord Ackerley gave him a supportive smile. Liam was thankful to have at least one friend on his side.

"Yes, we have everything under control for now. We'll let you know if we need your input on any decisions. But for now, we need you to focus on selecting your bride." Lord Willoughby pushed back his chair, signaling that their meeting was over.

Liam stood, thanking all of them. He walked back to the men's sitting room to catch up on some policy regarding trade agreements before Barrett returned from his honeymoon. With each step he took, two words kept reverberating through his mind.

Your bride.

Liam rubbed his temples after finishing his fifth chapter of the day in his current read, *Wistonian Policy of the Past and Present*. While it did not seem like too much to read in one sitting, reading five chapters of policy at once was like filling a toy dump truck with the entire sandbox: information overload.

Out of nowhere, soft, cold hands covered Liam's eyes from behind, making him jump.

"I have something special for you."

The hands left his face, and he turned around to see Piper holding a white porcelain plate with a single cupcake.

He really had enjoyed his one-on-one time with her a month ago, when they had explored a museum together. Piper had proven to be flirty but kind. He'd had a good time even though their conversation had remained on surface-level topics. Liam stood from the couch and walked over to her.

"I was told it's your favorite flavor." She smiled up at him, extending the plate in his direction.

Liam took it from her, eyeing the cupcake that appeared to be plain vanilla. Definitely not his favorite flavor, though he wouldn't tell her that. He was more of a chocolate guy himself…and not because it was the favorite flavor of a certain woman.

"Thanks." He held it up to her in a cheers motion and took a giant bite, not wanting to be rude. The vanilla flavor was warm and actually pretty pleasant, but there was a flavor he couldn't quite put his finger on. "What's in this filling?" Liam asked, his throat starting to feel scratchy.

"It's strawberry jam. Your favorite." She gave him a *duh* expression.

His eyes grew wide in alarm as he felt his tongue start to swell. "I need the doctor now," he said. But the words came out slurred and indistinguishable. Liam's heart began to race as he reached into his pocket only to find it empty. *Of course today is the one day I forgot to carry my EpiPen.*

Piper looked at him with a puzzled expression. There wasn't much time before he would go into anaphylactic shock. He pointed to his mouth where he could already feel his tongue and lips swelling.

She gasped in horror and promptly started freaking out. "Oh my gosh," she squealed. "Someone help! Something's wrong with Liam's mouth." The corners of her lips twisted into a grimace as she took a step back from him as if what he had was contagious and she might catch it. "I'm sorry. I can't be around any kind of sickness." Piper hurried from the room.

He was left alone as his hands started to tingle, and his body suddenly felt like he had stepped outside into one-hundred-degree weather. He could feel hives starting to climb his neck, and nerves settled in as his airway started to close. A wave of nausea hit him. *Is help ever going to come?*

A palace staff member rushed in with another blur of a figure moving behind her. "What's wro—oh, hold on, Your Highness," the young maid called out as she ran to a desk across the room and pulled an EpiPen from the top drawer. She rushed over to him but paused, seemingly unsure what to do. He held out his hand to her, but it shook too hard to get a strong enough grip to use the auto-injector.

As he felt his body weaken, Liam knew he might lose consciousness soon. He felt his whole body tremble in fear that this would be the end. Suddenly, a gentle hand was on his shoulder. He saw Charlotte standing next to him as his vision began to blur. She grabbed the EpiPen from his hand, removed the safety release, and pushed it into the middle of his thigh, holding it there and supporting him as he leaned into her. Charlotte's presence alone brought a calming sensation to him.

She pulled it out of his leg and gently rubbed the area where she had administered the injection. Liam noticed his allergic reaction was no longer worsening, and he finally felt like he could take a decent breath again. As the rush of adrenaline took over, he started to notice the scene around him again. Charlotte's hand still rested tenderly on his thigh with her other wrapped around him, supporting his weight as much as she could.

Her touch did something to his insides. It undid him. His heart was already racing because of the life-threatening situation. But he knew if it hadn't been racing from that, it would be racing from Charlotte's touch. From the realization that Liam was falling for her. And he wasn't sure his growing feelings for her were something that could be stopped.

His eyes found hers. "You saved my life."

"Let's not be dramatic. I'm sure it would take a lot more than an allergic reaction to bring down *the* Prince Liam," she teased.

He tried to laugh, but it turned into a cough from his still-shortened breathing.

Charlotte helped him over to one of the couches and instructed the maid to go fetch the palace doctor.

Liam leaned back into the leather cushion, trying to focus on each breath. "How'd you know how to use the EpiPen?"

"My mom is deathly allergic to bees. She taught me how to use one from a young age just in case."

"Remind me to thank her one day." He weakly smiled at Charlotte, the effects of the adrenaline rush starting to wear off.

She scooted closer on the couch and stroked his hair like his mom had when he was a young boy. The sensation made his eyes prick with tears at the memory, but he oddly felt a sense of comfort at the same time.

The door flung open, and Doctor West hurried into the room, rushing over to Liam.

He heard Charlotte explain the situation to him. After the doctor checked his vitals, it was decided that Liam would remain there rather than move to the infirmary so they could get medicine in him more quickly. The doctor inserted an IV and started pumping medicine into him. Charlotte promised Doctor West she would call for him if anything changed.

Once the doctor left, they were alone in the room together.

Charlotte scooted closer to him again, running her fingers through his hair. "You should rest. I'll stay here with you and make sure you're okay."

He leaned into her touch, resting his head on her shoulder. "You're always taking care of me."

"We take care of each other. It's what you and I do, remember?"

Her gentle, kind voice had him closing his eyes. Just as he was about to be lulled to sleep by the rhythmic, soothing feeling of her hands in his hair, he felt her lips press to his temple in a brush of a kiss—so light he wasn't even sure it happened. His body nuzzled against hers of its own accord, and then he drifted off, wrapped in the arms of the woman who was starting to feel like home to him.

Someone gently shook Liam's shoulder, pulling him from his deep slumber. He pried his tired eyes open to find that he was still in Charlotte's arms. Only now, his brother and new sister-in-law were standing in front of them, looking down with wide grins on their faces. They shared a conspiratorial glance that made Liam roll his eyes.

Liam grabbed the back of the couch and pulled himself up into a sitting position. Glancing back at Charlotte, he could see he'd left a circle of drool on her shoulder. *Lovely. That's attractive.*

"Sorry about the…" Liam pointed to the spot on her shoulder, but she brushed off his comment.

"You needed the rest."

"Yeah, you looked very…cozy there, brother." Barrett pressed his lips together like he was trying not to laugh.

Jules giggled as her eyes kept darting back and forth between him and Charlotte.

"I should head upstairs to my room to get changed for dinner and let you all catch up. I'll send for Doctor West to check on you." Charlotte stood and gave Jules a side hug before leaving them.

"Duuuude, you didn't tell me you had the hots for Charlotte!" Barrett grinned from ear to ear.

"Every part of that sentence sounded so wrong coming out of your mouth." Liam rubbed the sleep from his eyes. He swallowed a big gulp of water from the glass sitting on the coffee table, finding it was a lot easier to talk and breathe now that his allergic reaction had been stopped. The medicine must have all kicked in while he rested.

Barrett leaned forward and shoved his shoulder. "What's going on between you two? Is she the one you wouldn't tell me about before our wedding?" He pulled Jules into his side, and she melted into him, giving him a dreamy look.

"There's no such thing as 'the one.'" Liam made air quotes around the final words. "I'm enjoying my time with Charlotte, but it's too soon to say what's going to happen at the end of this."

"How many women are still here?" Jules asked.

"Nine."

"Why do you still have most of the women here? You need to start eliminating more of them and get serious about this. You only have a month left to find your bride." Barrett looked concerned.

Liam raked his hand through his hair. "I know, I know. I'm actually going to send one of them home before dinner tonight. Her birthday gift to me was an allergic reaction."

Why did someone tell her my favorite filling was strawberry? Surely she mistook them saying blueberry.

"What?" Barrett's voice boomed throughout the room. "Why wasn't I contacted?"

"It wasn't truly life or death. Piper gave me a cupcake with strawberry filling. Charlotte stabbed me with an EpiPen, and I was sleeping off the effects of that and Doctor West's medicine when you showed up. Otherwise, I would've already reached out to let you know."

Doctor West came into the room after a light knock on the door. He took Liam's vitals and unhooked him from the IV when he seemed pleased with the results. "Everything looks good, but please don't hesitate to call me if you feel any symptoms returning."

Liam nodded his thanks, and the doctor bowed before leaving them.

"I'm glad Charlotte was there to help you," Jules said with a wink.

"You two are the worst." Liam threw a pillow at his brother.

"You know you love us," Barrett cooed back.

"As for how many women are still here…I have the perfect idea of how I can help you," Jules said.

"You're allowed to do whatever you want." Liam stood and started walking to the door. "As long as my brother isn't involved," he yelled back over his shoulder.

He left behind a laughing Jules and sulking Barrett. Liam walked back to his room to get ready for dinner, stopping only to send Piper home along the way. She didn't take it well, but he couldn't risk having someone so careless as queen. If she couldn't think to check if he had any allergies, who was to say she wouldn't do the same for visiting guests?

As he got ready for dinner, he felt more sure of himself than he had in a long time. He was doing this. He was sending people home. He was starting to figure things out. And he was slowly gaining popularity with his people.

Maybe I can do this after all. And this time, he actually believed himself.

CHAPTER TWENTY-SIX
CHARLOTTE

You are cordially invited to a spa night in the women's sitting room this evening at seven o'clock. Hosted by Her Royal Highness, Juliette Alden.

Charlotte smiled at the words on the gold-embossed invitation in her hands. She had hoped she would get to spend more time with Jules before she and Barrett moved to their mountain estate a few hours away from the palace.

It was fifteen minutes until seven, but she couldn't wait anymore. Stopping in front of her floor-length mirror, she adjusted the collar of the emerald silk pajamas that had accompanied the invitation.

Jules's head popped up from behind a table of fancy appetizers and desserts when Charlotte walked into the women's sitting room. Jules squealed and ran over to her, pulling her into a tight hug.

"I know we already saw each other once, but you were a little preoccupied at the moment." Jules winked at her. "It's so great to see you."

"How was your honeymoon?" Charlotte asked once they had pulled apart, trying to change the course of the conversation. "But please, spare me the mushy details."

A blush climbed Jules's neck, landing on her cheeks. "It was wonderful. The more time I spend with him, the more I realize how perfect we are for each other."

"You truly are a perfect match." Charlotte walked over to the couch and sat down, Jules following closely behind. "What was your favorite thing about London?"

"I loved the private walking tour of Westminster Abbey. So much rich history has happened there. It gave me chills just thinking about it." Jules leaned her head against the couch. "Barrett also arranged a carriage ride around Hyde Park. I felt like I was being courted by a gentleman back in Regency times. It was magical."

Charlotte sighed. "If that isn't every woman's dream, I don't know what is. Now if only Mr. Darcy would walk through the door." She looked longingly at the door.

"I think you already found your Mr. Darcy." Jules gave her a knowing look.

"Liam isn't *exactly* like Mr. Darcy. He's definitely more flirty and less grumpy."

"Ah-ha!" Jules pointed a finger at her. "I didn't mention Liam's name." Jules waggled her finger in the air, still pointing it at her. "You *are* in love with Liam."

Charlotte sunk into the couch, putting her hands to her face. "What would you say if I was?"

"I would be ecstatic. We could be actual sisters." Jules bounced up and down on the couch cushion.

"That would be amazing." Charlotte reached over and squeezed her hand. "I don't want to get my hopes up, though. He may not feel the same way. I thought he was about to kiss me in the pond the other day, but I may be reading into things."

"An almost kiss in the pond? How did I miss so much? I wasn't gone that long." The words fell out of Jules's mouth so quickly it was like when Charlotte tried to listen to an audiobook at twice the normal speed. She had to listen hard to catch what Jules was saying.

Feminine voices came from the other side of the door. Charlotte stood, thankful for the interruption. "Looks like your duty calls."

"I'm not gonna forget about this," Jules whispered. "I'm planning on getting all the details from you later." Jules walked to the door with a large, genuine smile plastered to her face. "Come in, ladies. I'm so excited to spend the evening with you. After all, one of you will become my new sister-in-law." Jules spun back around, smiling at Charlotte and leading the other women into the room.

Charlotte joined the group, sidling up next to Rosalie as Jules showed them the setup for the night. There was a mani-pedi station where they could get their nails done. One corner had a massage table and another table for facials. Jules showed off the table of food that Charlotte had already scoped out. She rounded out the tour by showing them the couches facing a large television, where romantic comedies would be playing all night.

After Jules finished showing them around, spa workers walked in like clockwork, heading to their stations for the evening.

"Want to get your nails done?" Rosalie asked, bumping Charlotte's hip with hers.

"Let's do it."

Tiffany had already taken over the pedicure seats with her new bestie, Mariana. Since the other "TOP" girls—Olive and Piper—had been sent home, Tiffany had clung to Mariana at every meal.

Charlotte sat down next to Rosalie at the manicure table after she selected a pale-pink polish. One thing you learned at a young age growing up in the royal sphere is that women may only wear muted, natural-looking nail polish colors, if any at all. Charlotte's eyes widened when she saw Rosalie had selected a sky-blue polish.

Rosalie shrugged when she saw Charlotte staring at her. "Sometimes you have to take a dip into the wild side."

Charlotte laughed. "I think I'll stick with my…" She read the name on the bottle of nail polish in front of her. "Ballet All Day."

"Mine is… Sky's The Limit. Who comes up with these names?"

"I don't know, but they sure are creative."

After a few minutes of silence, Rosalie spoke again, her voice quieter than before. "I have a question for you that's a little forward."

"You've become such a good friend to me, Ro. Ask away."

"I was looking out my window the other day and could've sworn I saw two figures in the pond together. You wouldn't happen to know anything about that would you?"

She couldn't stop her mouth from falling open. "You saw us?"

A big smile covered Rosalie's face. "I knew it was you and Liam," she whispered.

Charlotte pressed her lips together. "Is it weird that we're both dating the same man?"

Rosalie waved a hand at her, blowing on it to speed up the drying process. "Not at all. I don't think Liam and I will end up together. I'm holding out for true love, and I think

Liam's eyes have always been on someone else." She looked at her with a sincere smile. "Besides, I'd like to think you and I are friends at this point."

"The best of friends." Charlotte reached out her hand on instinct. Remembering the wet nail polish, she pulled it back. "We'll find you the truest kind of love there is, Ro. Someone who only makes you shine even brighter because of his love."

Rosalie's eyes glistened with unshed tears. "You're the sweetest. I'm so thankful we've gotten close through this experience. Isn't it wild we've lived in the same country and known each other our whole lives but never been friends until now?"

"All it took was a reality dating show."

They both laughed and moved to the nail-drying station.

"Are you going to go home, then?" Charlotte asked, hoping her best friend wouldn't be leaving anytime soon.

"I would like to stay as long as I can. It's been nice to be in a palace that isn't empty ninety percent of the time and to be with friends. But the next opportunity I get alone with Liam, I'll share how I'm really feeling."

"I hope we're both here as long as possible. I'll miss seeing you every day, once the competition is over." Charlotte stood and pulled Rosalie into a tight hug now that their nails were fully dry.

"Me too." Rosalie squeezed Charlotte back just as fiercely.

They grabbed a plate of snacks and joined Sienna and Bridgette on a couch where they were watching *How to Lose a Guy in 10 Days*. It was one of the rom-coms Charlotte had seen so many times she could practically quote the whole thing.

"Isn't it so sweet that Jules set this up for us?" Sienna asked.

"It is," Rosalie said through a mouthful of bruschetta.

"She's probably undercover, too. You know, trying to get all the dirty details so she can report back to Liam on who isn't suitable to be the future queen," Bridgette added.

"You think so?" Rosalie gasped, holding a hand to her heart. Rosalie was always the optimist—the sunshine in every room she walked into.

"It's definitely a possibility." Sienna nodded, grabbing a mini apple tart from Charlotte's plate.

Mariana walked over and plopped down onto the couch beside them. "I used to think Matthew McConaughey was the most gorgeous man on the planet, but when I met Liam in person, I was proven very, *very* wrong."

"Right?" Tiffany said as she sat down next to Mariana. "Liam is totally a triple threat. Brains, brawn, and beauty."

All the girls started gushing about his looks, and Charlotte pressed her lips together in a firm line. It was one thing to sit with your girlfriends and gush about a man who was completely out of reach for all of you. But it was entirely different to hear a group of women gush about the assets of the man you were in love with.

"Ooh, this is one of my favorite parts." Charlotte pointed to the television, trying to quiet everyone else. Luckily, her plan worked. All the women quieted as they watched Kate Hudson show Matthew McConaughey a photo album of their "children." Charlotte smiled and popped a chocolate truffle in her mouth, savoring the burst of cocoa flavor.

A few movie scenes later, Jules walked over and motioned for Charlotte to join her at a table nearby. She ducked as she walked in front of the screen.

"This evening has been a real hit."

"Oh, I'm glad you think so." Jules clasped her hands together and sighed contentedly.

"What made you throw a girls' night?" Charlotte asked.

"I wanted to spend time with you, for one. But I also wanted to learn more about the other women. Make sure everyone is here for the right reasons, like those people on the dating shows always say."

"Did anyone seem like they don't have good intentions?"

Jules tapped her lip thoughtfully. "Maybe. But you don't have to worry about that." Her thoughtful expression turned wry. "For now, all you need to worry about is sharing everything about that almost-kiss you so casually mentioned."

"I don't even know how to explain what happened."

"Start from the beginning. And spare no details. I want 'em all."

"Well, one minute we were sitting on a blanket, having a picnic. The next, we were getting soaked by sprinklers. Then I tried to shove him into the pond because he was joking with me, and he pulled me in with him. We started out teasing each other, but then we ended up in each other's arms in the water, so close our lips were almost touching."

"And then...?" Jules's eyes were wide, urging her to go on.

"And then I freaked out." Charlotte shrugged. "I wanted him to kiss me, but I didn't want things to get awkward if it didn't happen, so I pushed him underwater."

"Let me get this straight. Liam almost kissed you. And you love him. But instead of letting him kiss you—which you wanted—you shoved his head underwater?"

"Well, it sounds silly when you put it like that." Charlotte threw her hands in the air and let them fall back on her lap.

"Love makes people do crazy things."

"It really does." Charlotte sighed.

"What are you gonna do about it?"

"What can I do? It's not my decision in the end."

"But don't you think Liam deserves to know all the facts before he makes one of the biggest decisions of his life?" Jules prodded.

"You think I should tell him I love him? Without knowing if he returns my feelings?"

"You deserve a shot at love. And so does he. Sometimes that might require putting your feelings on the line. Wouldn't you rather risk it all to potentially end up with the man you love than have him choose someone else, not knowing your feelings for him?"

"You make a good point." Charlotte held up a hand to cover her quivering lip. "I'm scared. I know I'd be okay eventually if he rejected me. But I'd be lying if I said I wouldn't be heartbroken."

"Anyone with eyes can see he has feelings for you. I honestly don't know the extent of them, but I wouldn't be telling you all this if I didn't think it would end positively." Jules pulled her into a side hug, making tears fill the corners of her eyes. "You deserve your happily ever after."

"Thank you." Charlotte blotted the corners of her eyes with the sleeve of her pajamas.

"Sorry to interrupt." Liana set her hand on Jules's shoulder. "I'm gonna go wash off these massage oils. I'll be back before the next movie starts."

Jules stood as Liana left the room. "We should go join the other ladies. And the end of the movie is coming up."

They joined the rest of the ladies on the couches and finished watching the final scenes of the rom-com.

As the movie credits rolled, the door slammed open, and they all turned to see Liana standing there in a robe. She held her hands out in front of her, and they looked like they had been dyed in black ink. Her typically sunny demeanor was gone—so was her blonde hair. Her hair was soaking wet and dark black, dripping onto the white robe.

"What happened?" Jules stood and crossed to her, concern written across her face.

"One of you did this to me." Liana held a finger out accusatorially, pointing it around the room. "Someone put black hair dye in my shampoo bottle. It's all over my hands. And don't even get me started on how my hair looks. I'm going home. There's no way I'm letting anyone else see me like this, but I wanted you to know I will get to the bottom of who did this to me." She stomped her feet with each step as she left, like a toddler walking to timeout.

The room was silent except for the song playing in the movie credits.

"We should probably tell Liam. We don't want accusations like that getting to the tabloids," Charlotte whispered to Jules. Her friend nodded and quickly excused herself, pulling out her phone and walking to the other side of the room.

Charlotte rose from the couch and walked over to the snack table, popping another chocolate truffle in her mouth.

After a few minutes, Jules returned and walked over to her. "Liam says he has a solution. But he needs someone to meet a guest at the palace entrance in ten minutes. Liana doesn't want him to see her like this. Will you do it? I would, but since I'm hosting, I should stay here."

"Of course I'll do it. Should I change?" Charlotte motioned to the silk pajamas she was wearing.

Jules shook her head. "You look fine."

"I'll head there now and come back later if everyone's still hanging out."

"You're a lifesaver. Thank you!"

Charlotte walked to the palace's large front doors, sitting on a bench near the entrance, awaiting the mystery guest.

As she waited, Charlotte thought about some of the strange mishaps that had happened at the palace throughout the competition. The mouse on the loose at the State Dinner. The changes to some of the menus at the garden party. The extremely salty cupcakes Sienna and Liam had made. The sprinklers turning on during her date with Liam. Liam's allergic reaction to the strawberry-filled cupcake. And now black hair dye being put in Liana's shampoo bottle.

As the events had occurred, she hadn't thought much about what had happened. She'd thought them to be unfortunate coincidences or accidents. But what if there was more to everything that happened? What if one of the women here was intentionally sabotaging other ladies in the competition, trying to get them sent home or so angry they would leave?

Charlotte shook the thought from her mind. A woman of royal standing would never stoop so low as to sabotage the competition. *Would they?*

She pulled out her phone and opened the *Kindle* app, starting a new romantic comedy by her favorite indie author. Times like these called for all the banter and romantic tension.

A few chapters into the new story, a throat cleared behind her. She spun in her seat, as she put her phone away, to find Wadsworth.

"I've heard our guest has arrived. If you'll excuse me for a moment." He bowed and walked out the front door.

"I heard someone has a hair emergency." A petite, middle-aged woman with teal-colored hair and an orange pencil skirt walked in the palace doors behind Wadsworth. She stepped over to Charlotte, extending her hand. "I'm Matisse, and you must be Lady Charlotte. I've seen those swoony pictures of you and the prince all over the tabloids."

Charlotte couldn't help but smile at the woman as she shook her hand. She admired how forthright she was. "If you'll follow me." She motioned down the hall, and the woman followed closely behind her. They walked up the stairs toward the guest quarters. "How do you know Liam? It sounded like he knew you personally."

"I've been the royal family's hairstylist for years."

"Ah, so you're the one responsible for cutting off his beloved locks."

"Guilty as charged."

Charlotte stopped in front of Liana's door. "I'm guessing Liam filled you in on what's going on?"

"Yes." Matisse held her hand to her heart. "That poor dear."

Charlotte nodded and knocked on Liana's door.

"Go away," Liana yelled.

"It's Charlotte. I have someone here to help with your…situation."

The door opened the slightest crack to where Charlotte could only see one of Liana's eyes. She smiled and waved at her, and finally, she heard a sigh as the door swung open.

Charlotte followed Matisse into the room, and Liana quickly shut the door behind them. She looked at Charlotte expectantly.

"Oh, yes. This is Matisse. She's Liam's hairstylist. He personally called her here to assist in fixing your hair."

Liana eyed Matisse wearily. "You really think you can fix this?" She held up a handful of her hair.

"Honey, there's nothing a master colorist can't fix." Matisse snapped her vinyl gloves like she was a world-famous surgeon of the hair world. "Let's head to the salon room. We'll get your hair fixed in no time."

"Will it look normal? My hair is usually light blonde."

"It will take a little bit of time, but Liam has arranged a room for me here—right next door to you, actually. That way, I can assist you until you're happy with how your hair looks before you leave the palace."

"Thank you." Liana pulled Matisse into a hug, and Charlotte could see the tension in her shoulders lift.

"Oh, hush. It's nothing. Anything for a friend of Prince Liam."

Charlotte backed toward the door. "I'll leave you to it. My room is the one right across the hall if you need anything, Matisse."

"Thanks, sugar. Have a good night."

"You, too." Charlotte closed the door gently behind her. As she walked back to the women's sitting room, she thought about how lucky it was they had been able to fix this problem before the tabloids caught wind of it. If the press had heard that someone's hair had mysteriously been dyed, there would have been news of sabotage in the headlines across all of Fenimore by morning.

She still wasn't sure if any of the mishaps had been intentional, but she made a mental note to be more cognizant of her surroundings moving forward.

CHAPTER TWENTY-SEVEN
LIAM

Liam stared at the book in front of him, though he couldn't focus enough to read the words on the pages. He couldn't help but let his mind wander back to what had happened to Liana last week. He still didn't know how black hair dye had ended up in her shampoo bottle.

Thank goodness Matisse had been able to step in. She truly had saved the day with her hair-styling abilities. After three days of Matisse working her magic on Liana's hair, Liana had felt presentable enough to leave the palace. She'd said as much when she'd stopped by his study on her way out to thank him for her time at the palace and for calling Matisse in.

He had Wadsworth send Matisse a gift basket immediately after she left. Truthfully, there weren't enough gift baskets in the world to convey his gratitude for saving his behind. If there had been any bad press about what had happened, he wasn't sure what would've happened to his public standing.

It wouldn't have been the end of the world, but it could have been a significant setback in gaining the trust and support of his people by the time he became king.

A knock sounded at the door, and Liam lifted his head to see Barrett walk into his study.

"Thanks for coming. I know it's early and you'd probably rather be with your new bride."

"You are correct." Barrett smirked. "But I'll always be here for my baby brother, too. What can I help you with?"

Liam held up the thick book in front of him. "Understanding this."

"Let's dive in, then." Barrett pulled out a seat at the round table in the room, and Liam joined him.

They talked through Wistonia's most integral political connections and how Liam could best maintain and further develop them until the sun shining through the window signaled it was late afternoon.

Liam stood and stretched his back. "Thank you. I feel at least a tiny bit better about all this. I need to go grab some food and prepare for the night's festivities."

"Is it weird that I'm actually excited about the ball tonight?"

"Who are you, and what have you done with my brother?" Liam jerked his head back aghast, his eyes wide, though a playful smirk pulled at his lips.

"This is what happens when you find a girl, fall in love, and want to spend the rest of your life holding her close. Or do you already know that feeling?" Barrett waggled his eyebrows. "You were pretty cozy with Charlotte the other night."

"Are you ever going to let that go?"

"Not if I can help it."

"Remind me why I didn't kick you out of the palace after you abdicated?"

"Because you'd miss me too much." Barrett laughed. "But what's really going on between you two?"

"You already know. She's one of the women here for the competition." Liam tried to act nonchalant, like there was nothing—absolutely nothing at all—to share.

"It's obvious there's something more there. And that's saying something, coming from me, since I'm about as observant as a tree when it comes to this kind of stuff."

"There's a possibility I might be attracted to Charlotte."

"We finally have the truth, folks. Bravo." Barrett clapped until Liam shoved his arm.

"It's not weird for you?"

"What's not weird for me?"

"Me liking Charlotte? You know…since you were kind of trying to date her last year."

"Bro, I'm married to the love of my life. Charlotte and I never even kissed. I think she only came here to help with the school renovation project. We were always better suited as friends. If you keep looking for reasons to not be with someone, life will pass you by, and you'll miss out on what could've been."

"I'm not looking for reasons to not be with her." Liam's tone turned defensive as he crossed his arms across his chest.

"Then what are you doing?"

"I only wanted to make sure my beloved older brother wouldn't feel uncomfortable if I were to potentially…please note the word *potentially*"—he emphasized the word again with a raise of his eyebrow—"choose Charlotte at the end of this."

"Thank you for your concern. But this is me giving you the green light. Go for it."

Liam should've felt relief at his brother's words. A green light to pursue his feelings, to see if there was something there with Charlotte, something deeper than their mutual attraction and chemistry. Instead, he felt a million butterflies swirling inside his stomach like a blustery winter blizzard.

♛

Liam stood in front of his bathroom mirror, adjusting the medals that hung from his white ceremonial suit. Tonight's ball was sure to be a showstopper. With guests coming from all around Fenimore, he was trying to prepare himself for all the conversations he would be having—and also all the questions other royals would surely have about the competition.

At least there won't be any eliminations tonight. That's one less thing to worry about.

He walked to the ballroom, arriving a few minutes early. Right as the ball was about to begin, Alec and the seven remaining candidates joined him in the hall outside the doors.

"Tonight is all for fun, ladies. No elimination ceremony. Just a ball with other royal guests and the chance for you to spend more time with Prince Liam. We'll still be filming sporadically throughout the ball to get some material for the next episode, but there's nothing specific you need to do." Alec tapped his pen on his clipboard. "Any questions?"

When the women had none, Alec gave the all-clear into his headset.

"Prince Liam, they have the cameras set up inside. You will be introduced first, and then each woman will be announced. You will escort them all down the stairs together, four women on one side and three women on the other."

"Every man's dream," Liam whispered in jest, and the ladies nearest him laughed. He walked over to the doorway, and a palace staff member immediately opened it for him, bowing.

"Presenting His Royal Highness, Liam Charles Frederick Alden, Crown Prince of Wistonia."

It still felt surreal to him whenever a footman announced his name, now that it came with the title of Crown Prince. And in less than a month, it would be *king*.

He stood at the top of the grand marble staircase, waving at the ball attendees that clapped from the floor below. Then he waited for the women to be introduced. One by one, they walked out as the footman announced them, and Liam thought about each of them as they approached him.

"Presenting Lady Tiffany of Meldovia."

She's a little forward and flirty, but I think she's sincere. Tiffany was close to some of the girls at the beginning of the competition, and it looked a little clique-y from what I saw. But she is well-spoken and has great connections, and I had a decent time with her on our individual date.

"Presenting The Honorable Mariana of Wistonia."

I still don't know too much about Mariana. Her family has supported our royal line for a long time, and that's really the reason I've kept her around so long. She's sweet and kind but a little bit quiet. I'm not sure if her more modest life has prepared her enough to lead Wistonia, though.

"Presenting Lady Sienna of Bristol."

Sienna is great. She's probably one of my best options here. She would make a great queen. And from our one-on-one date, it sounded like she wasn't sure she would find love again. We could have a marriage of mutual respect and lead Wistonia well together without the mess of love.

"Presenting Lady Bridgette of Westridge."

She's been kind and steady throughout the competition. Like Mariana, I still don't feel like I know her well. I mean, I know she's a good person, but I'll have to ask Jules what she thought about her. I think there are better options here for me than her.

"Presenting Lady Raina of Bristol."

The only reason she's still here is obviously because of her political ties. She'd probably flirt with anything that moved to get what she wanted. Not to mention that I'm not sure of her intentions. She's someone who would do anything to get the crown. Reminder to self: send her home soon, regardless of her connections.

"Presenting Lady Charlotte of Findorra."

Clearly, she would make a wonderful queen. She's beautiful, poised, generous, and respected. I know she would be a devoted queen, beloved by the people. And it's become obvious to me that I have feelings for her. To be honest, I'm not sure if my teenage crush ever went away. But I have…concerns. I know she said on our picnic date that she wasn't just here for her inheritance, but I can't help but worry that she would break my heart just like Mila did if I let myself fall for her.

"Presenting Her Royal Highness, Princess Rosalie of Findorra."

Rosalie is another great option. She knows exactly what it takes to rule and has been trained her whole life for what that looks like. There's no denying she's beautiful and that we get along. I'll need to have some conversations with her to see where she stands.

Only after all the women were introduced did Liam notice that he'd already dismissed all the ladies hailing from Glencrest, Rothwell, and Edgemont. He hoped the rulers of those kingdoms wouldn't be offended that they were no longer represented in the competition. Where the girls were from had no influence on his decisions, and he hoped it didn't appear like it had been a factor.

All the ladies had outdone themselves tonight, looking spectacular in their evening gowns. He had successfully avoided eye contact with Charlotte so far. But he hadn't missed her navy-blue gown. It dripped with sophistication, from its long, embroidered sleeves to the way the dress floated around her feet as she moved. The dress fit her body so well that it looked like it had been poured on her. Avoiding eye contact when she looked like that was most definitely necessary if he didn't want to make a fool of himself tonight.

He walked in step with the women down the grand staircase as everyone watched. Liam stood at his full height, attempting to look confident for the cameras aimed in their direction.

When they reached the first floor, the string quartet played classical versions of modern pop songs, and the dancing began. Liam hummed along to the first song as he observed those in attendance. When he spotted Barrett and Jules talking with his cousin, James, by the food tables, he made his way over to them.

James smiled coyly. "I would say I was surprised to see you with seven women dangling from your arms tonight, but it's not the first time you've been spotted with such a large entourage."

"Funny," Liam said without an ounce of humor in his tone.

"As much fun as this conversation is, I see someone I must talk to." James nodded and walked away.

"Does anyone else think he's been acting strange lately?" Barrett asked.

"Definitely," Liam responded. "Maybe he wants to be invited over more often?"

"Or maybe he's jealous that he's not the one currently dating seven women," Jules added with a shrug, making both men laugh.

"That's probably it." Barrett wrapped his arm around his wife.

Liam turned to his new sister-in-law. "I haven't had a chance to thank you for hosting a spa night for everyone last week. It sounds like they all enjoyed their time with you."

"Except Liana," Jules muttered, looking at the ground.

"That wasn't your fault in the slightest. Liana left happy, and that's what matters." Liam squeezed her shoulder in a brotherly manner. "I do have to ask, though. Did you find anything noteworthy about any of the women? It's getting more difficult to send people home at this point in the competition."

"I had individual conversations with every candidate. Obviously, you know I'm already Team Charlotte. I think Rosalie and Sienna would also be good fits for you. All three of those women are kind, strong, and well-loved, and I think any of them would help boost your popularity but also balance your personality. I thought Tiffany was going to be a typical mean girl at the beginning, but I think she is similar to you in that she can come off a bit strong at first but has a good heart when you get to know her."

"What about Mariana, Bridgette, and Raina?"

"They each have their positive attributes, but I don't ultimately see them ending up with you."

That confirms my opinions about each of these women. Jules is reiterating that I'm doing okay. That I'll end up with the right person at the end of this.

"Spoken like a true royal."

She smiled. "I'm working on it."

Liam nodded. "I'll take what you've said to heart before the next elimination ceremony. I think it's tomorrow night."

"You're doing great, Liam." Jules stepped closer, pulling him into a hug.

"We're both proud of you. Mom and Dad would be, too."

Barrett's words hit Liam right in the core. One of his worst fears was disappointing his mother. Even though she was no longer with them, he wanted to honor her memory by living a life she would be proud of.

"Thanks, man." Liam turned and hugged his brother. "I should probably hit the dance floor."

They waved goodbye, and he walked around the perimeter of the dance floor, trying to spot any of the contestants.

Finally, his eyes found Charlotte. She was on the edge of the dance floor, watching the couples currently dancing with a soft smile on her face. He took a deep breath as he approached her. She seemed so caught up in the moment that she didn't notice him walking over to her.

He nudged her shoulder when he reached her. Charlotte jumped a little and then smiled at him when their eyes met.

"Would you care to join me for the next dance?"

"I'll have to think about that." She tapped her finger on her bottom lip.

"Where has your sass been hiding all these years?" He extended his hand to her as the current song came to an end.

"I guess I just needed you to bring it out." She placed her hand in his, and tingles ran up his arm. Liam led her to the dance floor and pulled her close.

"Another waltz, Your Highness?"

Ignoring her question entirely, he whispered, "I like it when you call me Your Highness."

"I can't use that as your nickname for much longer. I'll have to call you Your Majesty before you know it."

"Wow. It's wild when you put it like that."

"I can still call you Your Highness if you really want."

"I think I still would prefer Hottie McHot Pants."

"And you're still incorrigible." Charlotte laughed, and he wished he could bottle up the sound to listen to whenever he was having a bad day.

The song came to an end too soon, and as she started to pull away, he grabbed her hand, stopping her. "Would you care to step out on the balcony with me? I could use the fresh air."

She intertwined her fingers with his and started walking. He could've sworn he heard her say, "I'd follow you anywhere." But maybe he was hearing things.

As they stepped outside, Liam breathed in the spring air, reveling in the chilly night. He let go of Charlotte's hand and placed both of his hands on the balcony railing, leaning over it and looking at the gardens below.

"Every time I'm out here, it brings me right back," Charlotte said.

"To the night you stood up for me?"

She nodded and wrapped her arm through his, leaning her head against his shoulder. They stood in silence for a few minutes, basking in the clear night sky and the fragrant smell of the budding gardens.

Charlotte released her hold on his arm, and he could feel her eyes on him.

He turned to look at her just as she said, "Can I ask you a question?" She played with the ends of her hair, which she had worn down for the night. Charlotte hardly ever wore her hair down. But he liked it. He couldn't help but wonder how it would feel wrapped around his hands.

"Anything for you." He winked at her.

"Why didn't you come say goodbye when I left after Barrett and Jules got engaged?"

Liam was taken aback. He had expected her to ask about…well…anything except that. *She deserves the truth.*

"I actually watched you leave from the window," he admitted, a slight blush climbing his neck.

"Then why didn't you come downstairs and see me off?"

"Because I would've wanted to do something really stupid."

"Like what?"

His mother's words from her most recent letter came back to him as a war waged within his brain. *Listen to your heart.*

"Like this."

A small gasp escaped from her as his lips crashed into hers. He could feel the smallest ounce of hesitation from her, but then she melted into him. Their first kiss was intense, each of them matching the other's passion with their own.

Her arms wound around his neck, pulling him closer to her. He cupped her jaw with one hand while he settled the other on her hip, holding her to him as his lips continued to explore hers. His hand moved from her jaw to her hair, winding his fingers through the silky strands.

One of her hands moved to explore his biceps, leaving a trail of fire along the path her finger traced. Liam kept his lips on hers as he gently pushed her back against the balcony railing. No longer having to support her back, he cupped her face with both hands, taking complete control of the kiss. He liked to be in control. And just in case this was his first and only kiss with her, he wanted it to be one to remember.

As the kiss slowed into something soft and sweet rather than fire and fervor, thoughts raced into Liam's mind.

What am I doing? I said I wouldn't kiss anyone until I made my final decision.

He pulled back, abruptly stopping the kiss. They both breathed heavily, evidence of what had just occurred between them.

"I shouldn't have done that." He angrily ran his hands through his hair, leaving it tousled as he started pacing along the edge of the balcony.

"What makes you say that?" She put her hands on her hips, drawing his attention back to her feminine curves.

He shook his head. "I said I wouldn't kiss anyone until I made my final decision at the end of this."

"You're saying that heart-stopping kiss was a mistake?" Charlotte's words were quiet and tinged with a bit of hurt.

"Yes." He stopped in his tracks and started pacing back in her direction. "I mean, no." Liam sighed and leaned against the railing again. "I don't know what to say. I can't promise you anything right now."

She placed her hand on his biceps again, making the hair on his neck rise in awareness. "I never asked you to promise me anything." Charlotte let out a small laugh. "I'd be lying if I said I didn't want you to kiss me like that again." Her cheeks turned a rosy shade.

Charlotte's hand slid down his arm and into his hand. He squeezed it and smiled at her.

"That kiss was a long time coming, wasn't it?"

She returned the squeeze. "It most certainly was."

CHAPTER TWENTY-EIGHT

CHARLOTTE

Holy guacamole!

Charlotte didn't think there was any other proper thought after the man she'd been crushing on for years had just kissed her as if his life depended on it.

And she had loved every passionate, mind-blowing moment of it.

If he didn't choose her at the end of this, she knew it would be impossible to find another man who could live up to the way Liam made her feel. His magical lips had ruined her forever. She could live a million years, and no one would ever come close to measuring up to Liam.

"I should head back inside." Liam's words pulled Charlotte from her thoughts.

"Right." She rocked on her heels. "You have other women waiting to dance with you."

He nodded and pulled her hand, which he still held, up to his mouth, kissing her knuckles and sending her heart racing again.

When she was alone on the balcony, she closed her eyes and took a deep breath, steadying herself before she walked back inside.

"I've been looking everywhere for you. Where did you run off to?" Sienna grabbed Charlotte's arm, pulling her over to a tall cocktail table full of mini desserts.

"I went out on the balcony for some fresh air."

"I grabbed some of your favorites." Sienna nudged the plate on the table toward her and took a mini apple pie for herself. "I'm glad I found you, though. How are you enjoying the evening?"

"It's the most wonderful ball I've ever attended," Charlotte said with a dazed, far-off look.

Sienna's eyes sparked with interest. Before she had a chance to ask any questions, Liam approached them and asked Sienna to dance. She accepted but sent Charlotte a "we'll talk about this later" look over her shoulder as she walked to the dance floor with him.

Charlotte selected a double-chocolate brownie from the plate and popped it into her mouth, enjoying the sweet fudgy flavor.

As the evening continued on, Charlotte talked to some of her friends and the other guests in attendance. But her eyes were constantly seeking out Liam. Watching him dance with other women still hurt, even though she knew it was part of the process.

Finally, the ball ended, and Charlotte headed back to her room. As she walked past the library, she heard the sound of books toppling off of shelves inside, catching her attention. Wanting to make sure everything was all right, she poked her head in, looking around the room for the source of the sound.

But when she saw what it was that had caused the noise, she wished she could erase the moment from her memory, turn back time and walk a different way to her room where she never would've walked past the library in the first place.

A woman was draped all over a man, kissing him as books toppled to the ground. She saw a red dress with matching red nails curling through the man's hair. It had to be Raina. But who was the man? He was taller than her and wearing a ceremonial suit.

Charlotte's heart stopped.

It was Liam.

The image of them kissing in the dim light of the room was one she would very much like to forget.

African Lily. Bellflower. Calendula. Delphinium. Evening primrose. Foxglove. Gardenia. Hyacinth.

That, very well, was the furthest she had ever made it listing off names of flowers. Because she had never felt feelings of anger quite this strong.

Liam just told me that he didn't plan on kissing anyone in the competition until he chose someone at the end. Is he simply throwing kisses around like candy? Have my feelings been blinding me to the truth of who he really is?

When she turned to leave, her heel caught on the door, echoing through the room. Her eyes darted up in a panic, hoping there was a chance they both had a momentary loss of hearing. Instead, her eyes connected with Liam's, sharing the same alarmed look. She turned to leave when he called out after her.

"Charlotte." His voice was filled with something she couldn't quite read.

But she didn't stop. Charlotte sprinted to her room—well, as much of a sprint as her heels would allow.

She quickly changed out of her dress and scrubbed her face clean of makeup before jumping in bed.

Charlotte ignored the knocks at her door and the weary sigh Liam made before he finally walked away. And for the first time in a long time, she allowed herself to cry. Charlotte continued to let the tears flow until she drifted off to sleep.

♛

She took breakfast in bed the next morning, having Maya leave it outside her door. If she showed up the way she currently looked, everyone would know from her puffy, bloodshot eyes that she had been crying all night. Then they would start asking questions. Questions she couldn't answer.

After wearing an ice eye mask all morning, she looked presentable enough to attend lunch. She successfully avoided eye contact with Liam during the meal. Charlotte could feel his gaze on her nearly the entire time, trying to get her attention, but she stood strong, not caving under his glances. As soon as the meal was over, she walked back to her room as quickly as her feet would take her.

"Charlotte, please stop," Liam called out, his voice sounding close.

Knowing she wouldn't be able to outrun him, she stopped and turned to face him, crossing her arms across her chest defensively.

"Can we talk?" Liam asked between deep breaths.

"There's nothing to talk about."

"Please." The one word held so much emotion that she looked up at him, instantly regretting it when she saw that his eyes were also bloodshot. Seeing him so upset—so undone—she couldn't ignore his request, even if she wanted to.

"Let's go to my room so there are no listening ears," she acquiesced.

Once they were both seated on the couch, he rubbed his eyes and sighed.

"Please, allow me to explain what happened after the ball."

"As I said, there's nothing to explain. You told me last night that you couldn't promise me anything. I should've known to expect this from *The Royal Heartbreaker*."

He winced at her words.

She bit her lip, mortified by the words she had said and the sting she knew they carried. Charlotte opened her mouth to apologize, but he held up a hand to stop her.

"Don't apologize. I deserved it." He closed his eyes momentarily. "Charlotte, I know what you walked in on looked bad, but it wasn't how it looked." Liam stood and began pacing back and forth in her sitting area. "Raina told me she had sprained her ankle while dancing with my cousin, so I was escorting her back to her room. She asked me if we could grab a book on the way, and when I turned around from grabbing a book off the shelf for her, she kissed me. I immediately pushed her away, but that was when I heard a sound by the door, and…well, you know the rest." He crossed back to the couch and grabbed both of her hands in his as he sat down. "You have to know it didn't mean anything to me."

Relief coursed through her. "You really didn't want to kiss her?"

"Not one bit." Liam shuddered.

Charlotte laughed freely, pulling one hand back to cover her mouth. "I shouldn't laugh."

"I used an entire bottle of mouthwash last night, if it makes you feel any better." His thumb brushed over her hand. "You are the only woman I have willingly kissed in the competition, Charlotte."

"I believe you." She pulled her hands back into her lap, wanting to think clearly. And the feel of his fingers brushing hers wasn't helping. "I'm sorry I overreacted. I didn't mean what I said."

"No apology necessary." He stood and extended his hand to her. "Care to go for a walk and put this behind us?"

She looked out the large window in her room, seeing the rain coming down outside. His gaze followed hers.

"A walk through the palace halls," he corrected.

"Sure." She wrapped her arm through his, and they started walking.

They made it up to the third floor without saying a word. Liam's voice finally broke the silence. "I think I should find Raina before tonight's televised elimination and send her home."

"You would do that?"

"Of course. I want you to know you can trust me. A man's word is his bond, after all."

She wrapped her fingers around his bicep, holding on to him more tightly. As they passed unused rooms, a voice behind one of the doors pulled her to a stop. "Did you hear that?"

"Hear what?"

Charlotte pulled him closer to the door so they could clearly hear the conversation occurring behind it.

"I've done as much as I can," the voice said. "I put black hair dye in someone's shampoo. I told another girl that strawberry was Liam's favorite flavor. And I even kissed him, and Charlotte saw. She was totally jealous."

It's Raina. Charlotte's head whipped to the side so she could look at Liam's reaction. Were they hearing…a confession?

"Raina tried to have me killed," Liam said. His mouth fell open as they continued to eavesdrop.

"He's such a nice guy. I feel bad about sabotaging him and the other girls here." Raina's voice turned into a whine.

Before Charlotte could react, Liam was pushing the door open. His anger was written across his face like a big, red, flashing warning sign.

Raina turned around at the sound, a small yelp escaping her mouth. Her mouth remained agape as she looked back and forth between them. "I'll have to call you back," Raina finally said into the phone before dropping it to her side. "Your Highness. Charlotte. How lovely to see you both."

"The jig is up, Raina. We both heard everything." Liam pulled his phone out of his pocket and tapped on his screen before holding it to his ear. "Yes, I need members of the palace guard to the unused quarters on the third floor immediately."

Guards arrived within minutes, and Liam motioned to Raina. "Arrest her—"

"Wait!" she cried out. "It wasn't my fault. It was Lord Howard and Prince James. They had this whole plan and told me if I went along with it, they would make me queen when James had the throne." Raina continued to share the details of everything that had occurred throughout the course of the competition and all her conversations with Lord Howard and Prince James.

The room stood still, everyone shocked by her confession and the information that she shared. Charlotte placed her hand on Liam's back, rubbing small circles. It couldn't be easy to hear the news that someone from the King's Council and his own cousin were trying to sabotage the competition to prevent him from taking the throne. And his cousin's betrayal could've killed him.

Once Raina was done speaking, Liam turned to the guards. "Arrest her and contact the authorities to have Lord Stephen Howard and Prince James arrested for treason against the crown and attempted murder."

"But…but…I'm innocent. They tricked me." She held her hands up in front of her. "Wait, I know more. Prince James and Lord Howard have something *big* planned. They didn't fill me in on the details, but they have a backup plan that they said was foolproof."

The guards continued removing her from the room when she yelled, "Please, I'm too pretty to go to prison." Raina's sobs could be heard even as she was escorted down the hallway in handcuffs.

Liam massaged his temples as Charlotte continued to rub his back.

"Have the authorities interrogate Raina to see if she knows more about this 'big plan' than she was letting on. And then interrogate James and Howard. We need to get ahead of this." Liam turned toward her. "If you'll excuse me, I need to go do some paperwork now and call a press conference before the elimination ceremony. Let me walk you back to your room."

As he escorted Charlotte back to her room, she prayed that the evening wouldn't be as eventful.

CHAPTER TWENTY-NINE
LIAM

The world around Liam appeared to continue moving, even though he felt frozen in time. He could hear the clicking of cameras and whispering of the paparazzi guessing what this big press release he was holding was for. But Liam's mind was still stuck in the moment when he and Charlotte had overheard Raina on the phone, talking about all the sabotage she had committed during the competition. When he discovered that his own cousin, Prince James, was in on the whole thing—or, according to Raina, that he was the one in charge of the whole plan.

Liam patted his hands on the sides of his face, trying to get his head in the game. He needed to show strength and control over this situation when talking to the press. The people needed to know they were safe and that he had things handled.

"Your Highness, Clark has some items he needs to brief you on before you speak with the press." Lindsay's heels tapped against the wood floor as she escorted Liam over to Clark, the head of the Royal Guard.

"Hello, Your Highness." Clark bowed to him. "We have both Raina and Lord Howard in custody and have interrogated them individually. Raina repeated all the information she already shared with you and the guards who were present at her arrest. Lord Howard lawyered up and refused to speak."

Liam nodded. "And James?"

Clark's eyes fell to the floor before he looked at him again. "Unfortunately, we have been unable to locate your cousin."

His eyes widened. *This can't be real.* "You're telling me James is still out there?"

"Sadly, yes. We have our best men searching for him and any clues as to where he might have gone. And we'll have more guards posted in and around the palace in case he tries to come there since we still haven't uncovered the 'big plan' Raina referred to."

"Let me know immediately if you have any updates. I don't care how late it is. I want to be the first to know," Liam said.

"Understood, Your Highness."

"What information am I allowed to share with the public at this press conference, then?"

"You can share everything I've told you," Clark responded. "Right after the press conference, we'll have local police put out a hotline citizens can call if they spot Prince James or know any information regarding his location or disappearance."

He turned to face Lindsay. "Is there anything else I should know before I go out there?"

"The paparazzi is going to scrutinize you and try to pick apart this situation to use it against you. Don't crumble under the pressure. Simply explain what's going on and show them that you're in control." Lindsay brushed her hands across his shoulders and adjusted his tie. "You've got this."

Liam took a deep breath before he stepped out from behind the curtain and onto the stage, stopping behind the wood podium. "Good afternoon, and thank you all for joining me today for this urgent press conference. We have discovered that my cousin, Prince James, along with a member of the King's Council, Lord Stephen Howard, and a contestant in the competition, Lady Raina Morrison, have committed treason against the Crown."

The flashing of all their cameras at once blinded him as he continued. "Lady Raina sabotaged other women and events throughout the course of the competition. She has been apprehended and will receive a sentencing in Bristol, where she is a citizen. Lord Howard and Prince James were the masterminds of the events that occurred. Lord Howard has also been apprehended and will sit before a Wistonian judge to face his charges." He pulled on his suit coat sleeves and ran his fingers through his hair. "Unfortunately, Prince James has yet to be detained. The Royal Guard and local police are diligently searching for him, but if any citizen has any information regarding his location, please contact the authorities."

Liam looked around at the press members in attendance. "I will be reaching out to formally apologize to the women who left the competition due to Raina's influence or sabotage. However, I stand by my decisions and am confident that one of the final women I have remaining in the competition will make a wonderful queen for Wistonia." He clasped his hands together in front of him. "Are there any questions?"

The room became utter pandemonium. The crowd was in an uproar, louder than it had been when they'd announced Barrett's abdication and his dating competition.

While that had rivaled the sound at a teenage heartthrob's concert, the noise level now was as loud as standing on an airstrip as an airplane took off right over your head. But here, instead of being hit with a whoosh of air, he was hit with a rush of strange questions—the press trying to turn all this on him.

"How could you be so brainless to not see what the girl was doing sooner?"

"How do you plan to lead a whole country if you can't even keep your own cousin in line?"

I will not crumble under their scrutiny. Liam stood tall and spoke with a tone of authority. "I appreciate your questions and concerns. I can understand how this all sounds alarming, but I assure you that I have the situation under control. My best men are searching for James as we speak, and he's not a threat to the general public. I will always do everything within my power to protect Wistonia and my people."

Lindsay came up beside him and gave him a reassuring nod. "That is all the time His Royal Highness has today. The Head of the Royal Guard will be out next to answer any further questions regarding the situation. Thank you."

She escorted him behind the curtain, and he released a long breath as soon as he was out of the public view. "You did great," Lindsay whispered to him. "I'm going to go introduce Clark, but your bodyguard is ready to escort you to your car."

Liam thanked her and walked with Marcus back to his black Mercedes sedan. On the drive home, he called both Piper and Liana, apologizing to them for the ways Raina had sabotaged them in the competition. Both ladies were understanding and acknowledged they were glad further harm hadn't been done.

He was grateful they were gracious about the whole situation. Liam could only hope that the two women he would have to send home at the third elimination ceremony this evening would react the same way.

CHAPTER THIRTY
CHARLOTTE

Charlotte wore a tight, closed-lip smile throughout the introductory filming of the third televised elimination ceremony. She blocked out everything Giovanni said, already knowing the drill at this point in the competition.

Right as the first song began to play, Liam approached her. "May I have this first dance, Charlotte?"

She accepted his hand, walking past the cameras to the middle of the dance floor. The fact that he'd asked her to dance first spoke volumes. It showed her that he wanted to prove he meant what he'd said to her. He was backing up his words with actions, demonstrating that he wanted her to be there. And she believed him.

"Are you okay?" she whispered in his ear near the end of the song as they swayed together to the music.

"I'm better now that I'm here with you." Liam spoke clearly and loudly enough that his mic had surely picked it up, but he didn't appear to care.

The way he looked at her made heat spread throughout her body. It was like his eyes saw straight into her soul. She felt seen. She felt understood. She felt cared for.

"I'm here if you need someone to talk to." She traced her fingers along the collar of his shirt.

"Thank you." He escorted her to the couches after the song ended and pressed a kiss to her knuckles.

Liam danced with Sienna next, and Charlotte gave her friend a hug when she sat on the couch next to her.

"I'm glad you're still here."

"Me too." Sienna smiled at her, a slight blush covering her cheeks.

"I know this is a little awkward, but I want us to be honest with each other. I'm so glad we've become friends throughout this journey, and I don't want that to change, regardless of the outcome of this." Charlotte bit the inside of her bottom lip.

"I don't want that to change either." Sienna took her hand and squeezed it. "I think I already know, but how do you feel about Liam?"

Charlotte glanced around to make sure no cameras or microphones were nearby. "I'm in love with him," she admitted.

"I figured as much." Sienna sighed.

"I haven't told him yet, but I plan to before he makes his final decision." Charlotte twisted her hands together in her lap. "What are your feelings for him?"

"I wouldn't use the word 'love,' but I care deeply about him. I'd be delighted to be the one he chooses." Sienna's eyes turned to watch him guide Rosalie onto the dance floor. "But I ultimately want what's best for him, even if that decision might hurt me."

"I completely agree. It will hurt if I'm not the person he picks, but I do want him to be happy. I know he'll make the best choice for him and for Wistonia."

"I'm glad we're on the same page." Sienna smiled at her as Rosalie approached them, giving them each a hug.

"He's only keeping one more person." Rosalie grimaced.

Charlotte looked over at the remaining women. Tiffany, Bridgette, and Mariana were shifting their feet, all looking nervous as they waited for Liam to select one of them for the final dance. When Liam offered his hand to Tiffany, Charlotte tried to bite back the emotions that someone from her friend group was going home. She hadn't expected their group of four would make it so far, but sadness still filled her at the thought that Bridgette would no longer be sleeping a few rooms away from her.

When she'd first joined the competition, she hadn't expected to make lifelong friendships with any of the other girls. But now she was honored to have three new close friends whom she knew she could always count on. Women who would support her no matter what. Everyone needed people like that.

After Alec announced they were done filming, Charlotte hurried forward and wrapped her arms around Bridgette. Rosalie and Sienna joined them, forming a large group hug.

"We're going to miss you," Charlotte said.

"I'm going to miss you, too." Bridgette hugged them tighter. "Promise me that we'll all still be friends after this?"

"Always," they all responded in unison. They said their final goodbyes to Bridgette and Mariana before Liam escorted them out of the ballroom.

"We're going to grab a snack from the kitchen. Do you want to come?" Rosalie and Sienna asked.

"I'm good, but thanks." Charlotte smiled at them and headed toward the women's sitting room, hoping she would find Jules there. When she poked her head into the room, she was pleased to see her intuition was right. "I thought I might find you here."

Jules turned around and clapped her hands excitedly. "I was hoping you would come find me tonight. I'm so excited for you."

"It's so surreal. It feels like the competition started only yesterday, and now there are only four women remaining."

"You're telling me. Time has flown by. But how are you feeling about everything?" Jules reached her hand out, and Charlotte walked over, joining her on the couch.

Charlotte bit her bottom lip. She didn't want to share things she promised Liam she wouldn't, so she asked, "What all did you hear?"

"About your kiss with him." Jules nudged her gently in the ribs with her elbow. "And about what you saw between him and Raina. And everyone knows about the evil plan she, Lord Howard, and James concocted."

A sigh escaped from her lips. "Oh, thank goodness you know everything. It's been hard not having anyone to talk to about all this. I can't believe they tried to sabotage the competition. Liam almost died." Charlotte held her hand to her chest.

"They'll be locked up for the rest of their lives. I hope they find James soon and all of that can be put to rest. But enough about them." Jules waved her hand in the air as if she were shooing away the topic. "I'm dying to know about your kiss and what you're thinking."

"I've fallen so hard for him, Jules. Our kiss only confirmed that the deep connection I feel with him goes beyond the mental and into the physical." A blush climbed her neck.

I think we could've started a fire with the heat from that kiss.

"Ohhhh. I'm so happy for you. Especially since he kissed you after he said he wouldn't kiss anyone until the end. That must mean he's feeling the same kind of things you are."

"I really hope he is. He kinda freaked out after the kiss and said he couldn't promise me anything. I know what he meant, but I'm so scared of the depth of my feelings for him."

Jules set her hand on Charlotte's forearm in a soothing gesture, giving her the strength to continue.

"I decided I'm going to tell him how I feel. It would be a disservice to Liam and myself to not see if my feelings are returned. I would rather end all this heartbroken than leave without trying. But that kiss has made me start to believe that what I've dreamed of for the past few years is finally within my reach—a deep, all-consuming love."

"That's wonderful." Jules smiled and squeezed her arm. "He said he wouldn't kiss anyone until he made his final decision, though…so do you think him kissing you was him choosing you?"

"It's obvious he returns the mutual attraction and chemistry, but I don't know if he truly loves me, if he loves every part of me for who I am. I want him to love my heart and my soul. I want to give love and be loved in return. And I'm scared my heart may never recover if he sends me home now." Tears filled Charlotte's eyes, despite her attempts to push them down.

Jules took both of Charlotte's hands in hers. "Everyone deserves a love like that. But especially you. You are so giving of yourself and your time to others. Liam would be a fool not to love you."

She leaned her head against her friend's shoulder, letting a few of the tears she'd been holding in fall down her cheeks.

Jules sighed. "Men can be clueless. He may not know what you're thinking, and he may be just as scared as you are to take a chance on love if he doesn't know his feelings are returned. I hope telling him how you feel will solidify everything for you. I hope everything ends in your favor, but please know I'm going to be here for you, no matter the outcome."

Charlotte pulled her friend into a hug and thanked her before excusing herself. She walked back to her room with a range of emotions coursing through her. But she knew one thing for certain. She would tell Liam how she felt before he made his final decision. Because a love like this was worth the risk.

CHAPTER THIRTY-ONE
LIAM

He wasn't proud of it, but Liam was avoiding Charlotte—or rather, he was avoiding the growing feelings he had for her.

Feelings that made his heart ache when she wasn't around. Feelings that made him question his promise to himself to never love anyone again. Feelings that threatened to fill every bit of his being if he let them. Feelings that scared the living daylights out of him.

Liam had thought avoiding her would help take all those feelings away. Instead, it had done the exact opposite. All his feelings for her were heightened. She was like a song he couldn't get out of his head. One which, no matter how hard he tried to not think of the tune, continued coming back into his thoughts unbidden.

He threw his covers aside and rose from his bed. Liam walked straight to his office, not bothering to change out of his sweatpants and t-shirt. Walking around a corner at the speed of light, he nearly bowled over his brother.

"Whoa." Barrett grabbed Liam's shoulders. "What's got you in such a hurry?"

"I'm going to read the laws regarding the judicial system." Liam tried to move aside, but his brother's hands held him firmly in place.

"You're in a hurry…to read…policy?" Barrett drew out the question.

"Why is that such a surprise?"

"It looked like you were running *from* something more than you were running *to* it." His brother let go of his shoulders, and he walked into his study with Barrett on his heels. "Is this about your press conference yesterday? I thought you were great. You set the story straight about what James, Stephen, and Raina did while reassuring the people that things were under control."

Liam paced in front of his desk, running his hands through his hair.

"Or is that not what you're freaking out about?" Barrett asked.

"What is wrong with me? Why can't I get Charlotte out of my head?" Liam cried out.

"Maybe because you're a man in love?"

"But I can't be." Liam paused and turned to his brother. "Do you know the vow I made to myself after Mila broke my trust and heart? I vowed that I would never love anyone again. Because becoming attached to someone like that would mean I had someone to lose, and I didn't know if I could endure that kind of loss again."

Barrett walked over and pulled him into a manly hug. "I know that was a really crappy situation. But not every woman is like Mila. The women left in the competition…they're here for *you*, not the Crown. It's okay to learn from every hard circumstance we face, but you can't let pain from the past hold you back from ever putting yourself out there again."

"How do I risk feeling that pain and betrayal again?"

"When you find someone you can't stop thinking about, someone who makes you the best version of yourself...isn't that worth the risk?"

Liam shrugged.

"Come on. Tell me what you like about Charlotte," Barrett prodded.

Liam stood and started pacing again. "She's smart. And generous and kind and loving. All the things that would make a great queen." He shoved his hands in his front pockets. "But I don't know if I could pick her."

"Why not? You sound like a man in love."

"She's too much like Mom." Liam's voice was quiet and clouded with emotion.

"You say that like it's a bad thing."

"Isn't it?"

Barrett smiled. "I always imagined you would end up with someone just like her. Someone who would be your opposite in many ways and balance you out. Mom loved Charlotte like she was her own daughter. She would be so proud of you, and I happen to agree that Charlotte would make not only a great queen but a great partner for you."

Liam walked over to his desk chair and plopped down into it, letting his face fall into his hands.

"You can't let the fear of loving someone keep you from ever opening your heart again. That's no way to live." Barrett came over and gave him a final clap on the back before leaving the room. "This isn't just about being a good king. It's about being a good man—a man our parents would be proud of—and it sounds like Charlotte makes you a better man. The country already is starting to see you for your true heart, Liam. You have nothing to fear. Trust yourself and what you have found with Charlotte."

His brother's words rolled over in his brain. Everything Barrett had said today was exactly what Liam imagined their mother would've told him. And he didn't know how to feel about any of it.

♛

Liam walked toward the cameras and stopped when he reached Lindsay.

"We have some reporters here today to write about your final group date," she said.

"Did they take my advice on this one?" He tried to peek around the cameras to see what date they had set up.

"They did, despite how your paintball suggestion turned out." Lindsay laughed. "The targets are set up over there for your archery date." She motioned behind the cameras. "And I made sure they were placed an appropriate distance apart so there wouldn't be any mishaps this time—especially with the reporters here. At least the cameras were no longer rolling when you got shot with the paintball last time."

"I can only imagine the fodder that would've been for the tabloids." Liam chuckled. "Thank you for handling everything, Lindsay. We're lucky to have you."

"Thank you, Your Highness." Her cheeks reddened the slightest bit before she slipped back into her polished role. "Let's get you over there so we can bring the women in."

Liam joined Giovanni by the targets, holding a bow in his hands as the cameras started rolling.

"You are sure to be royally entertained by our bachelor prince's final group date...archery." Giovanni shot a big smile toward the camera. "Now, let's bring out the final four ladies."

Liam couldn't stop the smile that crept onto his own face as he watched them approach. He hadn't been too excited about the idea of this competition, but looking back now, he was thankful for the time he'd gotten to spend with each of the women from the competition. Every one of them had helped teach him a lesson of sorts.

They'd taught him to stand up for those he cares about.

They'd taught him that people will always be there to assist you, even when you make mistakes.

They'd taught him to always ask what was in something before he ate it.

The experience had taught him the importance of patience and thinking before you speak.

And Raina...well, she'd taught him to never underestimate what a woman was capable of.

A tap on his shoulder brought him back into the moment. "Care to take the first shot, Your Highness?" Giovanni extended an arrow to him.

He took the arrow and walked a few paces away so he was the proper shooting distance from his target. Liam nocked the arrow and drew the bow, aiming it at the center of the target with the confidence of an experienced bowman. He shot the arrow and heard the thud of it connecting with the target, not even needing to look to know he'd hit a bullseye.

"Wow, very impressive, Your Highness. The perfect shot." Giovanni looked back to the camera. "I will now leave His Highness to his date, but keep watching at home to see if we have any other sharpshooters in our midst." He winked before walking off the set.

The women each hurried to grab a bow and quiver before walking to their stations.

"How do you do this?" Tiffany asked, holding the bow with pinched fingers as far out from her body as humanly possible like it was a dirty sock.

"You put the arrow in the bow, and you shoot," Liam deadpanned.

He heard Tiffany muttering behind him but didn't bother to turn around. She probably only wanted him to wrap his arms around her and show her how to use the bow and arrow like in a romance movie. He was definitely not about to do that on a date that was being filmed. The goal of all this was to have his people take him seriously, not to have them think he was there just to be close to as many women as possible.

Liam continued to walk between each of the four stations, encouraging the women as they shot at the targets. It came as no surprise to him that Charlotte was the best shooter in the bunch. She'd continually impressed him with her wide array of skills throughout the competition.

Walking to Rosalie's station, he saw that she was the only woman who had yet to even hit the target. "Would you care to take a break and walk with me, Rosalie?"

She sighed with obvious relief. "I would love that." Rosalie set her bow gently on the ground, and they started walking around the palace lawn together. They sat down on an oak bench as she spoke again. "I've really enjoyed my time here, Liam. It's felt like a bit of an escape, staying in a palace other than my own for a few months."

"I've been honored to have you as my guest." Liam tried to smile at her but failed. He knew she deserved more than this. Rosalie was the epitome of sunshine and kindness. She needed someone who could make her shine even brighter, not someone whose lack of romantic love would only dull her light. Sighing, he said, "I—you deserve more than I can give you, Rosalie."

She covered both of their mics with her hands before saying, "Like someone who's in love with me and not one of my best friends?"

His eyes shot up to meet hers.

"It's not rocket science, Liam. You and Charlotte will be amazing together. I've only stuck around to watch it all play out. It's not every day you get to watch two people fall for each other right before your eyes."

He glanced around, relieved to find that no one from the camera crew had followed them.

"I don't know that I am…I mean, I'm not…"

She placed her hand on his and gave it a friendly squeeze. "You may not fully recognize it yet, and that's okay. But I love how happy you make her. Just know you'll have me to go through if you ever hurt her." Rosalie attempted to shoot him an evil glare that made them both erupt in a fit of laughter.

"I'll be sure to keep that in mind."

"I'll pack my bags and head out once the date is over." She stood and pulled him into a hug before rejoining the other women.

How were his feelings so obvious to everyone but himself? He knew he cared for Charlotte, but his heart had been blocked off for years. Liam didn't know if he could allow himself to let his walls down and love someone again.

His brother's words from that morning popped back into his mind.

You can't let the fear of loving someone keep you from ever opening your heart again. That's no way to live.

Maybe today was the start of a whole new era in his life. Maybe today was the day he could open himself back up to living again.

Liam's nerves buzzed with tension as he thought about the people who would be welcomed into his home this evening. Tonight, he would be hosting a cocktail party for the families of the three remaining women in the competition. He'd had brief interactions with all of them in the past at balls or dinner parties. But it was a lot different to host them now, knowing that one of the couples he would be talking with tonight would become his future in-laws. That he would have to ask fathers for permission to potentially propose to their daughters.

No cameras would be present tonight. He wanted this time with Charlotte, Sienna, and Tiffany's families to be private. They needed to be able to have open and honest conversations, and luckily, Alec had obliged his request.

After giving a small toast, Liam walked around the room, playing the role of host.

When he saw that Charlotte's father was alone, he stood taller and took a deep breath. Liam cautiously approached him, his stomach twisting in preparation for the conversation. His interactions with him in the past had been short, but he knew enough to know that the Duke of Albury was a force to be reckoned with and that he was an intimidating man.

"It's an honor to have you here, Your Grace. I trust your travels went well?"

"It's not a long journey," His Grace, the Duke of Albury, grumbled. "I'm quite honestly surprised to be here."

"Why do you say that?"

"With all of the options you had, I'm merely surprised Charlotte has made it this far."

"May I ask why that would surprise you?" Liam tried to remain polite and cool despite the anger roaring inside him. His blood was sure to reach a boiling point soon.

"When you had beautiful, poised women like a princess and other daughters of dukes, I'm only surprised you would have someone here this late in the competition who was already rejected by the other Prince of Wistonia."

Liam heard a small gasp from behind him. Turning around, he saw Charlotte standing there, and from the looks of it, she had heard every cruel word her father had said about her.

"You should be proud of your daughter," Liam spouted before he could stop the words from coming out. "She is brilliant, considerate, and poised. Any man would be lucky to have her. Especially someone as imperfect as me."

The duke was quiet, probably in shock that someone had stood up to him. Heck, Liam had shocked himself by speaking his mind to the gruff Duke of Albury. But he couldn't let him degrade Charlotte like that.

Charlotte hurried away, and Liam was about to chase after her when the duke placed a hand in front of his chest, stopping him in his tracks.

"People don't speak to me like that."

Liam's heart stopped. *Am I about to get knocked out?* "I—"

Her father interrupted him. "But I can respect what you did. It's obvious you care about my daughter, even though I'm not sure she's good enough for the likes of a prince." Liam noted a flicker of acceptance in the duke's eyes. "Well, are you going to ask the question or not?"

"The question?"

"The one I'm sure you invited all the families here to ask." The duke's tone turned impatient as he tapped his foot.

"Oh." Liam cleared his throat. *This wasn't how I expected this conversation to go.* "Your Grace, if Charlotte is the final woman remaining at the end of this competition, I would like to ask for your blessing to marry your daughter."

"You have my blessing." He surprised Liam by extending a hand for him to shake. The duke squeezed his hand so tight Liam was sure his bones were about to break.

That was unexpected.

Alone again, Liam hurried in the direction Charlotte had walked, wanting to find her and make sure she was okay after her father's harsh words.

He found her sitting on a bench outside the room with a plate of chocolate desserts beside her. "I'm sorry, Charlotte. But I couldn't stand there and let him talk down about you like—" Charlotte wrapped her arms around him, pulling him into a tight hug and cutting off his words.

"No one has ever stood up for me like that—especially to my father. Thank you."

She pulled back slightly, leaving her arms wrapped around him. When he looked into her eyes, he saw admiration, respect, and...love?

He sputtered, trying to figure out how to speak again.

Words. Any words, Liam.

He gestured his thumb back, pointing to the doors. "Gotta go."

Not those words, you dummy.

Liam basically ran back into the cocktail party. He spoke with each of the other families in attendance, easily garnering both fathers' blessings for a proposal to their daughter should he choose them. Though he kept up his calm, royal façade, he was anything but calm on the inside.

His brain roared with thoughts. His heart bubbled with feelings and emotions. And even as he fell asleep that night, the image of Charlotte's adoring gaze still filled his mind.

CHAPTER THIRTY-TWO
LIAM

Liam lay on his bed, his clasped hands settling on his stomach as he stared at the ceiling. He hadn't even gotten ready for the day yet, and he already knew he wouldn't be productive at anything he attempted to do today.

His mind was filled with worries about the week. Mainly the fact that precisely one week from today would be his wedding day. Only seven more days before he would be a married man. Before he would stand before his bride—and the entire world—and say his vows.

Only eight more days before the coronation ceremony, when he would take his oath as king to protect and lead Wistonia for the rest of his life.

And only one more day until he would be proposing to the woman he would spend the rest of his life with.

He'd known these days were coming. *Everyone* had known these days were coming. But somehow, the fact that he was now down to single digits brought with it a new sense of realness.

There was a light knock on the door before Wadsworth walked in carrying a pot of coffee, a mug, and a plate filled with apple fritters.

Liam stuffed half a fritter in his mouth the moment after Wadsworth set it down, drawing a laugh out of the butler.

"I thought you might want to stay in your room this morning to work through things in your head."

"You thought right."

The butler cleared his throat. "I have a letter for you as well, Liam." Wadsworth reached into his suit coat pocket and pulled out a slightly yellowed envelope. "I honestly wasn't sure I would ever be delivering this one until the events of the last few months occurred. But here we are."

Liam gently took the envelope, running his fingers gently over the words written on it in his mother's script. *For my dearest Liam, when you are about to become king.*

His mouth fell open. "What? Is this supposed to be for Barrett?"

Wadsworth shook his head.

"How did she know?"

"She always had a way of knowing things before other people, didn't she?" Wadsworth said softly before leaving the room, allowing him to read the letter in private.

My Dearest Liam,

I'm guessing you asked if this letter was supposed to go to Barrett instead of you. But it really is intended for you. And though that may come as a surprise to you, it's never surprised me.

I had this feeling in my gut that you would be king one day from the moment I held you in my arms for the first time. I knew that you were born to be a leader. That you were born to do greater things than I could ever even begin to imagine.

As you grew older, I saw those inklings I had when you were just a babe come to fruition before my eyes. You were always so fearlessly forthright in sharing your opinions. You were never afraid to speak your mind and stand up for what you thought was right. You have grown into a young man with such strength.

There is power in your words, Liam. When you speak, people will listen. I know the people will believe in you as much as I do as they see your efficiency and smart decision-making skills over time.

If you are actually receiving this letter, that means the time for you to take the throne is near. That also means you're already married or are about to propose to one very lucky woman. I can only hope you've found someone who balances your weaknesses with her strengths. Someone who challenges you daily and who loves every part of you as much as I do.

I cannot wait to watch you lead our people. To succeed at what you do best—putting your ideas into action and inspiring others to do the same.

I'm so proud of you, my son.
I love you always,
Mom

Liam wiped away the tears filling his eyes. She'd had so much confidence in him. She always saw the best in him and believed in him more than anybody else.

But then a startling thought popped into his brain.

Charlotte believes in you.

She had told him as much multiple times over the past few months. Come to think of it, Charlotte had always stood up for him and believed in him.

While he didn't know if he could get past his aversion to love in a week's time, he knew that his mother was right in one regard. That he should find someone who balanced him. Where their strengths would balance out each other's weaknesses. And there was one woman still at the palace who definitely wasn't his perfect match.

After getting dressed for the day, Liam walked to Tiffany's room. He knocked on the door, and her lady's maid let him into the room.

"Liam, what a surprise. How can I help you?" Tiffany smiled as she sat down on the couch next to him.

"I've been doing a lot of thinking, and we both need partners who are different from us. Someone who's our opposite. Someone who can balance us out. Someone who complements us. Unfortunately, I think you and I are too similar to be a good fit." Liam pressed his lips together as he watched tears fill her eyes.

"I'm sad, but I understand. You and I both deserve to find the best fit for us. And obviously you're not my match if you don't want all of this." She ran her hand over the length of her body, drawing a laugh out of Liam. "Promise me I'll be invited to your wedding?"

"Of course you'll be invited." He stood and gave her a brief hug.

"Good luck making your final decision. You can't go wrong either way."

Liam thanked her and went back to his room, wanting to avoid human interaction for the rest of the day. Maybe if he sat in the silence long enough, he would be able to hear what his head and his heart were saying.

Liam still sat on his couch, his eyes pinched shut in thought, when a knock sounded at his bedroom door. He opened one eye and looked at his phone. Who would be knocking on his door a quarter after midnight?

He rubbed the sleep from his eyes and stretched his back before walking to the door. Liam opened it to find that no one was there. He poked his head out into the hallway and looked both ways, spotting Charlotte behind a large marble column.

"Charlotte? Is everything okay?"

"Oh," she squeaked, jumping out from behind her hiding spot. "Did I wake you?" Her steps toward him were tentative.

"No, I was still up. Did you want to come in?"

"I—" Her eyes darted toward the stairwell and back to him. "Yes, I'd like to talk."

He opened his door and gestured for her to come in. Liam closed the door, following her and her sweet, floral scent into his room.

"Isn't it funny that I've been here dozens of times and I've never seen your room?" She glanced around his room, and he suddenly felt self-conscious.

Should I have tidied up? He looked around at the pile of clothes sitting at the end of the bed and the books flopped open on the coffee table from his studying.

"It's so you." Charlotte smiled at him before sitting on his couch. He walked over and joined her.

"Thanks." Liam leaned back and placed his feet on the coffee table, crossing them at the ankles. "Are you going to tell me what brought you to my room at this hour?"

"Alec told Sienna and me after dinner that we're the only two women remaining. He also said that tomorrow night is the live finale. That you will be proposing to one of us in a final elimination ceremony out by the gazebo."

His heart dropped into his stomach as he nodded. "Yes, I'm sorry I wasn't at dinner. I've been in here...thinking."

"I don't want to change your mind if you've already come to a decision. Sienna is my friend, and she's wonderful. I don't know what your feelings are for her, but if you do choose her, she will make a wonderful queen." Charlotte stood and walked to his window. "But I don't know if I could live with myself if I didn't tell you the whole truth before you make your final decision tomorrow."

"The whole truth?" he asked.

"You asked me on our picnic date why I entered the competition. And the real reason I did is because I'm in love with you, Liam." She turned around to face him as she declared her feelings, causing a lump to form in his throat. "I think I have been for a long time. What started out as a crush on you a few years ago has turned into so much more." Charlotte came back to the couch and took his hands in hers. "I love that you bring out my competitive side. I love that you go after what you want in life. I love how you stand up for me and what you believe to be right. I love that you feel like a safe place to land. I love that you take action and care about your people. I love all the little things you do when you think no one is watching." Her eyes searched his like she was begging him to believe her words. "But I've always seen you, Liam. Even when I was here in the fall, helping with the school renovations, you were all I could see. You're strong and assertive and passionate and protective. I truly believe you're going to be the most wonderful king Wistonia has ever seen. And I would love nothing more than to rule beside you. I want to challenge you and be challenged by you for the rest of our lives." Her cheeks reddened as she added, "If you'll have me."

Liam was shocked into silence. He opened his mouth as if to speak, but no words or sounds escaped.

She placed her pointer finger against his lips. If he hadn't already been speechless before, he certainly would've been at her gentle touch.

"You don't have to say anything now. I know you need to think." She laughed breathlessly. "And I certainly gave you a lot to think about. I figured I may as well leave all my cards on the table so I don't leave with any regrets. I'm all in, Liam. I understand if you don't feel the same, but I thought you should know."

Charlotte stood and walked to the door, giving him one more shy smile over her shoulder before leaving.

The sound of the door shutting pulled him out of his dazed state.

She loved him.

Charlotte really, truly loved him.

Her love declaration had awoken something inside of him. He felt like his heart was truly beating for the first time in a long time. And that scared him more than anything.

CHAPTER THIRTY-THREE
CHARLOTTE

Charlotte's heart raced as she leaned back against her bedroom door, needing the strength of it to hold her up. She had done it. She had finally laid all her feelings on the table. Liam knew that she was in love with him.

She hadn't known what she was going to say to him in that moment. Charlotte had struggled to find the right words to express the depth of her feelings. So, she had stopped thinking and let her heart do the talking.

Now it all came down to him and his final decision.

Her stomach twisted, knowing that the other person remaining was one of her friends. She would be happy for Sienna if Liam picked her, but her heart would break at the same time.

Sienna had told her at dinner yesterday that she was starting to fall for Liam, which made Charlotte feel even worse about the whole situation. *I'm either going to get my own heart broken or see my friend get hurt.*

Once she had changed into a pair of silk pajamas, Charlotte slipped under the covers. She grabbed her phone from the end table and continued reading the book she'd started while waiting for Matisse to show up after Liana's hair emergency. When she finished the final page of the story, her heart was full and broken at the same time. Reading romance usually filled her—she was a hopeless romantic, after all. But tonight, it filled her with a sinking feeling in her stomach. She lived for happily-ever-afters in novels, and she could only hope she would have the happily-ever-after to her story tomorrow.

Charlotte turned off her lamp and lay down, closing her eyes, but she knew she wouldn't be able to get much sleep tonight. Because all she could think about was how tomorrow would either be the absolute best day of her life—or the absolute worst.

CHAPTER THIRTY-FOUR
GIOVANNI GERALDO

"I can't believe we've already reached this moment in the show." Giovanni smiled brightly at the camera. "I'm pleased to interview the final two contestants on *Royally Yours*—Lady Charlotte and Lady Sienna. First, I will be speaking with Lady Charlotte. Let's bring her out."

Charlotte approached him, and he kissed her on the cheek before she took her seat on the chair across from him, sitting with all the poise of a queen.

"You look stunning—practically glowing. Can you believe that, by the end of today, you might be engaged to Prince Liam? I remember the start of the competition like it was yesterday."

"Thank you." Charlotte smiled at him. "It's very surreal. The competition has flown by, and I'm simply honored to have made it to this point."

He nodded along understandingly. "It really has. I must ask. In every reality dating show, we see romance, of course. But we also often see friendships and rivalries form between the contestants. Did you personally experience either of those throughout the filming of *Royally Yours*?"

"I believe everyone knows about the sabotage that occurred during the competition, so I won't comment further on that. Regarding friendships, I have met a few women who I believe will remain some of my closest friends, no matter where life takes us."

Giovanni pressed his hand to his heart. "The news that broke about the conspiratorial plans against the Crown was very disappointing." He leaned forward in his seat. "But tell me, who are these close friends you've made?"

She smiled, and he could tell it was genuine. "Right from the start, I instantly connected with Rosalie, Bridgette, and Sienna."

His eyebrows raised. "Oooh, Sienna. How does it feel to be in the final stage against one of your best friends?"

"It's a bit strange." Charlotte twisted her lips to the side. "We've spoken about it, though, and we'll both be happy for the other person regardless of whom Prince Liam chooses."

He turned, looking right into the camera with a wide grin. "Don't we all love a good supportive friendship?" Facing Charlotte again, he asked, "Now, let's cut right to the question that everyone in all of Fenimore is asking. Are you in love with Prince Liam? Sparks seem to be flying whenever you two are on screen together."

"All I'll say is a picture is worth a thousand words." Charlotte winked at him.

Giovanni waggled his eyebrows at the camera. "Take that as you want, everyone, but I think that means we may have a love match in our midst."

She shot him a winning smile. "That's the beauty of photos, right? A picture means something different to everyone who looks at it."

"You're already speaking like a true royal."

"I take that as the highest compliment. Thank you."

"Now, can you tell us anything about the gown you will be wearing this evening?"

Charlotte pressed her finger to her lip thoughtfully. "I don't believe I'm allowed to give any specifics, but I will say that I'll be representing Wistonia proudly this evening."

"Wistonia, not Findorra?"

"Yes. Although I will always love Findorra, if Liam decides to propose to me this evening, I want to be wearing a look that represents my future. One that shows my love for Wistonia."

"Very well said, as always. I believe I speak for all of Wistonia when I say we would be lucky to have you as queen."

"You're going to make my eyes puffy if you keep talking like that, Giovanni." She leaned over and swatted his arm playfully.

He laughed boisterously. "We wouldn't want that! It's time we let you go get ready. Thank you very much for joining me today, Lady Charlotte. I wish you the best of luck this evening."

"It's been wonderful. Thank you for having me, Giovanni." She smiled at him before rising from her seat and giving a final wave to the camera before leaving the room.

♛

Giovanni only had a few minutes for a quick water break before Sienna strolled into the room.

"Let's welcome Lady Sienna."

Sienna walked over and shook his hand, and he pressed a kiss to it. Taking her seat across from him, she looked elegant and regal, her legs crossed at the ankles.

"It's a pleasure to meet with you today, Lady Sienna. How are you feeling now that the end of the competition is here? Especially knowing that you might be engaged to Prince Liam by the end of the day."

"I truly can't believe it's the final day. I'm excited and nervous, knowing my whole life could change today." Sienna sighed but continued wearing a soft smile.

"That's understandable. It's wild how a single day can change the course of your life forever," he said. "Now, I finished interviewing Charlotte earlier, and she shared that you have become close friends during the competition. How does it feel being in this position against someone to whom you've gotten close?"

Sienna dropped her gaze as she pressed her lips together. "I think it's difficult for both of us. Neither of us wants to see the other one get hurt, but we both want the same ending—for Liam to choose us. It's a tricky situation, but I'll be happy for her regardless of the outcome tonight."

"That's a true friend right there, folks." Giovanni grinned ear-to-ear at the camera. "But let's not skim over the big declaration in what you said. I heard you say you want Liam to choose you tonight. Please expand on that for me. Are you in love with Prince Liam?"

"Love is a strong word, but I have great respect for him and care about him a great deal." She wrung her hands in her lap. "I think I'm starting to fall for him, but I can't let myself fully get there without knowing where his heart is."

"I completely get why you would want to hear how Liam is feeling first." Giovanni leaned over and patted her arm. He could tell she was getting uncomfortable, so he effortlessly changed the conversation. "Can you tell us anything about the gown you will be wearing this evening?"

"I will be wearing a lovely cream-colored dress, but you'll have to wait until tonight to see it." She smiled shyly.

"I cannot wait to see it. It's time we let you go get ready. Thank you for joining me today, Lady Sienna. I wish you the best of luck this evening."

Sienna stood and gave him a hug. "Of course. It was lovely talking to you, Giovanni."

CHAPTER THIRTY-FIVE
CHARLOTTE

"Tonight is the night. Tonight is the night," Maya said in a sing-song voice, jumping in place.

Charlotte giggled with her. Her lady's maid's child-like exuberance lifted her spirits as she prepared for what she hoped would be one of the biggest moments of her life.

She sat in a chair in front of her vanity mirror as Maya did her hair and makeup. Her dark-blonde hair was curled and then pinned up into a loose, low bun with sprigs of baby's breath placed into it.

"Okay, Charlotte, you can open your eyes."

Her eyelashes flitted open, and she gasped when she took in her reflection in the mirror. Maya was a wizard with a makeup brush. She looked mature yet youthful. All her facial features were enhanced. Her eyes were brighter, cheekbones sharper, and lips plumper. And her face was framed by soft curls falling down in wisps on either side of her face. "It's perfect, thank you."

"Now there's only one thing left to do." Maya rushed out of the room and came back holding a large gown bag. She removed the emerald-green gown from the bag in a flourish.

Charlotte was stunned into silence at the sight of it. Even though she'd already tried it on last week for a fitting, seeing it today made it feel more magical. She was honored to be representing Wistonia by wearing the main color from their flag.

Her lady's maid worked to undo the zipper before holding it open for her. Charlotte stepped into it, and Maya zipped her in.

The shoulder straps were crafted out of tulle, and they—along with the whole top half of the dress—were covered in deep, emerald-green lace flowers. The skirt fell softly to the ground in layers of emerald-green tulle. It would look beautiful, floating around her in the late-spring breeze.

She looked like a Disney princess come to life. But today, she hoped to be the princess of her own story.

"You look absolutely stunning, Charlotte. For what it's worth, I hope he picks you," Maya said.

Charlotte stepped into her gold strappy heels. She ran her hands along her dress as she stood. "Thank you for everything." She pulled her in for a quick hug.

Standing tall and putting on a brave face, Charlotte walked out of her room and headed to the first floor. As she walked past the men's sitting room, she overheard Liam and Barrett's voices. She thought it would be nice to talk to Liam so she would be prepared for what was coming tonight. Charlotte raised her hand to knock, but her hand stopped short of touching the door when she heard his next words.

"She told me she loves me. I'm not sure I can return that kind of love."

That was all she needed to hear. Charlotte slowly backed away from the door, her breathing as heavy as if she had just run a marathon. *Am I that unloveable?*

When her brain connected with her feet, she hurried to the back of the palace and out the doors leading to the garden. She breathed in the sweet, floral aroma when she arrived, but even the scent of the flowers couldn't calm her.

Angelonia. Black-eyed Susan. Cosmos.

She turned around to go back inside. *I need to pack. I'm going home. What's the point of staying out here to get rejected on kingdom-wide television?*

"There you are. We're about to begin filming." Lindsay sighed, grabbing her arm and pulling her to the gazebo.

No, I can't do this.

When they arrived at the gazebo, Lindsay left her next to Sienna. Charlotte looked around and saw the camera crew was already there, set up for the decision ceremony. She needed to find a way out.

"Hey." Sienna glided over to her, looking like a goddess in a cream dress that perfectly contrasted her dark hair. "What's wrong?"

Charlotte shook her head and put on a fake smile. "I'll be fine," she whispered back.

Before Sienna could respond, Alec approached them, going over the details of what would happen. Charlotte tried to listen, but she only caught a few words of what had been said.

"We'll begin rolling when Liam walks out." Alec turned to the camera crew. "Let's double-check all the camera angles and get ready to begin filming."

As they all were focused on their tasks, Charlotte's feet slowly pulled her backward until she was out of the gazebo.

I can't be rejected by the man that I love.

When she was sure no one had seen her leave, she spun around, picked up the skirt of her dress, and ran as fast as her heels would carry her. Charlotte ran past the horse stables, waving politely at the stableman standing outside, and continued running until she couldn't anymore.

She reached a field of newly bloomed flowers and sat down, sucking in sharp breaths.

Maybe she shouldn't have laid all her cards on the table. Maybe telling Liam the depth of her feelings would be the exact reason he didn't pick her. Because maybe she had been horribly wrong. Maybe he didn't feel the same way she felt after all.

CHAPTER THIRTY-SIX
LIAM

Liam sat on the couch in the men's sitting room, constantly running his hands through his hair.

"If you keep doing that, I'm going to have to call Matisse to come fix your hair before you start filming."

Liam lifted his head slightly to look at his brother, wearing an amused expression.

"I thought you'd already made your final decision. What has you so nervous?"

"Charlotte came to my room last night. She told me she loves me. I'm not sure I can return that kind of love."

"Why do you say that?"

"I haven't loved someone in so long." Liam's chin quivered as he dropped his head. "What if I'm not what she needs? What if I'm not enough for her?"

Barrett came over and placed his hands on Liam's shoulders. "Look at me."

Liam lifted his head only enough to look his brother in the eyes.

"You are more than enough. Your worth isn't defined by what anyone else says about you. It's not measured by what the King's Council says or what the Wistonian people say. You have to believe in yourself. I know you will work your butt off to be a better man and to love her even more every day. That's why you will be what she needs."

"I'm scared to let her in."

"Love requires risk. It requires sacrifice. It requires selflessness. It requires us to take a leap of faith and put our hearts on the line. But when you give love and are loved in return, it's one of the greatest feelings in the world."

"Thank you." Liam stood and pulled his brother into a tight hug, holding onto him with everything he had.

Barrett ruffled his hair. "Now go fix your hair and get outside. You look like you rubbed a hundred balloons on your head."

Liam laughed and walked to the nearest bathroom, fixing his hair in the mirror. Looking at his reflection, he whispered, "You can do this."

He checked the time on his watch and hurried outside. When he was walking up to the gazebo, Alec stopped him.

"Don't start filming," the producer yelled to the cameramen. Turning to the production assistants, he asked, "Where's Charlotte?"

"Right there, of course." One of the ladies motioned to the gazebo, her eyes wide when she saw only Sienna standing there. "What happened? Where'd she go?"

"Charlotte ran toward the stables," Wadsworth called out, running toward them from the palace doors.

Liam sucked in a breath. He had two options. He could propose to Sienna and not risk his heart. Or he could set aside his pride and chase after Charlotte, following his heart.

The decision for him was surprisingly easy. "You may want to start rolling," Liam said to Alec. Jogging over to Sienna, he took her hands in his. "Sienna, you're an amazing person. I know you would make a wonderful queen, but you deserve to find someone who can give you his whole heart. Someone whose heart isn't already with someone else."

She squeezed his hands and pressed a light kiss to his cheek even though tears slowly started spilling from her eyes. "Go get your girl, Your Highness."

He didn't need to be told twice. Liam ran to the stables. He had to find her. When he arrived, he found the lead groomer brushing the horses. "Lady Charlotte," he rasped. "Have you seen Charlotte?"

"You just missed her. She came through here a few minutes ago," the man called out. "She went that way." He pointed toward the forest behind them.

Liam paused for a mere second and composed himself. Who knew how far she could've gotten by now? He would never catch her on foot.

A war raged within his mind. Fear screamed that something awful would happen if he got on a horse again. His mind jumped back to the moment he'd watched his mother fall from her horse and hit her head on a rock.

He couldn't lose another person he loved.

Yet his heart screamed all the louder that something awful would happen if he didn't. He thought of what it would mean—what it would feel like—to lose Charlotte forever. His heart shattered at the mere thought.

He *wouldn't* lose the woman he loved.

I can't live without her.

"Please prepare my horse for me."

The groom's mouth opened in shock. He quickly recovered and began moving. "Right away, Your Highness."

After his horse, Zeus, was saddled, Liam walked toward the animal. His heart raced more with each step.

Listen to your heart.

I can do this.

Without another thought, he mounted the horse, sliding off a little at first before righting himself. Liam took in a few deep breaths, then he kicked his heels into Zeus's sides, pushing him into a full gallop, gripping the reins so tightly his knuckles turned white. Riding again scared the living daylights out of him, but losing Charlotte scared him even more.

He continued pushing Zeus deeper into the forest. His heartbeat sped up at the sight of Charlotte in the midst of a field of wildflowers. The flowers themselves were probably beautiful, but all he could see was her.

The woman in the emerald-green ball gown.

The woman he loved.

Liam jumped off his horse, tying the reins to a tree before rushing to her. He stopped a few feet away and whispered her name in a husky voice. "Charlotte."

Her head whipped around, and her eyes found his. He could see she'd been crying, but she still was the most stunning woman he had ever seen. "Hello, angel."

She dabbed her fingers beneath her eyes. "What are you doing out here, Liam? I thought you would be engaged to Sienna by now."

He hurried to her, cupping her face in his hands. Liam gently wiped away her tears with the pads of his thumbs.

"How could I be engaged to her when I'm in love with you?"

CHAPTER THIRTY-SEVEN
CHARLOTTE

How could I be engaged to her when I'm in love with you?
The words echoed in her mind.

"What did you say?" She searched his eyes, wanting to make sure she'd heard him correctly.

"I said I'm in love with you." Liam helped her to her feet and cupped her face again. "I love you, Charlotte. It scares the living daylights out of me. But it's true."

"You love me." Her eyes darted back and forth between his, filled with hope.

"And you love me." He brushed his knuckles along her cheek, making her breath hitch.

"But I heard what you said to your brother before I came outside. You said you weren't sure you could return my love." She pulled back from his touch.

"And right afterward, I told him I was scared. Scared of loving you but not being enough for you." She opened her mouth to speak, but he held up a hand. "I'm not scared anymore." He gestured behind him, and she turned her gaze to where he pointed.

A gasp escaped her lips at what she saw. A horse. Liam's horse.

He rode a horse to come find me.

He loved her. He really, truly loved her. He'd faced his biggest fear to follow her. If that wasn't true love, she didn't know what was.

"You rode a horse to come find me? But you haven't ridden—"

"Since my mother died. I know. I didn't know how far you'd run. I couldn't risk not finding you." He moved closer, wrapping his arms around her. "I couldn't risk losing you. So this is my grand moment—or whatever they call those big scenes in the romance novels you love. I literally got back on the horse for you."

"A grand gesture?"

"Yeah, that. This is me trying to prove to you that you are worth fighting my deepest fears. That there is nothing I wouldn't do to be with you. I can't promise I'll be perfect. I know there will be times I'll fail, but I promise never to be too stubborn to say I'm sorry or that you were right. I promise to push myself to grow and be a better man. I promise to remind you every day how much I love you."

Tears slipped from her eyes again, but she didn't bother to wipe them. She stared in awe at the man she loved sharing his heart with her.

"As king and queen, we will make an oath to put Wistonia first. But I want you to know that you will always be the queen of my heart. I will make sure there are at least three chocolate desserts at every event we plan. And I will do my best to love you the way you deserve to be loved. Sacrificially and unconditionally."

Charlotte couldn't hold back any longer. She threw her arms around his neck and pulled his lips to hers. Their mouths crashed together in a kiss that defied time and gravity. If she'd thought their first kiss had been magical, this one was extraordinary. Phenomenal. Otherworldly.

Their lips moved together in perfect harmony, making a beautiful chorus to a song of their own. One that only they knew and that she wanted to spend the rest of forever making with him.

He pulled back slowly, his eyes looking longingly and lovingly into hers.

"Now, angel, I have a very important question for you."

She gazed up at him with happy tears glistening in his eyes.

Liam got down on one knee and pulled a small velvet box from the pocket of his suit jacket as tears rolled freely down her cheeks. "Charlotte Elizabeth Croft, will you marry me? I don't think I can live another day without you by my side. You are the air I breathe and the keeper of my heart. Please be my wife."

"Yes, I'll marry you, Prince Hottie McHot Pants."

He threw his head back and laughed fully. "All it took was me finally proposing for you to call me that?" He pulled the ring from the box. "This ring was made from diamonds I selected from my mother's collection. I hope you like it."

Liam slid it onto her finger, and she finally got a closer look at it. The center stone was a large pear-cut emerald. It was surrounded by a halo of small diamonds, all on a thin gold band.

"I'll cherish it forever. Now I can always have her close to me." Charlotte gazed at the ring in adoration before looking back to Liam—her fiancé. "I can't wait to marry you."

"Well, that's a relief, because our wedding is this weekend." Liam squeezed her sides, making her squirm and giggle.

Suddenly, Giovanni popped out in front of them with all the camera crew. "I'm so grateful we ran through the forest to catch all that."

Liam jumped. "I'm impressed you were able to keep up with me. You never cease to amaze me, Giovanni."

The host chuckled and patted him on the back. "That's what golf carts are for, my friend." Giovanni smiled at them both before continuing, "That was the most beautiful proposal of all time. I believe I speak for the whole continent of Fenimore when I offer my sincerest congratulations on your engagement and upcoming nuptials. I think everyone could see the connection between you two from the beginning. Prince Liam, when did you first know you loved Charlotte?"

"Deep down, I think I knew from the moment I watched her walk down the stairs at the beginning of the competition that she had a hold on my heart."

"Why didn't you propose to her right then and throw the competition out the window?"

"I wanted to see the process through. And, truth is, I can sometimes be a bit stubborn, Giovanni. It took my head and heart a while to get on the same page. I closed off my heart for a long time, but I've learned we can't let hurt from the past keep us from living in the present. Life passes us by way too quickly. And I ended up realizing that I would rather spend the rest of my life with Charlotte, whom I love, than spend my whole life wondering what it would've been like with her."

"I can already hear all the women in Fenimore swooning at that comment, Your Highness."

"It's the truth." Liam wrapped his arm around her back, and she nuzzled into his touch. "And not only am I confident that she will make the most amazing wife, but Charlotte will make a wonderful queen."

"And Liam is going to make a magnificent king—the king Wistonia needs," Charlotte added, hugging his side tighter. Liam responded by kissing her temple.

Giovanni smiled at them knowingly. "I think we should give our newly engaged couple some space to celebrate. Be sure to tune in Saturday at three o'clock to watch His Royal Highness, Prince Liam, marry Lady Charlotte. And tune into a special episode Sunday at nine in the morning to witness their coronation ceremony. For everyone watching at home, thank you for tuning in to the season finale of *Royally Yours*. I, for one, know you were royally entertained by that dramatic, heart-warming ending. Goodnight."

When the recording light turned off, Giovanni turned and pulled them into a group hug. When he pulled back, a warm smile was on his face. "Congratulations to both of you." Leaning in toward Charlotte, he whispered, "I was rooting for you from the get-go." With a wink he walked off, calling for the camera crew to follow him.

When they were alone again, Charlotte turned and wrapped her arms around Liam's midsection.

"Can you believe this is all real?" Liam asked, looking at the field of beautiful wildflowers around them.

"It feels like a dream," she said, looking only at him.

She let out a happy sigh when his lips met hers again. Liam's kiss told her everything words couldn't say. Charlotte wasn't sure how long they stayed out in the field kissing and talking…and kissing some more.

Liam was her dream. And now she would finally get to live out the greatest fairy tale of all time.

Theirs.

After dinner, Charlotte basically floated to her room. She had yet to come down from the dream-like haze she'd been in since Liam had proposed to her that afternoon. Not many people got to say they were going to marry the man they'd been attracted to for years but had always believed was out of reach. Visions of their wedding day were already running rampant in her mind.

"Lady Charlotte, I have a note for you." Maya ran around the corner. "From your fiancé." She waved the little piece of paper in front of her.

Charlotte quickly took the note from her, reading Liam's words.

Angel,
Meet me in your favorite place at ten.
I love you,
Prince Hottie McHot Pants

She held the note close to her chest, letting out a happy sigh. Ten o'clock couldn't come soon enough.

Charlotte went to the bookshelves in her room and selected a cozy mystery from them. Cuddling up with a blanket on the couch, she dove into the story. She didn't feel the need to read any romance stories today. Her love story was far better than any she could find within the pages of a book.

Half an hour before she was supposed to meet Liam, she set her book down and perused her closet for something to wear. She settled on an emerald-green blouse and jeans, wanting to go for a classy-casual look. Charlotte fluffed the wispy hairs that framed her face and applied a layer of lip gloss before heading to the greenhouse to meet her man.

She waved off the guards at the palace's back entrance who offered to escort her to her destination. "I'm just going to meet Liam at the greenhouse."

As she approached the building, her heart rate increased, beating to a rhythm that only Liam could stir. When she saw a figure around the side of the greenhouse, she started to wave, but then she noticed another figure approaching from behind in a menacing manner.

Charlotte ducked as the figures stepped into the light. She bit back a gasp as she saw Prince James hold a knife to Liam's back. James hardly looked like the man she knew. His blond hair was covered in dirt, and strands of it hung over his face in muddy clumps. The clothes he wore were grungy, like he'd been wearing them for days straight. He looked frenzied and delirious, and Charlotte didn't know if she'd ever forget the deranged look in his eyes.

She could hardly look at Liam without feeling like she was going to get sick. He wore a calm expression, but she could see the fear in his eyes.

Charlotte dug around in her pockets, pressing her lips together in frustration when she realized she'd left her phone in her room. *I should've had the guards escort me. I can't lose Liam. Not after we are finally together. Not after I finally get to be with the man I love.* All she could do was watch the scene unfold as she tried to think of how to save Liam.

"Why are you doing this?" Liam asked.

"You robbed me of what is rightfully mine," James growled. His voice was different—crazed.

"What are you talking about?"

Charlotte watched as James pressed the knife harder against him, and Liam winced.

"My father should've been king. He was born a mere seven minutes after yours. My father knew what it took to lead a country, better than yours ever did. The crown should've been his," he hissed. "Then I would be the one ascending the throne. The throne should be mine." His mouth pulled up at the corners in a wide, evil grin. "And it will be mine after I get rid of the only thing standing in my way—you." James forcefully led Liam away from the greenhouse, walking farther from the palace and toward the forest.

Charlotte slowly followed them, taking careful steps to not snap any twigs. She had to save him, but she didn't want to make any sudden moves and lead James to do something rash. James came to a sudden stop behind the groundskeepers' storage building, jerking Liam to a halt with him.

Maybe there's something in here I can use to save him.

She carefully turned the doorknob, grateful to find it unlocked. Once inside the dimly lit structure, Charlotte's eyes darted around frantically, trying to find something—anything—she could use to help Liam. In the corner of the room, she finally spotted something that made her feel like she could breathe again.

A paintball gun.

She grabbed the gun, seeing there were still a few paintballs remaining—but all she needed was one shot. Charlotte tiptoed out of the room and pressed her back against the building, moving slowly toward where James was holding

Liam hostage. She continued listening to the conversation, trying to find her opening.

"Can't we just talk, James? We're family. Why don't you put the knife down? Then we can have a conversation." Liam tried to reason with his cousin.

James's evil laugh reverberated in the air. "This conversation won't be continuing for much longer." He twirled the knife in his hand.

Their entire future flashed before Charlotte's eyes. *This can't be happening.* She clutched the gun tighter in her hands, waiting for her opening.

"There's no good way out of this, James. All of Fenimore is looking for you. If you kill me, you'll only be in prison longer. There's no way for you to be king now. You need to give it up."

"You're wrong," James snarled, whipping around so he now stood face-to-face with Liam. "The people will see what I have done and put me on a pedestal—honor me. They will see how powerful I am and all bow before me."

Charlotte's breath hitched. This situation was escalating quickly. *James has lost all sense of reality. I need to act now...before he does.*

Adrenaline coursed through her body as she moved closer now that James's back was to her. She caught Liam's attention and held a finger to her lips. He gave the slightest nod of acknowledgment.

Charlotte analyzed the situation and decided the back of James's head was the best place to shoot. It would catch him off guard and give Liam time to move out of his hold.

She held up the paintball gun and took her aim. Charlotte released a slow breath and hit the trigger. James let out a roar in pain as she hit him squarely on the back of his head. That split second gave Liam the opening he needed to disarm James, taking the knife from him.

Charlotte called out for the palace guards as Liam forced James to the ground. The guards came rushing from the back of the palace, weapons drawn. They quickly apprehended James, putting him in handcuffs and patting him down to make sure he had no additional weapons on him.

She raced over to Liam and launched herself into his arms, holding him as tightly as she could. Charlotte pulled back, holding his face in her hands and searching his eyes. "He didn't hurt you, did he?" She spun him around and helped him lift up the back of his shirt, finding a few puncture wounds that lightly dripped blood where James had held the knife firmly against him. "You're bleeding."

Charlotte called over a guard who quickly cut off a piece of his own shirt, wrapping it around Liam and tying it tightly until they could get him inside and to the palace doctor.

"You'll regret this," James hissed, his eyes darting around until they found Liam. "I'm the only one who has what it takes to be king. I'll make my father proud if it's the last thing I do." His maniacal laugh hung in the air, even after the guards had dragged him away.

"That was not the evening I had planned with you." Liam let out a breathy laugh, wrapping his arms around Charlotte.

"I would surely hope not. Otherwise, our life together would be filled with a lot more action than I bargained for." She rubbed her hands up and down his arms.

He leaned in close, brushing his lips over hers. "You saved me again," he whispered against her mouth.

"It's what we do." She pulled back and gave him a stern glare. "But let's maybe keep the saving from life-threatening situations to a minimum."

"Does taking your breath away count as a life-threatening situation?" Liam raised an eyebrow and smiled coyly at her, pulling her even closer to him.

"I think I can make an exception for you." She winked at him right before his lips collided with hers. Charlotte wrapped her hands around his neck, savoring the moment with him.

This night definitely hadn't turned out how she'd planned. But Liam was okay—more than okay, from what his kiss had told her—and the people who had been attempting to hurt him had all been apprehended now.

She pulled back and smiled up at him. Their love story was far from perfect, but as long as she could be with him, she was exactly where she wanted to be.

"Cream or eggshell for the linens and napkins?" Felicity, the royal wedding planner, asked, flipping to another page in a binder that was so large it probably weighed more than a small child.

Charlotte looked between the two options. "Cream."

"And for the centerpieces? I was thinking of a tall display of white roses."

"Could we add in some forget-me-nots?"

"What's this about forget-me-nots? Are you going somewhere?" Liam walked into the room and kissed her on the forehead.

"You can't get rid of me that easily." Charlotte narrowed her eyebrows playfully. "We're making some selections for the wedding." Liam tried to moonwalk back out of the room. "You're not getting out of this."

He let out a sigh, even though she could see the smirk on his face. "For you, I'd suffer through just about anything."

"Who said anything about suffering?" She shoved his shoulder once he sat down next to her.

"I think wedding planning had to have been used as a mild form of torture in the past. I mean, how many shades of white are there, really? They all look white to me."

Charlotte patted his shoulder. "And that's why you gave me full control of all the wedding details."

"Well, that and I want my future wife to have everything her heart desires. Happy wife, happy life, right?"

"I have everything I need right here." She wrapped her arm through his and leaned in to kiss him.

After a moment, Felicity cleared her throat, making them both pull back.

Color flooded Charlotte's cheeks. "I'm sorry. Please continue, Felicity."

"No, that's quite all right. Why don't you go through the next few pages on your own and let me know your decisions via text? I'll give you some alone time." The wedding planner shot Charlotte a conspiratorial smile before handing over the gigantic binder and leaving them.

Charlotte turned to face Liam. "Do you know what I could go for right now?"

He leaned in so their lips were only a breath apart. "I think I do." Liam waggled his eyebrows.

When he leaned in to kiss her, she turned her face so his lips landed on her cheek. "I was going to say we should go taste-test the cakes."

Liam groaned. "We both already know you're going to pick the chocolate one."

"No," she drew out the word. "I might've had Chef Lorenzo make three different kinds of chocolate cake."

He laughed as he tugged her to her feet. "Okay, we'll go taste-test the *three* different chocolate cakes." Liam took her hand in his, interlocking their fingers as they walked toward the kitchen. "And just so you know, angel, I accept payment for my time in the form of kisses."

Charlotte giggled and wrapped her free hand around his bicep.

Of course, she planned to thoroughly kiss her fiancé later. But right now, she wanted to soak in the moment.

The feel of his hand in hers. The dazzling smile he shot her way. The look of adoration in his eyes as they roamed over her.

Charlotte couldn't wipe the wide grin off her face. She knew she'd found her place. She was home. Liam was her home. And she wouldn't have it any other way.

EPILOGUE
LIAM

Six Days Later

Today was *the* day. The day all of Fenimore had been waiting for. His wedding day.

Liam would've laughed if someone had told him a year ago that he would be looking forward to this moment. If someone had told him he would be marrying the woman who had his heart. His heart that he had *willingly* given her.

Yet, here he was. Giddy that he would get to call Charlotte his *wife* in about eight hours.

Life had a funny way of turning out differently than you planned. But it also had a way of giving you more than you'd ever thought to ask for.

"How're you feeling? Today's a big day." Barrett clapped Liam on the shoulder.

"I've never felt so sure about anything in my life."

His brother stopped and stared at him. "She really has done a number on you."

Liam shot him a glare.

"No, no, no. I mean in a good way. Charlotte has changed you for the better. And I couldn't be happier for you. Mom and Dad would be thrilled for you, too."

Liam bit back the sting of tears in his eyes. He adjusted the medals on his white ceremonial suit and brushed his shoulders before running his fingers over the cufflinks Barrett had made for him at the beginning of the competition. As his fingers ran over the "I love you" engravings written in his parents' handwriting, he felt more at peace, knowing they were at his side. "Let's go to my wedding."

They were both quiet on the ride to Brookside Abbey. He thought about his life and all the moments and people who had shaped him. And he also thought about the future—what life would look like as king and, most importantly, what it would look like with Charlotte by his side.

Their car came to a stop at the church. Thousands of people stood outside a perimeter the Royal Guard had set up.

Goosebumps covered Liam's arms when he stepped out of the car and the people chanted his name and waved Wistonian flags. He had done it. He had won over the Wistonian people. There would, of course, still be those who didn't support him as king. But his popularity had grown. He had gained the trust and support of his people by letting them see the real him, and that made it that much sweeter. He waved back before entering the church.

"You might even be more popular than I was." Barrett raised an eyebrow and nudged him in the shoulder.

They both removed their white gloves to shake hands with the archbishop. Liam handed his gloves to Wadsworth, who stood off to the side in a suit, tears glistening in his eyes. He pulled their butler into a tight hug.

"Thank you for everything," Liam said.

"It has been my life's greatest honor to serve your family." A few tears slipped onto Wadsworth's cheeks as he stepped into the background.

Liam stood tall as the music began flowing from the organ. He followed the archbishop down the aisle with his brother at his side in slow, measured steps just like they had planned in the rehearsal. He smiled politely at the guests seated in the pews on either side of the aisle as he passed. Almost all the women from the competition had returned for the occasion. And the entire King's Council—minus Lord Howard, who would be sitting in prison for a long time alongside Prince James and Raina—were also in attendance along with the other kings, queens, and high rulers of Fenimore.

When they reached the altar, Barrett hugged him and then went to sit beside Jules.

Liam's heart pounded in his chest so hard he could feel it in his throat. It was time to see his bride.

Charlotte walked down the aisle on her father's arm, and she truly lived up to the nickname he'd given her. She floated down the aisle, looking every bit like an angel sent straight from heaven above.

Her dress was the embodiment of elegance. Floral lace covered a sheer, high-necked bodice and long sleeves. The lace cascaded down onto a tulle ball-gown skirt that swayed gently as she walked toward him. She wore a matching veil, which was carried by her lady's maid, Maya. When she got closer, Liam could see how her makeup emphasized all her features in the best way possible.

She was the picture of grace and beauty—just like his mom had been. And that thought didn't tear him up inside anymore. Instead of feeling pain and sadness, Charlotte brought about joy and hope. Being with her helped keep the memory of his mom alive.

Today just so happened to also be Charlotte's birthday, which meant she should be receiving her inheritance after all. Her father was trying to fight them on it, saying she needed to be married *by* her thirtieth birthday, not *on* her thirtieth birthday. Liam didn't care much for semantics. They didn't need the Duke of Albury's money. He could have his sauna or theater room or whatever. Liam got Charlotte, and that was all that mattered.

"Who gives this woman to be married to this man?"

"Her mother and I." Charlotte's father placed her hand in Liam's. The duke gave Charlotte a stiff hug and Liam a firm handshake before moving to his seat in the first row next to Charlotte's mother. Liam helped her move up to the altar and adjusted her train for her.

Repeating after the archbishop, they said their vows about how they would take each other from this day forward. For better or worse. For richer or poorer. In sickness and in health. And how they would love and cherish each other until their final days.

The archbishop cleared his throat and turned to face him. "Liam Charles Frederick Alden, will you have this woman as your wedded wife, to live together according to God's law in the holy estate of matrimony? Will you love her, comfort her, honor and keep her, in sickness and in health, so long as you both shall live?"

"I will." Liam beamed at her.

The same words were read to Charlotte, and she also said, "I will."

The archbishop blessed their rings before Liam slid a thin, gold band onto Charlotte's finger.

"With this ring, I wed you. With my body, I honor you. And all my worldly goods I share with you. In the name of the Father, and of the Son, and of the Holy Spirit."

Charlotte again repeated the same words and slid a gold band onto his finger.

They kneeled together before the altar as the archbishop prayed over them and their marriage. When they stood again, the archbishop joined their hands as he said, "Those who God has joined together let no man separate. I pronounce you man and wife."

He knew sharing a kiss wasn't traditional in a royal wedding ceremony, but Liam walked over and whispered a question to the archbishop, who nodded his consent with a smirk on his face.

Liam hurried back to his wife. He leaned in, dipped Charlotte, and kissed her fully on the lips, before God and all their family and friends and people. He was hers, and she was his.

One Day Later

Liam took a deep breath, trying to calm the butterflies swarming inside him. He adjusted the high collar of his velvet cloak and stood tall as four servants from the palace staff lifted his long train, and he began the slow walk down the large aisle in Brookside Abbey.

He kept his eyes straight ahead as he walked, knowing all eyes were on him. Liam sat when he finally reached the throne.

The archbishop stood before Liam. "Are you willing to take the oath?"

"I am willing."

Liam held a Bible in his hands as the archbishop asked his next questions.

"Will you solemnly promise and swear to govern the peoples of Wistonia according to its laws and customs?"

"I solemnly promise so to do."

"Will you, in your power, cause law and justice to be executed in all your judgments?"

Liam found Charlotte's eyes in the back of the church, and she smiled at him, giving him all the courage he needed.

"I solemnly promise so to do."

Three high rulers of the church approached him and presented him with an orb and a scepter. He took them and sat still as the archbishop came and placed the crown on his head. In Wistonia, the orb, scepter, and crown were known as the three Crown Jewels. While the crown was sometimes worn for other events, the orb and scepter were only used in the event of a coronation.

He got on his knees and declared before God and his people, "The things which I have promised here, I will perform and keep. So help me God."

All of those in attendance bowed before him, paying homage to their new king.

A footman sounded a horn and hit a staff on the ground. "May I present His Royal Majesty, Liam Charles Frederick Alden, King of Wistonia."

"God save the king," the room said in unison, and goosebumps covered Liam's body.

He walked back down the aisle as the new king of Wistonia, and those in attendance applauded. Liam stood in the back of the church as he observed Charlotte being crowned Queen Consort. She took her own oath to govern Wistonia alongside him. She answered the same questions he had as Liam watched her in awe.

In awe that she was his wife.

In awe that he had been able to open his heart to love again.

In awe of how absolutely regal she looked sitting on the throne.

When he let the reality of the moment truly sink in, he knew how proud his mother was of him. And Charlotte would serve as a reminder of her every day with her class and wisdom.

He knew that, every day, they would do their best to lead Wistonia well. To protect their wonderful country and honor it.

"May I present Her Royal Majesty, Charlotte Elizabeth Alden, Queen of Wistonia."

"God save the queen," Liam said with the rest of the room as his eyes met Charlotte's.

As she left the throne, Wistonia's national anthem began playing, and everyone in attendance sang along.

Charlotte smiled widely at him as she walked down the aisle toward him.

When she reached him, Charlotte wrapped her hand around his arm, and they walked out of the church as king and queen, as husband and wife, and into their future together.

Read the paintball scene from Liam's point of view when you sign up for my emails at https://dl.bookfunnel.com/d52fh9a0ir.

Keep reading for a bonus epilogue!

BONUS EPILOGUE
ROSALIE

Rosalie watched as the scenery outside her car window changed from the mountainous backdrop of Wistonia to the lush green fields of Findorra. She would miss her time at the Wistonian Palace. Really, she would miss her friends.

As a princess, true friends were hard to come by, and she hoped that the friendships she'd made throughout the competition would continue even when they were all back in their own kingdoms. She especially hoped she'd remain close to Charlotte.

Rosalie smiled at the memory of the coronation ceremony from this afternoon as she'd gotten to watch her best friend be crowned Queen of Wistonia. Charlotte and Liam's wedding yesterday had been beautiful, but watching a coronation ceremony in person was like something out of a fairy tale. She'd never witnessed anything quite so magical before.

Her phone started vibrating in her lap. She glanced down and answered when she saw it was her mother calling—her parents only called her directly when it was an urgent matter.

"Mom, is everything okay?"

"Rosalie, you need to return home immediately."

They'd left in a car a few hours before her while she stuck around to spend more time with her friends in downtown Brookside before returning home.

"I'm only about an hour away." She hesitated, unsure if she wanted to know the answer to her next question. "What's wrong? Has something happened?"

The long pause on the other end of the line sent her mind wandering. "It's not something we would like to discuss on the phone. Meet us in your father's study as soon as you get here."

"Okay," Rosalie whispered, but her mother had already hung up.

She placed her phone back on her lap as nausea began to swirl in her stomach. Rosalie let out a long, slow breath.

What could be so bad that they won't tell me over the phone?

Ideas ran through her mind that were likely far worse than whatever was actually happening.

Findorra's going to war.

Someone in our family passed away.

Before she could think of any other terrible things, a sound chimed from her phone that sent her fidgeting with her hair as another wave of nausea rolled in. The specific ringtone that sounded was for the *Royal Inquisitor* news app on her phone. Normally, the notification sound didn't worry her, but after what her mother was—or wasn't—saying, she was scared for whatever news article she might see.

Rosalie closed her eyes and took a steadying breath before flipping her phone over. She nearly dropped her phone after seeing the words on the screen. She clicked on it, opening the app and rubbing her eyes to make sure she was seeing things clearly.

The words remained on the screen. She'd only been gone for three months. It couldn't be true.

Findorra in Financial Trouble.

She quickly read the article explaining how the country had a few bad economic years that had led to them going deeper and deeper in debt—more debt than any country in Fenimore had ever seen before.

A sinking feeling filled her gut. There was only one reason her parents wouldn't tell her what was wrong before the story broke. There was something else going on. Something bigger. Something that involved her. And something deep within her knew it was far worse than the financial troubles Findorra was apparently facing. It was something that would change her life forever.

♛

You won't want to miss Rosalie's story in A Royal Arrangement. You can get it at https://www.amazon.com/gp/product/B0C6V4WD37.

BY AMANDA SCHIMMOELLER

Royal Hearts Series
A Royal Obligation
A Royal Competition
A Royal Arrangement

ACKNOWLEDGMENTS

To my husband, Wade — Even though this book is dedicated to you, I couldn't help but mention you in my acknowledgments as well. You're the absolute best. Thank you for working so hard to allow me to live out my dream.

To my mom, Lori — You've bought more copies of my books than I can count! Thank you for supporting me in all my endeavors, but especially in my author journey.

To my editors, Emily Poole and Jenn Lockwood — Y'all are a dream team! Thank you for your feedback on my story. You helped make it shine and catch all the pesky typos that always seem to slip through the cracks. I'm so grateful to have you on my team.

To my beta readers, Ashley, Hailey, Kathryn, Kimberly, Madi, Megan, and Steph — Thank you, thank you, thank you!!! Your feedback and suggestions were absolutely wonderful. You helped me take the beginnings of a good story and shine it up into a gem!

To Kimberly — You inspired so many of my favorite scenes in this book! Thank you for all the time you put into helping Liam's story be what it is today. I never want to write a book without you!

To Ashley — I can't believe you read my book TWICE. I appreciate all the feedback you provided more than you know. Thank you for always checking in and giving me the encouragement to keep going! Having you on my side throughout the writing process has meant the world to me!

To Lindsay and Matisse — Thank you for helping me find all the typos in A Royal Obligation! I hope you enjoyed reading the characters named after you in Liam's story!

To my readers — I've said it before and I'll say it again, you all are the reason I do this and you make every hour spent on writing so worth it. Thank you for reading my book and making my dream of being an author become a reality!

To my Savior, Jesus Christ — Thank you for putting a love of stories in my heart and for giving me the ability and words to write this story. All the praise and glory goes to you!

ABOUT THE AUTHOR

As a child, Amanda Schimmoeller had two loves: writing and Disney. She now combines the two by writing stories of true love, broken hearts, and happily ever afters while surviving on copious amounts of iced chais and binge-worthy tv. You'll find her plotting her next great love story and living out her own fairytale in Knoxville, TN with her husband and their dog.

To stay connected with Amanda, you can sign up for her newsletter at https://www.authoramandaschimmoeller.com/newsletter.html.

You can also follow her on Instagram at https://www.instagram.com/authoramandaschimmoeller or join her reader group at https://www.facebook.com/groups/amandaschimmoellerreadergroup.